VORO

———————

M.M. PERRY

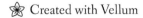

PROLOGUE

S arah huddled into the letterman jacket with a violent shiver.

"Why is it so cold? It's August."

"It's night?" George offered helpfully. "I'd give you my jacket, but..."

He gestured at her with a lopsided smile that Sarah couldn't help but be warmed by. She returned with her own shy smile before fidgeting with the heavy letterman jacket she wore. She loved wearing George's jacket; it made her feel petite and cute huddled inside the excessive amounts of cloth.

Her fingers traced the edging of the newest letter that had been sewn onto the jacket while she waited patiently for George to sort through the beat-up cooler at his feet. Always conscious of the fact that he could be looking her way at any time, she tossed her red hair over her shoulder elegantly, making sure to keep her best side toward him. She hoped he looked at her as often as she looked at him, particularly since she put so much effort into every move and gesture, maximizing her potential attractiveness. It had taken far too long to get his attention, but now that she had it, she aimed to keep it.

He handed her a can of beer before joining her on the slightly damp log. Sarah stifled her annoyance when George forgot his chivalry – her nails were too expensive to risk on a pull tab. He opened his can and took a deep draft before turning to her. She held her beer so it didn't look like she was waiting for him to open it, but he wouldn't be able to miss that she wasn't drinking, either.

"Here, you goofy girl. I'll save those precious nails of yours."

He took her beer and opened it, slurping the foam off the top before handing it back. It was the little things, Sarah thought, that made George so special. He might have taken forever to ask her out, but it was worth the wait. She took the beer back and allowed herself to be tucked under his arm.

She snuggled into the warm spot against his body while his hand rubbed her shoulder. These were her favorite moments: the quiet ones when Jay wasn't around to foul up the place, when Jessie wasn't there to draw attention away, when it was just her and George.

She felt George fumbling in his pocket and stiffened.

"What are you doing, silly?" she asked, even though she knew exactly what he was doing.

"Just wondering where the rest of the guys are."

Sarah put her beer down, trying her best to look casual. She wrapped her arms around George and kissed him lightly on his earlobe.

"Do we really have to rush them?" she asked breathily. "I'm sure we can find a way to pass the time before they get here."

Her distraction worked, and George took his hand back out of his pocket without the phone. As he kissed her, Sarah smiled. He didn't need to know she'd texted Jay and said they would meet them at eleven instead of ten. She'd make sure that by the time the others got there, George wouldn't mind her little trick at all.

Five of the most pleasant minutes of Sarah's life went by before George pulled away from her, a disgusted look on his face.

"Do you smell that?"

Sarah turned away from George, worried he was talking about her breath. She frowned angrily. She'd told the pimply-faced cretin behind the counter to hold the onions on her burger earlier, but when she'd taken her first bite the bitter taste had been overwhelming. The dork hadn't held the onions; he'd trebled them. During the ride out to their special spot, Sarah had surreptitiously chewed three pieces of mint gum in succession to try to cover up the sour taste in her mouth, spitting each out into the foil rectangle that originally held them before sneaking another piece.

She tucked her hands into her pockets, her fingers trailing across the cold, foil-wrapped balls. She counted them up to make sure she'd remembered correctly. She was about to risk the embarrassment of breathing into her hand to check, when she caught a whiff of something that was definitely not her own breath. Her face wrinkled into a look of revulsion, the stench so overpowering she forgot that George was still watching her.

"What the hell is that?" she asked. "Did the park service put a new port-a-potty out when we weren't looking?"

She pinched her nose to hold back the reviling smell.

"If they did, someone died in it," George said. "That's not the smell of a hundred shits. That's something else. I think maybe an animal died out here. Something big."

Sarah jumped up. Suddenly she no longer wanted to be

alone. Suddenly she hoped Jay and his idiot friends, and even Jessie, would show up early.

"George, if we can smell that—"

"I know," he said. "I don't want to meet a hungry bear in the woods, either. Let's go. It's not safe here. We'll have to find another place to hang until whatever's stinking up the place gets cleared."

He got off the log, fished his phone out of his pocket, and turned on the flashlight. Sarah leaned in close to him while he pointed it out into the woods. The light made it even worse in her mind. It blasted all the dark details of the forest away from everywhere but inside the narrow cone of light. Her heart raced, fearing the beam would catch a pair of eyes.

"I don't see anything," George said. "But we should still go. Hopefully, a dead pile of meat is more enticing than the living."

He was fiddling with his phone, pulling up a list of contacts, when Sarah stopped him.

"We'll call them from the truck, George. Let's just get out of here."

"Yeah." George reluctantly put his phone back away and took another look around them. "Okay. Let's go."

They'd travelled the path to their secret spot so many times, Sarah could do it with her eyes closed. Yet, this time, the fear made the route feel foreign, as if she'd never traveled it before. She stumbled and cursed, George holding her arm tight to keep her from falling. The smell was getting worse, not better.

"George?"

"I know," he said. "Just keep moving. We get to the truck, it'll be fine."

Sarah clutched his arm tighter. The strong muscles she felt under her fingers didn't comfort her as much as she'd hoped they would. She stared in the direction of the truck, willing it to appear.

"Hey."

The voice was unfamiliar, male, and very close by. Sarah's heart stopped.

"Jay?" George called out.

The nervousness in George's voice made Sarah panicky. She clutched him ever tighter.

"Hey."

Another voice, female this time, rang out. It was equally unfamiliar.

"Jessie? Are you guys fucking with us?" George shouted. Sarah felt George tense up with a mixture of anger and fear. "It's not funny."

"George," she whispered, her voice shaking.

"Get out here, assholes. I mean it."

"George," Sarah said, this time more insistently.

"What?" he snapped.

She hardly had time to feel upset that he'd shouted at her.

"It's not a bear."

"Thanks, genius," he said.

She stopped him from taking another step forward, clutching him like a vice.

"It's not Jay or Jessie, either," she said.

The smell invaded every part of her mind. It was so strong, she felt like it was clouding her vision. But she could still hear, and something was moving right in front of them.

George must have heard it, too. He pulled Sarah closer to him, though she had the strong sense it wasn't to protect her; it was out of fear. He was holding her out of fear. Her thoughts reeled. George was big and strong, and he was clutching her like a boy would his blanket.

"Jay?" George whispered, desperation drenching his voice.

That was the last thing Sarah ever heard George say. It would be an annoying thought that would plague her until her dying breath. He called out Jay's name, and then he died. Jay's name, after everything she'd given him – her heart, her body, her mind – and Jay's was the last name that George would say before he died. Or at least, she thought he died. She was pretty sure he died. She was sure no one screamed quite like that unless it was the last scream they'd ever make.

She was alone in the dark. Her mind raced through thoughts with reckless abandon – mindless, inconsequential, insipid thoughts. She couldn't stop them from flooding through her. She should have run; that thought came and went like a lightning bolt before her body started to shut down from the terror of not being able to control her sanity. One second, George had been there, clutching her for comfort. The next, he'd been yanked away like a rag doll. And then the scream happened. And some sounds – sounds she didn't want to think about too long lest her brain add a picture. Picturing those sounds was the last thing Sarah wanted to do.

She took a deep breath, forcing control. The feeling she was having was not unlike the feeling she'd had when the first pep-rally of the year came around. She had to perform a new routine and she was the one chosen to be the flyer. She was the smallest, since Sissy had graduated, so it made sense, but she'd never done it before. Her first ever basket toss as the flyer, and she'd been terrified. Months of summer practice hadn't calmed her nerves when she stood in formation in the crowded stadium. She remembered she'd panicked then, too. It hadn't helped that George was watching and that everyone knew they'd just started dating.

The sounds she was avoiding paying attention to started to

diminish. She knew that was a bad sign; a sign that meant she didn't have much time. She hoped George hadn't locked the truck. As the fear threatened to crowd into her brain again, she did the only thing she could think to do and sang the song that got her through that first rally.

"The wheels on the bus go round and round," she began.

Her voice shook, and she could hardly breathe, but she found the strength to move one foot.

"Round and round."

Another foot moved forward.

"Round and round."

She took three more steps, finally finding the path she remembered so well.

"The wheels on the bus go round and round."

She started running. The path spread out before her like a lighted runway strip. Her mind focused and she couldn't hear or smell anything but what was in front of her. She imagined coming around the last cluster of ancient trees and seeing the edge of the campground, George's shiny, white truck tucked behind the state park sign where it wouldn't be easily seen by the rangers. But she knew it was there, and that was all that mattered. She pictured it, like she'd pictured the perfect basket toss.

See it. Make it happen. Coach Simpson had said it a thousand times. Sarah pictured the truck. She pictured opening the door and getting inside, locking out whatever was tearing George apart in the darkness. George, whose last word was "Jay."

"All through the to—"

ONE

The motel was one of the kinds you see on television or in the movies – the kind that screams "stay away." From the road, Casey could see a single line of pastel, metal doors with numbers on them, interrupting the pale-yellow siding plastering the building. It looked more like a motel he'd expect to see in California than Michigan, the color scheme evoking tacky warmth.

Casey walked along the gravel parking lot, counting down the numbers as he passed by them. A sign stretched up over the corner of the motel, marquee letters spelling out the name in more yellow – Sunset View Motel. He glanced out over the road curiously. The land sloped gently away from the adjacent highway, covered in dense trees green with life. Wind rustled through the leaves, showing hints of yellow and some orange. It was, indeed, a view of the west skyline, unhindered by the earthbound landscape.

Accurate, at least, he thought as he looked back up at the sign. The neon flickered, the few letters that still lit up buzzing when Casey got close to them. It reminded him of the sound his head made when he thought too much about what he had to do. He became lost in thought beneath the sign for more than a minute, the sound droning into him until his toes vibrated with it.

A car passing at speed broke him from his trance. They had the windows rolled down, a thumping beat escaping them that reverberated through Casey. But it wasn't the sound that startled Casey out of his reverie – it was the scent that came on the blast of wind accompanying the speeding vehicle. A thick, oily smell rolled off the car's wake. Casey's nostrils flared as his mouth turned into a grimace. More memories came with the smell, but he didn't have time for them.

Casey hefted his duffle bag onto his shoulder before taking a breath and straightening his T-shirt. He didn't think whoever manned the desk at this old motel would care that he hadn't showered in more than a day, or that his shirt wore the wrinkles and dust of a day's ride in a pickup bed, but his mother had always stressed the importance of first impressions. There weren't many lessons imparted onto him as a boy that he continued to practice, but this was one he always kept as a habit, even when it felt as futile as it did just then.

A bell chimed pleasantly against the glass door to the motel's office as he opened it. The sound cleared his mind. He stepped up to the desk and waited for the surly-looking, young woman glued to her phone to notice him. She was pretty in an angry way, defiantly frowning through her highlighted bangs and heavy mascara. Casey pegged her as in her mid-thirties, somewhere in the middle range. He couldn't be one-hundred percent sure, since she wore so much make-up. Her clothes were trendy but well worn. She didn't look like she belonged in the motel office at all – certainly not a motel pulled from a

Stepford world where pastel palettes reigned even in the commercial district.

While Casey waited for her to acknowledge him, he set down his bag. When she finally looked up, her frown deepened. She pulled a piece of light-green gum out of her mouth and hastily wrapped it in the tiny bit of foil that had originally held it.

"You need a room?"

He gave her one of his million-dollar smiles. It usually worked on women, and often on men. It didn't work on this woman. After a few beats she crossed her arms and glared at him, as if daring him to flirt with her.

"Uh," he stammered, unsure why his casual charm had failed him this time. "Yes."

The woman got up and tapped a few keystrokes into a laughably out-of-place, modern computer. He scanned her shirt looking for a nametag, hoping if he used her name it might ingratiate himself to her. He'd read that in a book once about getting people to like you but had never really had enough chances to practice it to say if it actually worked or not. It would go better, he knew, if he could win her over.

He needed more than just a room. At best, the clerk, or manager – Casey was still unsure on that point – was neutral toward him. Though, when he considered her sour look, he downgraded that assessment to something more realistic; he was an annoyance to her, he could see that much. One final furtive check and he came up empty. She had nothing pinned to her shirt and he couldn't find any nameplates on the desk.

"One bed or two?"

"One is fine."

"How long are you planning to stay?"

Casey brushed back his dark hair as he pondered his answer.

"Well, I might be here a bit. I was wondering if you had weekly rates?"

Her eyes rose from the screen and met his. He smiled again, but she only responded by picking up her phone and tapping on one of the contacts. Casey mulled over the possibility of finding another ride before dark that would take him into town, fearful this motel wasn't as good a choice as he thought it would be. Before he could think on it too long, the woman began speaking.

"Max, guy here wants weekly rates. Yes, I'm being nice. What do you mean I don't sound nice? I sound perfectly nice. You don't—"

The woman pulled the phone away from her ear and looked at it in disgust before setting it back on the counter. She forced a smile onto her face and looked up at Casey.

"The manager will be here shortly to discuss those rates with you. I'll get everything else set up. What name should I put the room under?"

"Casey Pierson. P-i-e-r-s-o-n."

The woman tapped away on the keyboard a few seconds.

"Payment?"

Casey shoved his hands into his jean's pockets. He looked around to see if the manager was coming. He didn't think this woman would be helpful with his next request, nor did he relish having the discussion with her.

By the look on her face, it was obvious she'd expected him to pull out a wallet. When Casey didn't, her frown returned.

"The weekly rates won't be zero, you know."

"I know. I was hoping someone here might be able to point me to some local work. Something temporary while I'm in town.

I can do a lot of things. Handyman type stuff. Yard work, house—”

“Are you a fucking hobo or something?”

“Anne!”

Casey felt the sweat that had started beading up along the back of his neck abate with the manager’s entrance. She bustled into the office with an apologetic look on her face. She was taller than average for a woman, but still a few inches off Casey. She was lean in the way teenage boys can be, small chested and athletically built. Her hair was tied up behind her head, a handkerchief knotted around her brown hair, stained with sweat. Even though the woman behind the counter had painted her face on, it was obvious the two were related – they shared similar noses, and both had a slight cleft in their chins. Other than that, they were as different as could be. The manager’s clothes were practical: jeans and a tank-top, sneakers that looked more lived in than the oldest house Casey had ever seen. And she didn’t seem to have a speck of makeup on, or, if she had, the sheen of sweat that coated her skin had washed it away.

“I’m sorry for my insensitive sister—”

“Calling someone a hobo isn’t insensitive.”

Casey could see the muscles tense in the manager’s jaw. She wet her lips and began speaking again, ignoring Anne’s protestation.

“I’m Max. I manage the motel. Let me check you in.”

“He doesn’t have any money, Max.”

“Anne, let me handle it.”

“It’s not just your decision, Max,” Anne said, drawing out Max’s name. “He left it to both of us. I get a say, too.”

“Go hire a lawyer then,” Max said.

Max leaned against the counter as if waiting for something to happen. Anne threw up her hands. She stalked out of the office, her phone close to her face as she furiously tapped into it. Once Anne was gone, Max walked around the counter and greeted Casey properly.

"Welcome to the Sunset. I hope you're still interested in staying."

"Yes," Casey said. He pulled out his most winning smile again. "I just... can't pay right now."

Surprisingly, Max was also unaffected by Casey's charm. She turned to the computer to check the screen, hardly noticing Casey desperately trying to keep eye contact with her.

"Mr. Pierson—"

"Casey. Please."

She looked up from the screen, giving Casey a second chance to smile at her. He leaned forward onto the counter, hoping he looked as unthreatening as possible – just a nice fella down on his luck. The corner of Max's mouth tugged up a little, but her eyes slid away from Casey's before it could become a full-blown smile.

"You actually work? Or do you always just flirt your way into a free fresh bed?"

Casey chuckled. Max wasn't going to be won over so easily. He switched tactics, deciding honesty, where possible, might work where charm hadn't. It was tricky – Max would have to be the type of person who cared about strangers. He launched into his tale, hoping she was.

"I work. I'm not above vacuuming and doing laundry either. But I do need a place to stay for a while. I can work in trade for a room."

Max drummed her fingers on the counter top. With each tap, the knot in his stomach that Anne had caused loosened. Casey was fairly confident Max would let him stay, but it wasn't because of his charm. If she wasn't a sympathetic woman, she

14

would have already decided to turn him away. Her indecision was a marker of a decent person. Besides, he thought, it would take someone sympathetic to put up with Anne.

She looked back to the computer, her mind made up, and tapped a few more times.

"Road noise bother you?"

Casey started. It was one thing to have confidence she'd let him stay, and another to have it actually happen. She looked up at him when he didn't answer right away.

"No," he said once he'd gathered his thoughts back. "But headlights might keep me up. Do you have blackout curtains?"

"We do. But I'll put you in a room that shouldn't have that problem in any case."

Max tapped a few more strokes on the keyboard, then turned to grab a key from the wall behind her. She gestured for Casey to follow her. He hauled his bag up to his shoulder and trotted out of the office after her.

He hadn't realized there were more rooms than the ten across the front of the building, but Max led him around the edge of the office to another row of rooms that stretched away from the road. They passed by a red pickup truck – not old, but not very new either – and a silver sedan of such a generic nature, Casey couldn't say with authority what make of car it was.

He hadn't seen any other cars in the lot, but he wasn't surprised by that either. Based on the way the motel looked, they weren't likely to have much by the way of reservations, and probably less from walk-ins. He followed Max almost to the end of the row of rooms. She stopped at the second to last room and fitted the key into the lock, opening the door.

"This one's yours," she said, handing him the key.

Casey marveled at the metal in his hand. Actual keys, and

not plastic cards, were a rarity, even among the older places like this motel. The thick plastic keychain reminded him, and anyone else who might see it, that the key belonged to the Sunset View Motel.

"Not much of a view of the sunset from these rooms," he joked.

"No," Max said. "But on the upside, not much of a view of the sunrise. Which happens right around seven a.m. whether you want it to or not. I'm guessing if the light of cars keeps you up, you're like me and the tiniest ray of sun is stronger than a cup of espresso."

"Thank you. I appreciate it," Casey said.

He entered the room and dropped his bag on the bed. The inside was surprisingly modern. He'd expected a wash of mustard yellows and pea greens: outdated shag carpet or linoleum, bedspreads that could stand up on their own, a bathroom with more mildew than grout. Instead he was greeted with fresh white linens, modern carpeting in an inoffensive beige with, if not luxurious, at least commercial grade pile that could withstand lots of traffic before losing its cushion. The walls were eggshell with wine-colored highlights. Ripples of light danced across one wall and Casey excitedly rushed to the back of the room where long blinds hung open, framing sliding glass doors.

"You have a pool!"

Max entered the room and joined him at the back. She slid open the blinds, then the door, leaving only the screen between Casey and the crystalline water glistening beyond. Casey was surprised he hadn't smelled chlorine the second he got off the pickup truck.

"I had it put in when I got the place," Max said.

"It's gigantic for a motel," Casey said without thinking. He turned to her quickly to apologize. "I'm not bashing motels or anything."

Max held up her hands to stop him.

"I wouldn't blame you if you were. Motels aren't known for their luxury. I get it. But it's the turd I was given. I need to shine it up good and offload it onto somebody who actually wants to run one."

Casey stepped away from the window and took in his room again. Now the look of it made sense; it'd been recently updated.

"You're selling," he said.

Max nodded.

"I've seen those home shows on TV," Casey said. "All that staging stuff. I didn't know motels did staging, too."

Max leaned up against the wall, pulled a cloth out of her pocket and started cleaning a smudge off the glass door.

"Kind of," she said. "I tried to sell it as soon Anne and I got it. I don't want the hassle of running a motel, and if it wasn't already obvious, Anne is not exactly well-suited for the hospitality industry."

"You don't say."

She shared a genuine smile with him, then went back to cleaning the door.

"No one would buy it," she said.

"I don't know much about this kind of thing," Casey said, "but it does seem like a weird place for a motel. What are we, five miles outside of the next biggest town?"

"Ten," Max said. "I suspect the reason my dad picked this place is the land was cheaper here than closer to Manistee. Even so, I hoped someone would see potential in the place. Campers stopping on their way to the UP. Families heading to the lake. And then in September, the leaf peepers show up."

"Leaf peepers?"

Max eyed Casey before answering.

"You aren't from around here. I thought that might be the case."

"I've been in Michigan before. But I wouldn't call myself familiar, exactly."

At least not with lingo, he thought. That would require hanging around somewhere long enough to make friends.

"Peepers are people who travel to see the changing leaves in the fall," Max explained. "Thousands go on driving tours through this area just to see them."

She tucked her cloth back into her pocket and put her hand on her hip. Everything about her expression told Casey something else was running through her head, something she didn't look inclined to share with him, even though it was clearly weighing on her.

"Anyway," she said. "The place needs a lot of work if it can even begin to attract that kind of crowd. That's where you come in, if you're up for it."

"Me?" Casey glanced around the room. "What else could you possibly do? This room looks immaculate. Exactly like the kind of room I'd expect from a nice, clean motel. Unless you mean the outside of the place?"

"I do, but not right away," Max said. "The rooms come first. Come on, I'll show you."

Max led him out of his room to one of the neighboring rooms. She fumbled in her pocket before fishing out a set of keys and opening the door. She nodded at Casey, indicating he should head in.

Before he'd even turned on the light, he had an idea of what he might see. The smell told him more than his eyes would in any case. Years of sweat and sex lingered in the air. Each step he took on the thin carpet beneath his feet kicked up remnants of tenants from years ago, along with an assortment of spores and molds.

He flipped on the light and blew out his breath in a rush.

"I didn't know they made shag that color," he said.

"I'll have you know that was a special request by my father," Max said. "He said sunshine made people spend more. Sunshine yellow carpeting. Sunshine yellow bedspreads. Sunshine yellow trim. If the sun has an asshole, it probably looks like this."

"The lighting's probably better, though," Casey said.

He looked over at her, a grin already plastered on his face. For a second, he thought he might've taken too familiar a tone with her. He'd been feeling like she was warming to him. But her expression remained blank, making him doubt his read of her – that was, until she started laughing so hard tears sprung to her eyes. With immense relief his feeling of mirth returned. He joined her, and they continued giggling for almost a full minute.

He would have stayed longer – cracking jokes about the hideous décor would be an easy way to get Max to warm up to him – but his nose began itching as if the air in the room was actively attacking it. He left, Max following him out, more to give his nose a rest than for any other reason.

"You could have put me up in one of these instead of the remodeled room," he said.

"No. I couldn't have. That's a crime against humanity. And the mattresses..." Max looked like she might say something else, but she broke eye contact again and focused on the closed door. "Anyway, this something you might want to do? I'll give you a decent hourly rate. Does sixteen sound alright?"

Casey couldn't answer right away. He was too surprised. After he regained some of his composure he cleared his throat.

"No one's ever—" He stopped himself. He didn't need too many questions. "That seems high. You could hire real workers at that rate."

Max smiled before heading off toward the office again.

"Pretty sure the work you do is real, too, Mr. Pierson."

"Casey," he said, calling after her.

She just waved her hand in the air in response. He watched her walk away longer than he should have, but she disappeared around the corner without a look back. She hadn't even asked him to start immediately. Another thing no one had ever given him – the benefit of the doubt. He'd always been asked to work first before being given anything of value.

He went back to his room and clicked on the AC. It hummed to life, filling the room with cool air that smelled faintly of plastic. Max really had updated the rooms, he thought. He slumped onto the bed and took off his dusty shoes before peeling off his sweaty socks and tossing them as far away as he could. Both his feet were covered in fresh blisters – one stretched across the surface of the ball of his left foot such that he could barely see where his foot ended and his toes began. He touched it gingerly, wincing in pain.

A ripple of light from the pool caught his eye and he looked out the sliding door before looking at his feet again. He rummaged through his bag and pulled out a suitable pair of shorts.

"I guess we wait a night before I begin the search," he said as he took one last look at his feet.

The sun had set more than an hour before Casey finally pulled himself out of the pool. He plopped down and stretched languorously on one of the bamboo lounge chairs. It was such a small luxury, but laying beside a motel pool at that moment made him feel like a rich man, if only for a short time.

The pool was surprisingly large for a motel, or a hotel for that matter. He didn't think he'd ever been anywhere that had a true Olympic-length pool, but here, at this dingy roadside motel, was a beautiful rectangle, complete with tiled blue lines making up four lanes. It wasn't even a standard chlorine pool – it was one of those exotic saltwater setups. He could smell chlorine, but only faintly. It was nothing like the overpowering chemical assault he'd encountered at every other dingy pool he'd visited. His eyes burned from the memory of those mildly toxic waters. It must have cost Max a fortune to install, and Casey wondered at the wisdom in such a decision.

The pool was surrounded on three sides by motel rooms. A small clearing with a swing set and a slide sat along the back – not much for families, but enough to put in a brochure. Beyond that was nothing but hills and trees. The whole setting was peaceful. The highway in front of the motel wasn't heavily travelled, and the building buffered the pool from too much noise. The glass doors to the rooms with their clean white curtains, the fluffy white towels stacked near the entrance, the bamboo furniture and the summer heat, together lent the whole place an almost tropical feel. He could imagine a family, landlocked in the Midwest, finding a lot to like about the motel.

As his mind drifted, he played with the drops of water pooling in the ridges on his stomach. The evening lighting around the pool made his olive skin look darker than normal. He liked the dramatic look it gave his abs, as if they'd been painted in rich oil colors. He ruffled up the dark curls trailing down from his belly button into his shorts to dry them out in the warm night air, then traced the shape of his muscles dreamily, half in and out of sleep.

When he heard a noise, he looked up to see Max coming toward the pool in a fuzzy white towel. He tried to wave hello, but his hand wouldn't move. He could only watch as she opened the gate in the wrought iron fencing surrounding the pool. He found he couldn't even turn his head, having to strain his eyes to follow her as she approached.

She stood beside the pool close to where he lay, smiled at him, then shrugged off the towel before diving in. Casey wasn't even surprised she was naked. It seemed right. He watched her for a while, swimming in the water playfully, until the air suddenly cooled. His skin prickled up into goosebumps. He moved to grab the towel Max had brought only to find it was gone.

The wind rustled through the leaves of the trees and Casey saw something out of the corner of his eye near the swing set. He stood slowly, checking the pool for Max. She was still there, smiling up at Casey as she drifted toward the edge where he was standing. A noise drew his attention back to the playground. One of the swings was moving as if a child had recently jumped off it. The sound of the metal chains swaying was far louder than it should have been.

"Max, go inside," he said.

But when he turned back to her, she was gone. A dark stain spread across the tiled rim of the pool where she'd been. It moved sluggishly, like it was thickening as it spread. When the stain reached the edge of the pool, it bulged, threatening to drop into the water.

"Max!" he shouted.

He was reaching down to touch the stain when a scream echoed out from the trees. He bolted upright and ran to the swing set, vaulting over the wrought iron fence. He stopped at the tree line, his every muscle tense. The faint, but clear, scent of lemon wafted through the air.

"Max?"

The only answer was the sound of clapping leaves. His nostrils flared. He smelled rot, festering and putrid, filling the air and suffocating his senses, destroying all hint of anything else. Under it all he searched, looking for some tiny sign of life he could trace.

He took a step into the woods. A low, unnatural growl came from the blackness under the trees. Casey took a shuddering breath.

"Luca?"

He waited a few seconds with no response.

"Noah?"

His voice was barely above a whisper. He stepped forward again, reaching into the darkness to feel his way. His hand brushed something cold and damp.

Casey screamed as he fell out of the poolside lounge chair. He looked up to discover Anne standing there, a confused expression on her face.

"You shouldn't sleep so close to the water," she said. "Especially if that's how you wake up."

Casey rubbed his face before glancing back at the playground. The swings were still.

"I was asleep."

"Yeah. I know," Anne said testily. "That's what I said. And we don't need the insurance hassle if you drown in our pool. Don't do that again. Also, I hope you showered before you got in there. It isn't a bath. It's a pool."

Casey clambered up from the ground. He glanced around the pool, looking for evidence of Max. He still couldn't be sure when the dream had started, but it was looking more and more like the whole thing was a figment.

"Did you need me for something?" he asked, trying to remain civil as he walked over to grab one of the towels.

He noticed Anne's annoyance at his use of the services the motel had to offer and grabbed a second one. She glared at him, but managed to bite back what she was going to say. She straightened up and examined her nails.

"Max wants to know if you have any dietary requirements."

"Dietary requirements?"

"Yes, asshole. Jesus. No wonder you need to hike around looking for nice, stupid people like my sister to take advantage of. Dietary requirements. Are you vegetarian? Vegan? Or maybe you just imbibe all your nutrients."

Casey tossed one of his towels over his shoulder, shooting her a smirk.

"No, I'm not a vegetarian."

"But the drunken homeless thing. You're not denying that?"

Casey smiled in answer and tried to walk past Anne. She stepped in between him and the gate, looking challengingly at him.

"How old are you, Anne?"

"What? What the fuck does that have to do with anything? I'm not jailbait, if that's what you're fishing for, you fucking creep."

Casey had difficulty not laughing in her face.

"No one will ever confuse you for jailbait, Anne."

It took a split second for his words to have an effect. Anne turned beet red and stormed away, slamming the gate as she went. With every step he took back to his room, Casey regretted letting Anne get under his skin. He hadn't intended to be mean to her. She was just really good at rousing his ire. He couldn't remember the last time someone had annoyed him so much he'd lashed out at them.

The cool air from his room hit him as he opened the sliding door. The clash with Anne disappeared from his mind as goosebumps broke out over his body. He looked back at the woods beyond the swings.

They can't know I'm here. Not yet.

After a few more seconds of staring, he closed the door on both the courtyard and the thought. He caught sight of himself in the full-length mirror as he dried off. Casey turned to get a better look at the tattoo on his back, touching the decades old ink. He wasn't worried Anne would think anything of them. She'd probably write it off as prison tattoos. He smiled at the thought as he pulled on a clean T-shirt.

A relaxed sigh escaped him when he finally fell back into the bed. He flipped on the TV. There was nothing on, as usual, but the droning sound was enough to lull him back into a light, dreamless sleep, which was what he was looking for. The knock on the door came before he had succumbed to a deeper resting state, and he grumpily got up.

He expected it was Anne, who had probably spent the last thirty minutes attempting to think up the wittiest and most biting of retorts and was now ready to deliver it. He was determined to let her say her piece without comment, so he could get back to being left alone for the night. When he opened the door to Max, standing there with a box of pizza and a six pack of root beer, his face cracked in a grateful smile.

"I'm sorry about earlier. With Anne," Max clarified as she handed him the box. "I'd just mixed a batch of mortar and you gotta use that stuff fast. Anne wanted to make the pizza call right then. So I sent her to you. I promise, that's the last time I'll do that, mortar be damned."

Casey was happy she'd come by. His head buzzed in a pleasant way as he stepped back from the doorway to let Max in, a huge grin on his face. She hesitated.

"Come on," he said. "I can't eat all this alone."

Max raised a lone eyebrow, causing Casey to laugh.

"Okay, okay. I could. I don't want to."

Max took one last look down the line of rooms before relenting. She came in and sat on the bed, cross-legged. Casey was glad she'd picked the location before he could suggest it. He wasn't looking forward to cramming around the tiny table nestled in the corner of the room, and asking her to sit on the bed with him sounded sleazy. He dropped down next to Max and opened the pizza box. A square pepperoni pizza steamed inside, still hot from the delivery. Max had come straight over with it.

"Here," she said, fishing some napkins out of her pocket. "We ran out of paper plates yesterday and I haven't gotten into town to get more yet."

Casey grabbed a slice while Max sorted the drinks. He balanced a can between his feet while Max chose her piece, picking one of the corners.

"Thanks for this." Casey popped open his root beer. The TV continued to babble on in the background. "I'm not sure it's fair that I'm already benefiting from our arrangement and you aren't. I'm ready to lend a hand right away. I'm good with mortar. You tiling?"

Max picked a piece of pepperoni off her pizza and popped it in her mouth. She was looking anywhere except into his eyes. Casey was suddenly afraid he'd made her uncomfortable by inviting her into his room. In fact, he wasn't exactly sure why he'd done it. He didn't typically try to make friends with the people he did odd jobs for. He was never around long enough for it to be worth the effort.

"Yes, I'm tiling," she said. "But I don't mind you resting up. You were in no shape to work today. I saw you get here, climbing out of the back of a pickup, limping like you'd been on your feet for days. You needed a break."

"I'm fine," Casey said reassuringly. He moved his soda and held up one of his feet. "My feet, as you can see, are also fine."

He patted the bottom of his smooth, pink foot. Max looked unconvinced, so he showed her the second one, too. Both looked healthy and strong.

"All right," Max said. "If you wanna work, I won't stop you. But you do need to eat something. I know you must be starving."

Casey bit into a piece of pizza with relish, earning a smile from Max. The pizza in the box slowly disappeared as they ate in silence. They'd polished off more than half the box by the time Casey was onto his second can of root beer. Max pushed the last two pieces toward him, and he took them gratefully. He finished them, then leaned back against the headboard and stretched his legs.

"I appreciate the work. It's very kind of you," he said. "Not many people would hire a guy who tumbled out of a truck bed without a hundred questions first. And even after I've answered them, most still decide I'm not worth the trouble."

He'd hoped to gauge her reaction – maybe get a little insight into why she'd been so generous to him. But her eyes were inscrutable; that was a particular kind of maddening that Casey wasn't fond of. He was used to knowing what people thought of him. On the road, with only the kindness of strangers to get him from one place to the next, it was essential he knew if someone had sinister intentions before he got into a car or went to their house.

It wasn't that he thought Max meant him harm, but he was bothered by the fact that she might think the reverse was true. His concern came not only from the knowledge that fearful people were less predictable, but also from a nagging notion that he wanted her to like him.

In a rare instance of connection, she held his gaze longer than normal. He felt as if she was scouring his brain, perhaps trying to figure him out as much as he was trying to figure her out.

"I think I'm a pretty good judge of character," Max said, finally breaking eye contact. "Anne disagrees. That's mostly because of my ex. About a year ago he left me. In Anne's view, that's proof I don't know people all that well."

"All because of one misjudgment?" Casey asked. "Seems unfair."

"She might have a point." Max looked at her left hand as if there was still a ring there. "But, I got fourteen good years before it went bad. I figure, even if I am wrong about you, I won't find out for fourteen years. Seems a pretty safe bet for me."

Casey shook his head with a smile and closed his eyes.

"What?" Max asked. "You about to tell me you're a monster?"

"No. Just imagining still working on this motel in fourteen years. That would be some kind of hell right there."

"The worst kind," she said with a chuckle.

An awkward silence filled the room. Casey wasn't sure if it was the direction the conversation had turned or if Max was just waiting for a good chance to see herself out.

"I'll do my best not to remind you of your ex," he said.

"I wouldn't worry about that," Max said. If the conversation about her past was too personal or bothered her, it didn't show. "You strike me as the kind of person who'd worry about real problems. My ex was the kind of guy who worried about things like... getting old."

"True enough. Everyone gets old," Casey said, "and there's literally nothing you can do about it. I like to tackle the things I can do something about."

"Basically what I told him. He still took off."

"Because he was scared of getting old?" Casey asked.

Max tugged at the bedspread absently. She looked guilty about something, and Casey had the strong sensation it was because she was speaking ill of her ex. It was a strange thing for her to feel guilty about, considering the guy left her.

"That's just my resentment coming through, maybe," Max said. "It makes it easier to accept, I suppose. Thinking it's fear that drove him off. It's easier to imagine that than it being a failing of mine. So I say he just got old and scared. Instead of a sports car or a risky hobby, he traded in his wife. At forty, I was too much a reminder of his mortality or something. So he picked out a new model. Twenty-four. Same age I was when we met. Maybe it makes him feel like he went back in time."

Casey shook his head in disbelief. The things people were afraid of always shocked him. Getting old was the last of his concerns. Leaving a person for no good reason was a privilege he couldn't even dream of.

"I expect he'll regret that decision in time," Casey said.

"Bold statement to make," Max said. "For all you know, I'm a monster."

"I think I'm a pretty good judge of character," Casey teased. "And I have a supernatural ability."

"You do, do you?"

"I can smell monsters. You aren't one."

"And my sister?"

"I can't smell bitches," he said without thinking.

It could have been a step too far, but fortunately, Max found it funny and full-on laughed. She stood and collected the garbage before walking to the door. Casey wished he could think of something to say to keep her from leaving. He'd been having fun chatting with her. Most of the people he met in his travels weren't as warm and open as Max. It wasn't just that, though; he'd actively enjoyed her company. But he could also feel a change in the room. Max had given him all she was willing to for the night. Casey didn't feel put off by it. She'd already spent a lot of time with him considering she didn't know him from Adam.

She turned to him just before leaving.

"I'm sorry about going into my personal stuff," Max said. "I swear I don't talk about my ex all the time. It's just..." She looked at her ring finger again. "Weird timing. It was my anniversary today."

"I liked it," Casey said, waving his hands to ward off the apology.

His statement was met with a quizzical expression from Max.

"That sounds creepy," Casey said, chuckling. "I mean, real talk. I don't get much of that. I mostly get all the inconsequential stuff people store up for when they meet someone they don't know. 'Where'd you go to school?' 'What do you do for a living?' 'Sure is hot these days.'"

This drew a knowing smile from Max.

"It's nice to have a real conversation with someone," he said.

Max didn't respond directly to his compliment. Casey couldn't tell if she was bashful or just uncomfortable with what he said. She just nodded and opened the door.

"Good night, Mr. Pierson. I'll be by in the morning around eight if that's okay with you."

"Casey. And yes, that sounds great." The door was almost closed when Casey remembered something he wanted to tell her. "Max?"

"Yeah?" Max said, popping her head back in to the room.

"Your sister's right. About trusting people who come wandering up out of the blue. Not everyone is just a guy looking for work and a place to stay. Some people mean you harm."

"They can give it a go. But I'm pretty good at handling trouble."

"Yeah," he said. "I bet you are. Good night."

Casey stared at the door for several minutes after it closed. He frowned as a sour feeling filled the pit of his stomach. He closed his eyes until it passed, rolling over and gripping his pillow between his arms. Thoughts swirled through his head with abandon, making sleep hard to reach. He kept returning to the dream. Try as he might, he could not dislodge the feeling that he was putting Max and Anne in danger by being there.

His concern made no sense – he'd just arrived. They couldn't know he was near, and even if they suspected he was close, they wouldn't know exactly where he was staying. They'd have to track him down faster than he tracked them down.

Still, he worried. Maybe it's because he was starting to get to know Max. In the past, he'd avoided such complications. He'd always assumed his stays in places were temporary enough no one he'd met would become collateral damage. He wasn't used to caring so much.

He rolled onto his back and forced himself to breathe evenly, focusing on what he had to do. Tomorrow, he'd keep his head down and do his work. He could do that. He could ignore Max and concentrate on the work. Then tomorrow night, he'd start the search.

In the abstract, it didn't seem like a hard thing to plan out.

At least until he closed his eyes and let all his mental processing power be consumed by his nose. The pizza smell was still overpowering, but his nose wasn't distracted by that. It found the faint lemon scent in the chaos of the motel room and focused on it. Casey put his hands behind his head, eyes still closed, and smiled wistfully. He was exhausted enough that he slipped into a semi-conscious state within seconds. After an hour of pleasant, dreamlike thoughts that Casey was only peripherally aware and in charge of, he finally fell into a deep sleep.

TWO

The light didn't manage to creep into Casey's room until full on dawn. He woke just after seven, the crust in the corner of his eyes alerting him to the fact that he should have showered after his swim. He tipped the standard issue motel clock upright, allowing the glowing red numbers to alert the world that it was seven fifteen.

An ache in his foot let Casey know he'd had fitful sleep. The bedsheet had twisted completely around his leg from his tossing and turning. As he unwound the sheet and massaged his calf to get the blood flowing into his foot properly, a shadow passed by the door to his room. He wrapped the sheet around himself as a makeshift robe before peeking out the window. Max was retreating toward the office, her back to him, her wet hair tied up in a pony tail, ready for a day's labor.

He leaned against the door wearily, rubbing his face, and bolstering his mind for the day ahead. Concentrating on his upcoming tasks was already difficult – he couldn't stop thinking about how little time he might have to find anything of note before they spooked and moved on. He couldn't let them get away again. Feeling anxious wouldn't help him, he finally decided. It was time to get to work and show Max her trust in him wasn't unwarranted. He tossed the sheet on the bed and went to the shower.

Like the rest of the room, it was modern and fresh looking. Beige tiling with brown accents lined the floors and walls. There was no tub, but the glass-walled shower was large. Perfect, white, fluffy washcloths were folded into decorative cones on the counter. Casey tugged at one and it unfurled. As his fingers ran over the soft terry cloth, he imagined Max preparing the bathroom, placing each towel and cloth just so. He smiled at the thought, and suddenly realized he hadn't had a chance to see the un-remodeled bathrooms. They were probably washed in more yellows to match the rest of the rooms. He'd never really thought about how garish something could be made to look just by overloading on one color.

He hopped into the shower and kept the temperature tepid. Mid-August was one of the warmest times for the Midwest, and the day was already proving to be no exception. He felt too warm, even with the AC going and the water running over him. The idea of a hot shower was completely unappealing.

The water woke him better than a cup of coffee. He finished quickly, eager to start the day on the right foot. He was nearly dressed when the knock came at his door at a quarter after eight on the dot. He shuffled to the door in bare feet.

"Breakfast by the pool," Max said, after he opened the door. "If you're interested that is."

"I am," Casey said with a grin.

"You sure? Anne's there, too."

Casey leaned on the door frame, crossing his arms. Max had

been more than accommodating. She'd been outright generous. It felt petty of him to complain too much about Anne.

"She's your sister. I'll do my best to be friendly," he said, pausing. "For your sake."

His response elicited a wry look from Max.

"If I don't have to like her, you certainly don't," she said. The casual mirth that danced in her eyes was replaced with a stern air. "But she is my sister, which means so long as she doesn't commit some heinous crime against another person, I'll love her until she dies. That means I can't let people pick on her unprovoked. Or, you know, threaten her in some way if she pisses them off."

The look she was giving him made Casey uncomfortable. He could tell she was waiting for a response that would satisfy her – that would quench a fear he could smell in her. She was heavily hinting that something was wrong, and it took Casey a few seconds to puzzle it out. Anne must have said something to Max about the conversation they'd had at the pool the night before.

He'd been unkind to Anne, but he hadn't been violent or threatening. He recognized it was possible that Anne felt differently about the altercation and might have passed that on. Fear that Max would give him the boot blossomed in him. He didn't want to leave – for several reasons, a couple he didn't want to confront just then – but he knew for certain he didn't want to leave.

Max was giving him a chance to fix it – another round of generosity he didn't think he deserved. He wasn't about to waste it. He nodded, trying his best to show his sincerity.

"I didn't want to be mean to her. I promise. It was a long day and—"

Max held up her hand to stop him from explaining further.

"She won't tell me what you said."

A silence hung in the air between them.

She thinks I've threatened Anne, he thought.

He could imagine several things a person might say that would inspire such fear – something so dreadful that it may as well have been an assault. He'd heard enough threats over the years that he was familiar with their power.

There was no doubt in Casey's mind that Max was worried she'd made a mistake and was reconsidering letting him stay. He had to fix this.

Honesty was the only way forward. Casey hesitated before telling the whole truth – not because he didn't think it would work, but because he was concerned it might hurt Max personally.

He recalled their conversation over pizza from the night before. Max had suggested her husband had left her because she'd gotten too old. Her confidence could be a front, disguising insecurities about any number of things. Casey decided it was a risk he had to take. Lying now, when Max was so agitated, would only further undermine the trust she'd given him.

"I might've... I implied she was old," he said.

It took several seconds for Max to react. A slow smile spread across her face as she rubbed her forehead with one hand. Casey hadn't fully realized how tense she'd been until that moment, when her whole posture relaxed. The relief came out of her in a laugh mixed with a sigh.

"You told her she was old?"

"Uh... kind of. She suggested I was a pedophile who was after her. I told her no one could confuse her for jailbait."

Saying it out loud again, Casey blushed. He was embarrassed he'd let Anne get under his skin, and even more embarrassed Max now knew about it. It was a juvenile jab. He should've known better.

"I'm glad to hear it," Max said.

"You're glad I called her old?"

"I'm glad you didn't threaten her."

"Oh." Casey considered Max's face carefully. He spoke his next words with a raw honesty that couldn't be mistaken. "No. I would never."

"I see that now," Max said. "You might want to steer clear of the old thing from now on though."

"I will. To be honest, I didn't think it would cut that deep."

Max sighed in a way that made Casey think it was something she had heard way too much about.

"She's on the other side of the 'cusp.'" Max said, using air quotes when she said "cusp."

"The cusp?"

"It means, at thirty-six, she's closer to forty than thirty. And apparently that means her life is over."

"I guess I better get to living before I die." Casey looked at an imaginary watch on his wrist. "Let's see. I have a few months left before my life is over, too. I'll have to check my bucket list and get started on that."

"I hope remodeling a motel is on that list."

"No," Casey said. "But ridding the world of sunshine yellow shag carpeting is."

He pushed his hands into his pockets and gave Max a playful look. The last of the tension between them vanished as Max smirked.

"I'll see you by the pool, Mr. Pierson."

"Casey."

"Sure." Max started to go but stopped as if she'd just

remembered something. "Don't mention you're younger than Anne. It won't go over well."

"It's just a few months."

"All the same, not a good idea."

She walked away without another word. Casey let the heavy door close on its own as he stepped back into his room. He dumped the contents of his duffle bag onto the bed and sorted through the clothes until he found a pair of cleanish socks. They were the least crusty of all his socks, yet still stiff enough that it took some effort to pull them on. It was disgusting, but the rest of the socks were as bad as the pair he'd discarded in the corner of the room. He'd need to find a place to do laundry – something else to ask Max about.

Casey wandered out of his room through the poolside door to find Max and Anne sitting at a patio table under a pastel umbrella. Max greeted him with a smile. Anne did her best to avoid looking at him at all. If there was any breakfast banter before he'd arrived, he'd killed it simply by showing up.

He took the seat closest to Max, leaving a comfortable gap between him and Anne. Her icy, sullen look told him he'd made the right choice. Several paper wrapped packages were in the center of the table. He double-checked before he made his choice; both women already had something in front of them. He picked up what looked like a burrito and sniffed it before unwrapping it. He chewed quietly, trying not to draw attention to himself lest he inadvertently start an argument with Anne.

He popped on a pair of dark sunglasses, in part because the morning sun baked the tidy courtyard unhindered by any cloud, but mostly because it allowed him more freedom when looking over his breakfast companions. He didn't feel the need to dodge Anne's eyes from behind the mirrored lenses, which made eating less strained.

The two couldn't be more different, he thought. Anne was meticulously made up. Every stroke of makeup was perfect, every strand of chestnut hair in its place. Casey didn't even want to imagine how long it took her to do it. He'd only ever tried to style his hair once. After thirty minutes he'd given up trying to look like the man in the glossy magazine picture he was using, even though he was certain they had the same kind of hair. Once again, Anne was clad in trendy clothes. He watched enough television in his wandering he was capable of recognizing brands that were hot, though they were just a bit faded for something so current.

Max was more comfortable looking in her cargo shorts and tank top. Her clothes were stained with paint and construction materials. Her light brown hair was tied up in a messy ponytail and her lean, pale legs stretched out in the sun, her feet in sneakers that looked like they'd seen the end of the world and come back again to tell the story. In contrast to Anne's deeply tanned skin and carefully pedicured toes peeking out from tiny, pink flip flops, Max's comfortable practicality was more attractive to Casey.

The silence dragged on. Normally, Casey wouldn't have been bothered by it. Surprising even himself, he spoke up in an attempt at cordiality.

He poked the steel cable that attached the table to the wrought iron fencing around the pool.

"I've always wondered why hotels and motels tied their tables down. Is there a black market for run of the mill patio furniture I don't know about?"

He looked between them both, sporting a friendly smile, but Anne pretended not to hear him.

"We didn't do it so much to keep them from being stolen," Max said. "The insurance asked us to do it. For the pool. The guy said people hurt themselves in pools like this, dragging everything they can into them. So, it all has to be tied down."

"People take the tables into the pool?" Casey asked.

Max shrugged in reply. Then things went back to being quiet again. His inoffensive banter hadn't had the effect he'd wanted; Anne hadn't even looked up from her phone once.

He looked away from them both as he drank down a miniature carton of juice, focusing on the woods beyond the swing set. So much of his effort was concentrated on the woods, he didn't even hear Anne get up to leave. When Max tapped him on the arm, he almost fell out of his chair.

"Didn't mean to wake you," Max joked. "We should get started on the rooms. I've already started the AC in room six. Should be ready for us to lay some tile."

Casey followed Max through the poolside doors into room six. Unlike the bright yellow room she'd shown him yesterday, room six was already gutted. The carpeting had been torn out, leaving only the cement foundation behind. The walls had been painted over, but there were no furnishings or lighting other than the ceiling fixtures.

"Are you doing them one at a time then?" he asked.

"Kind of. Half the rooms are completely done, like yours. The rest are in various states of destruction, with a half dozen I haven't even touched yet. I choose what to do based on what I can stand. First I tear out all the stuff from a room and toss it in the dumpster. Then the paint. Then the tiling and fixtures. Once all the dusty work is done I put the carpeting down. Then all the furniture comes in."

Max stopped explaining and looked around the empty room.

"Sometimes, when I feel like the mold from the carpeting I've torn up and the chemicals in the paint I'm putting on the wall are fighting over who gets the scraps of my brain matter, I need a break. So I switch to slowly petrifying my lungs with grout dust." She looked over at Casey and patted him on the shoulder. "Sixteen an hour is not overpaying you. But if you're willing to help out for that, I'd be happy."

In answer, Casey picked up a dust mask and fitted it over his nose and mouth.

"Where do I start?"

Most of the day was gone, the sun hanging low in the western sky. It was well past lunch and quickly running in to dinner time, but Casey hadn't even noticed. He'd spent the morning helping Max out, back buttering tiles and mixing mortar and grout. He'd been enjoying it – more than he'd wanted to. He'd mostly kept the conversation light, trying to concentrate on the work. He never brought up anything personal, keeping to small talk about what he knew and needed to learn when it came to being a handyman. Max was easy to listen to, and she seemed happy to have the company.

He'd been happily toiling for a few hours before Casey realized a real problem was growing, nurtured by the close working conditions between him and Max. A feeling he'd been willfully ignoring up until then drew his eyes to a drop of sweat near Max's hairline. She was bent over in front of him, placing tiles. The drop edged down her neck until it hit her shoulder, diverting down her clavicle. Casey managed to tear his gaze away before Max caught sight of him staring, but that hadn't stopped the room from feeling too small, the temperature from being too high, and the air from being too stuffy.

Silently cursing, he made a hasty retreat, citing the need for some fresh air. Max helpfully suggested he could move furniture to the dumpster, which would give him some time outside. It was too convenient an out for Casey to dismiss it.

Being outside had helped bring his focus back to his task, so much so that Casey was able to write off his leering as a side effect of being alone on the road for too long. Covered in dust, mold and sweat, he hauled carpet and mattresses to the oversized, industrial dumpster around the side of the motel. He'd completely cleared out three rooms before Max came to find him.

He was on the fourth room, tearing up a chunk of carpet when he heard the door open. Max stood there with a brown paper bag in her hand. She went to the AC unit and clicked it on.

"You didn't turn on the AC? You're gonna get heat stroke," she scolded him.

She tossed him a rag from her pocket. He drew it across his brow before pulling off his dust mask.

"I'll be okay. Been making sure to drink." He tucked the rag into his jean's pocket and walked over to her. "You need help with something?"

Max held up the paper bag. The word "Lunch" was written on it in marker.

"Last I saw you, you were in eight. I left this on the table in there. Not a fan of ham and cheese?"

Casey took the bag with an apologetic look. He opened it to see a bag of chips, a soda and a sandwich.

"I'm so sorry, Max. I didn't even see it. Or maybe I did, since I took that table out of the room, but I don't think it registered."

"It's okay. But you must be starving."

"I always am," Casey said, pulling the sandwich out of the bag and opening it. "I'm used to ignoring it though."

In his rush to eat, he missed the concerned expression that crossed Max's face. By the time he looked up at her to smile in thanks, she was checking out the room.

"You worked hard today," she said. "A ham sandwich isn't gonna cut it. Let's stop for the day and get something more substantial in you."

"Actually," Casey said around a mouthful of sandwich, "if it's at all possible, I'd appreciate a lift into town. I can grab something while I'm there."

"Manistee?"

"Yes," Casey said. He could tell Max was confused by the sudden request. "I—You're worried what I'm up to."

Max shrugged, but she didn't deny it. Casey knew this was bound to happen eventually. Max had been more tolerant than most, perhaps even the most tolerant person he'd ever met. But he guessed she also knew people in Manistee – was maybe even close to some of them. She didn't really know him at all.

"Have you looked into me yet?" he asked, keeping his voice even.

He knew the answer. Max wasn't foolish.

"You know I did," Max replied. "I found your mugshot. But trespassing in a state park after dark is hardly something that follows someone. And you're a man who looks like he's being followed. But it's not my business. Not unless you want help."

She paused, clearly waiting to see if he'd take her up on her offer. When he didn't, she continued.

"I let you stay here because I can handle whatever comes up that road after you. But I know the people in this area. They don't need more trouble."

He wished he could reassure her, tell her she had nothing to worry about, and that the people of Manistee needn't worry either, at least not about him, but he knew there was no way he could lie to her. Even if he could get over the fact that lying would make him feel like complete shit, he was sure she'd see through it. She was shrewder than she let on, more observant that most and worst of all, she was being kind to him despite his shady circumstances.

Her willingness to help him, knowing so very little about his situation, ate at his conscience. Her generosity would only get increase the closer they got to true friendship. Her confidence would blind her to the full danger of doing so.

She probably could take on most trouble coming down the road. Everything about her pointed to the fact that she was tough and resourceful. The problem was, the trouble that followed Casey wasn't typical at all. Casey wasn't sure anyone could handle it – not even Max.

He straightened. Knowing what he had to do didn't make it any easier, but it had to be done. He could already tell that Max was the type of person who would put herself in danger to help others. She'd offered just that not minutes before. If he stuck around, she'd get into trouble.

It hurt him to do so, but he had to distance himself from Max. He had to make himself someone she no longer wanted to help out. She wouldn't be safe otherwise, and that was something he was unwilling to live with. His desire to shield her from his troubles gave him the strength to do what he did next.

His back stiff, his gaze cool, he brushed past her.

"I'll need my pay for today," he said, his tone harsh. He grew uncomfortable as the words left his mouth, but he soldiered on. "I can pick it up at the desk, then I'll be out of your hair. We agreed on sixteen an hour but I only need fifty bucks. The rest should cover the room for the night I stayed."

He started toward his room without looking back. His teeth ground together, punctuating his unhappiness with himself and his situation. Max didn't call after him or try to stop him. He was glad of it.

He loathed being mean, but it was better this way. He was too close to the end of his nightmare – he'd spent too long on the hunt to throw away all the ground he'd gained over selfish reasons. As fun as it was to imagine whiling away the evenings with a friend, he had to finish the job he'd started. And if Max died because he put her in danger, he'd never forgive himself.

When he got back to his room he showered up, taking time to scrub every part. If he wanted to keep what little cash he'd earned up, he'd need to resort to alternative means of earning his lodging – means that would be hindered if he didn't look and smell his best. It wasn't his favorite way to earn his keep, but it was faster, and despite the physical intimacy it often required, sleeping with someone usually came with less questions, not more.

Before he left the room, he tidied it until it looked like no one had been there, aside from the dirty towels. He considered asking about the laundry facilities, thinking he could at least toss the linens in so Max wouldn't have that trouble, but decided against it. He was trying to be brusque, after all.

He left his room, his duffle bag over his shoulder, and headed to the office. The red truck wasn't parked near his room. He hoped that meant Max had taken off. His thoughts seemed to be confirmed when he got to the office. Anne was the only one there, and, for once, he was glad to see her.

"Checking out?" she asked.

Oddly, she didn't seem happy. Casey had been sure she'd at least gloat about it. But Anne was surly as ever, as if his checking out was no better than his staying.

"Yes," he said, setting his room key on the counter. "Did Max—"

Anne grabbed an envelope from somewhere under the counter and snapped it open with a flick of her wrist, cutting him off mid-sentence. She pushed a button on the cash register – an old fashioned one, the buttons raised up high off the keyboard. Casey didn't catch how much she grabbed; she'd flipped through the bills too quickly for him to keep up before hastily shoving them into the envelope. With a glare, she slammed the drawer shut and slid the envelope across to him.

Casey opened it up and counted out seven twenties and four ones.

"You're counting it? Don't trust me?"

"This is too much," he said, trying to hand it back.

Anne wasn't having any of it. If anything, her glare grew harsher.

"You're not only an asshole, you're an idiot. Good to know. Max said you worked eight hours. You agreed on sixteen an hour. That's a hundred forty-four. Paid in full."

Anne snatched the key from the counter and hung it on the wall. She turned back to face him, crossing her arms defiantly. Casey just stared at her. He started to correct her but thought better of it. It was best not to antagonize Anne further when all he wanted was to leave.

"How much for the room?" Casey asked, doing his level best to remain unagitated.

"The room was part of the deal. You were getting to stay here free as long as you helped out. It was a sweet deal for you, but your dumb ass thinks you can wing it out there on a hundred forty bucks. Good luck with that."

Casey folded up the money and put it in his pocket. He looked guiltily around the office, not sure why he was dallying. This was what he wanted, after all.

"Will you tell Max thank you for me?" he asked.

Despite being futile, he made the gesture. Even if Anne told her, Casey had little hope Max would think much of it. And it was unlikely Anne would pass on the message in any case.

"Tell her yourself. She's waiting out there to give you a ride into town."

"What?"

"Yeah. She's nice. Too fucking nice for the likes of you."

Casey paused in the doorway. He glanced to the left towards the highway and, sure enough, the red pickup was sitting there, idling.

"You know what, Anne? You're right about that."

Anne sneered before returning to whatever was so absorbing on her phone. Casey was about to head out when he realized he needed to know where to go. He had a feeling Anne would be more familiar with the type of place he was looking for than Max. He turned back around and leaned on the counter, relishing the look of disgust on Anne's face when he did so.

"What now?"

"I'm wondering if you could suggest a place I might go to… meet someone."

Casey didn't think it was possible for Anne's face to scrunch up any tighter.

"What?"

"I'm sure I don't have to spell this out. Not to you."

"Go. To. Hell."

"So you do know what I'm asking about," he said. "Good. Where should I go?"

"Don't you have a phone? Use Tinder, fuck face. I'm not going to help you find a hook-up for the night."

"You're such a charming woman, Anne." Casey's voice dripped with faux geniality. "I do not have a phone. But I've learned that, in little towns like these, you don't really need one. You just need to know where to go."

Anne looked like she might pick up the whole countertop and smash it over his head. What she didn't look like was someone who planned to help Casey out for one second – not for anything.

"I guess I'll ask Max then. Thanks for all your help."

Anne's face turned red. Casey spun around and headed for the door again, counting down his steps. He'd hoped he gambled correctly. He hoped, that despite the way she acted, Anne wouldn't want his question to land at Max's feet. Sibling love was a thing he understood well.

"Wait," Anne said. "Arnold's. Off fifth street. Don't tell Max that's where you're going. Have her drop you at the supermarket off the highway. It's six blocks away. Just head north from the parking lot."

"Thanks, Anne. You're a peach."

He heard a faint, "asshole" float his way before the door closed behind him.

The sun was almost completely gone from the sky. Cicadas and frogs filled the air with song. The sounds were a comfort to Casey; they meant all was right with the world, even if he was actively tearing down any goodwill he'd earned. The tiny creatures going about their nightly routine reminded him of his duty – one normal night, eating pizza on a bed with pleasant conversation would have to be enough for now. He just had to make it through the ride into town without endangering anyone any further. Just the one ride, then they'd both be safe again.

THREE

Casey approached the truck. The engine hummed, as healthy a sound as a vehicle could make, but Max wasn't inside. She'd opted for a no-frills model based on what Casey could see of the interior. It made him smile to think of Max at the car lot, explaining to a salesman that no, she knew exactly what she wanted, and no, that did not include heated seats.

"Ready to go?" Max asked.

Her voice startled him. Casey looked up to see her standing near the driver's side of the truck. She looked even more distant than usual, and it pained him to think he'd hurt her feelings. He started to smile, his body unconsciously trying to undo the damage to what little relationship they'd built, before he remembered he'd wanted it to be like this. He nodded curtly then tossed his duffle bag in the back of the truck. He hopped inside and tried not to overthink things.

He kept his eyes forward and buckled up while Max got in. When the truck didn't move, he was forced to look at her to see what was wrong, only to find her staring at him intently.

"You have a destination in mind?" she asked.

"Uh..." he stumbled. He wasn't sure what he expected from Max. Cold indifference wasn't on the list, he was sure of that. "Anne said there was a grocery store off the highway. She said you'd know it."

"I do. That where you want to go?"

"Yes."

Without further question, Max put the truck in gear and pulled onto the lonely two-lane highway in front of the motel. The minutes flitted by in silence feeling more like hours. Casey thought he could make the trip – he thought he could sit in the air-conditioned cab of the truck and not say a word the whole way – but when confronted with the reality of it, he discovered the idea that Max might be angry or upset at him was an unbearable weight.

"It's ten miles to Manistee?" he asked.

"Closer to twelve," Max said.

She offered no further conversation. Now Casey was sure she was upset with him. His concern morphed into annoyance – not at Max, but at himself. He couldn't understand why it bothered him so much. He hardly knew her. He'd been doing this for nearly twenty years and he'd never cared who he left behind, or who he'd upset before. There were likely dozens, if not hundreds in his wake that felt betrayed, or taken advantage of – people who he'd needed until he didn't anymore. Max was just another in a long line of well-intentioned people.

He stared out the window at the passing trees. At night, they took on the form of a single dark shadow looming over the highway. He let the silence stretch out between Max and him and solidify into a wall. He had to convince himself, once again, that this was the best and only way forward. His impulses were to do the opposite, and he struggled with why that was. By the time they pulled into the parking lot of the supermarket, the war being waged in his head caused the ache in his chest had grown into full blown pain. He practically fell out of the truck in his rush to get away from the silence within.

He'd just grabbed his bag from the truck bed when he felt Max come up beside him. Reluctantly, he lifted his eyes to meet hers. Her face looked hard, but not angry. There was something else there, something he couldn't quite read, but he knew anger enough to know that wasn't it.

"You don't have a phone," she said.

"No. When you're living like I do..."

He shrugged, knowing she'd understand without more of an explanation. When she handed him the yellow-jeweled brick, it took him far too long to register what it was, exactly. He turned it over in his hand before it dawned on him what Max was giving him.

"It's been a long time since I met someone who didn't have a phone," Max said. "Even for a drifter like you, it's a little weird."

"I just... Why is this so yellow? And shiny?"

"It's Anne's old phone. She's an accessorizer, so the phone matches the motel color scheme. It's not that old a model, but she had to get rid of it before the summer started. The jewels, if I recall correctly, are passé. Or something. She follows that stuff, I don't. Her new phone is less dazzling than that one."

"Aren't you afraid I'll rack up charges on it?" Casey asked. "Drive you broke?"

"I think the only way Anne could spend more time on her phone is if she could use it in her sleep. There's no way I'd get a phone plan that wasn't unlimited everything. It's paid up through the month. After that, you'll have to sign it up yourself. There are stores here, or everywhere for that matter, where you can buy another month."

Casey turned the phone over in his hand. He wasn't completely unfamiliar with them, having used them from time to time. He pressed a button on the side to light up the screen. A variety of icons he didn't think he'd ever use surrounded the only one that he thought he would. In the middle of the screen was a picture of Max standing in front of the Motel. He touched it, causing the picture to fill the screen. She was smiling in the shot.

Max's phone blared out a singsong ringtone that Casey didn't recognize. She pulled it out of her pocket and answered.

"As you can see, that's me," she said into her phone.

She put her phone back away while Casey stared at the picture.

"I don't deserve this," he mumbled.

"It's got nothing to do with deserving, Mr. Pierson. There's been some trouble around here this summer." Casey looked up at this news, his interest piqued. "I don't mean the kind of trouble that normally comes to places like this," Max said. "I mean the kind of trouble where that happens."

Max pointed at a woman who was posting missing persons signs up near the front of the store. Casey looked from the signs to Max. For a practical woman, she seemed wildly overconcerned about something unrelated to him.

"There are missing people everywhere," Casey said. "And men aren't typically abducted. Healthy men in their thirties even less so. I don't think you need to worry about me."

"So you say. I'd rest better knowing you could call if you got into trouble."

"Okay," Casey said. He looked at the phone one more time before shoving it in his pocket, secretly pleased she'd given it to him. "And really, you can call me Casey."

"No. I don't think so. You've made it pretty clear you'd like to be Mr. Pierson to me."

Her words felt like a punch to the gut. He flinched when she closed the door to the truck. She was truly upset with him. He could feel it now, coming off her in waves. Her reaction was stronger than it should have been considering they'd only barely approached the edge of friendship.

The too personal talk – that had to be it, he thought. He'd encouraged it. Another uncharacteristic bit of behavior from him. Why had he done that? It complicated things under the best of circumstances.

It bothered Casey to no end that her anger continued to dominate his thoughts. He'd wanted her to be upset with him; he'd forced the issue. It was simple cause and effect. It had worked like he wanted. So why was it so hard to move past it?

The tug of war inside his head was confusing and unexpected. Becoming attached to people, especially so quickly, was unfamiliar territory for him. For the first time he could recall, his motivations were murky. He had no clue what he wanted from her, and even less clue what she might want from him.

He briefly wondered if all his feelings could be explained by Max's unreadable nature. Normally, reading women was his strong suit. But asking Max point blank if her anger was due to more than misplaced empathy would only dredge up something he wasn't prepared to deal with.

This emotional limbo was why he purposefully never made friends. There was no controlling how attached people got and, obviously, despite how intently he was trying, it was hard to ignore natural chemistry. This was why he didn't normally invite people into his room or have meals with them. He made a mental note not to flirt so much in the future.

No, that wouldn't have worked, Casey thought, finally admitting what he'd been denying since he met Max. He'd have ignored that rule the second he met her.

Max gave him one last look before heading into the store, as if to give him a chance to change his mind about leaving her generous offer of work and a place to stay on the table. It wasn't an option for him – not anymore. If his suspicions were true, and he was attracted to Max, it would only make things more dangerous for her. He had to push on with his plan, no matter how tempting it was to apologize to her and head back to the motel. He only needed to recall the ill omen from the night before to know that was true.

They were close – closer than they'd ever been. The dream had all but confirmed it for him. And if he was dreaming about them, they were surely dreaming about him. It wouldn't take them long to find him. He couldn't risk sating his curiosity about something so nebulous as a potential relationship, especially one with so little evidence of even existing – not when they were so near. Yes, he could admit to himself the idea of spending more time with Max might result in something far more meaningful than hooking up with a random townie from the local bar scene. Whether or not that would evolve into something any more meaningful than a fun roll in the hay was not worth the chance that more people would die.

Especially if one of those people ended up being her, he reminded himself.

"Don't forget the paper plates," he said, finally making up his mind.

Then he breezed past her toward the store. It was unkind, but it had to be done, though he did mentally curse himself for choosing a grocery store as his drop off point. He decided in that moment he'd have to carry on with the charade and go inside and buy something. He couldn't very well walk north toward the bar Anne had pointed him to – at least, not without Max finding out he was being deceptive.

Being mean enough to keep Max safe was one thing but being cruel was a line he wasn't willing to cross. There was a tiny chance things could all work out. He was shocked to find himself even thinking about it, but there it was: a pinprick of hope nestled in his darkly entangled mind. That thought, far-fetched as it was, kept him from burning all his bridges back to Max.

He mentally made a list of things he could pick up in the store that might be useful but wouldn't degrade his financial situation significantly. Condoms were on the list, but he decided that was another thing he'd rather Max not see him buy. He could meander until she was done. That was his best option.

A stack of hand baskets teetered near where the woman was posting the missing person signs. He stopped to grab one when the woman turned and smiled. He was confused by the look of recognition on her face, until he realized she was looking past him toward Max.

"Max, I'm glad you're here. Would you—"

The woman's hand shook as she held out several flyers with a young man's picture on them. The boy was in a letterman's jacket. He looked to be about sixteen or perhaps seventeen, based on the number of letters on the jacket and what Casey vaguely remembered about high school. He was brown-haired and blue-eyed, and Casey imagined he would have been popular with the girls. The smile on his face was cocky, the kind of assurance that comes naturally from being a young man with good looks. Casey knew the look well.

"Of course, Miriam," Max said, taking the flyers.

Casey pretended to fiddle with the baskets, buying time so

he could listen in. The woman, Miriam, looked haggard and on the verge of tears. Her pockets bulged with crumpled paper. He watched quietly as Max reached up and touched the remnants of a flyer that had been torn down.

"Miriam?" she asked.

Miriam, who bore a striking resemblance to the young man in the flyers she was putting up, began to break down.

"They think my George killed her, Max. They say he's on the lam. I don't know what to do. All my friends ignore my calls. I don't know what to do. Bob is the only one who'll let me put these up anymore!"

Miriam fell into Max, her face already streaming with tears. A man came rushing out of the store. He was stocky, but in that way some men get when they've settled down. A little soft to cover the hard, but underneath the pumping blood of a teenaged sports star still flowed somewhere, waiting for any opportunity to rise to the occasion and be the local hero again.

"Miriam," the man said, running up to her. He hardly noticed Max. "Is everything okay?"

"I think she could use some coffee, Bob," Max said.

Bob appeared to see Max for the first time. He looked up at her and nodded mutely before ushering them both into the store. The automatic doors closed behind them, leaving Casey outside alone. He looked up at the bulletin board covered with notices and approached it.

A couple of prominent missing persons signs hung alongside the standard announcements of sales and church dinners. They were of the same girl – Sarah Linkman. Like the young man in the other flyer, she was attractive, a youthful glow shining out from her smile. In her picture she was in a cheerleading uniform, sitting in the grass, the pleated skirt spread out to show off the alternating navy and gold colors of each segment, a pom-pom in each hand. She had red hair, green eyes and a dazzling smile.

Missing: Sarah Linkman

Description: Age 17. Red hair. Green eyes. 5'4". 112 pounds. Wearing men's letterman jacket from Manistee High School, jeans and a green blouse.

Last seen August 9th: Sarah was last seen heading to Bear Track Campground in a white 2015 Ford F-150. Her travelling companion was George Cunningham, age 18, brown hair, blue eyes 6'1", 203 pounds.

Casey skimmed past the section about who to call if Sarah was seen, searching for more pertinent details, only to find nothing of interest. He'd studied many such posters over the years. They never had information relevant to his search, but he always looked, just in case. He started to head into the store when he noticed a crumpled piece of paper on the ground. He picked it up and spread it out.

It was one of the missing person's flyers Miriam was posting for her son, George, only this one had been defaced. Someone had crossed out "Missing" and written "Murderer" in its place. Several other unpleasant things were written over George's face. Casey balled it up and tossed it in the trash just outside the doors.

He continued into the store, casting about to see if Max was anywhere near the section he needed the most. Casey spied her at the front with Miriam, Bob and another man he hadn't seen come in. He made his way quickly through the store. After finding the condoms, he hustled to the front to check out, hoping Max wouldn't be nearby when he did. When he got to the front of the store, she was nowhere to be seen, but Miriam was still there, sitting on a bench, a cup of something steaming in her hand.

Casey recognized the look of despair on her face. He'd seen it too many times to count them up. There was nothing he could do for her – nothing he could do for any of them, but, still, the guilt crept up his throat like uninvited bile. He paid for his goods with the cash he'd earned, ignoring the snickering of the young teenager checking him out.

On his way out of the store, he noticed a small office with three people in it; Max, Bob and the unknown man. He made sure he was out of sight of the occupants of the office then paused to tie his shoe, tilting his head to catch any stray conversation. The unknown man was in uniform, and the last thing Casey needed was a police officer stopping him for questioning.

"I've known George since he was a tiny thing," Bob said. "I coached him all through middle school. He worked here every day over the last three summers. Never late. Always courteous. He saved every penny for that truck of his."

Bob paused as emotion audibly tinged his words. Casey heard a muffled sniffle and imagined the store manager was collecting himself.

"He was gonna be big," Bob said, his voice wavering. "He just needed to get outta this tiny place, so he could spread his wings. The people in this town make me sick. No loyalty at all."

"Bob, calm down. People are just scared. This is a small place. Two beautiful, young people have gone missing. They're just trying to put a period on a sentence that has a question mark on it. The unknown of it all scares them."

Casey assumed this was said by the second man, the police officer. He didn't recognize the voice.

"Still, it ain't right," Bob said. "We got all kinds of travelers from all kinds of places up here. Places that aren't so decent, either. We all know it. We deal with it, same as we always do. We clean the graffiti, scoop dirty condoms and beer cans out of the rivers and off the lakeshore. We ignore the open immorality of all those that come through. We've protected our own from all that and remain good people. Why on Earth would people assume George has done anything wrong? If it isn't some slur that he murdered that girl, it's that he's run off with her because her father didn't approve. None of it makes sense. Where's George gonna go without his truck? Why would he throw his life away?"

"I'm with you, Bob. Trust me, I am," the officer said. "But this is the age of the amateur detective. Everyone with an internet connection thinks they're a private eye. Don't worry. I promise, when we get to the bottom of this, George's name will be cleared up."

There was movement in the office, signs that whoever Bob and Max were talking with was about to leave. Casey finished tying his shoe and stood, ready to head out of the lot and away before Max could see him.

"Come outside with me, Max? I have something I want to talk to you about," the officer said.

"Sure, Frank." Max's voice was getting closer. "Take care, now, Bob."

Casey slipped through the doors like a shadow. He scouted the dark parking lot as best he could in the short time he had. A police cruiser was sitting in a parking spot, near Max's truck. It hadn't been there when they parked, and Casey assumed the unknown man, Frank, must be the cop. A row of grocery carts lined the front of the store. Casey skirted along the shadows enveloping the carts until he melted into them.

Max and the cop didn't take long to leave the store. They stopped under the brightly lit sign advertising milk and produce. It wasn't particularly close, but in the still night air with few people around, Casey had no trouble hearing them.

"Saw a fellow with you when you drove up here," Frank said.

Casey could tell Max was uncomfortable with the line of conversation from the strain in her voice. It was subtle, and he hoped the officer missed it.

"That's just Mr. Pierson," she said. "I hired him to help out at the motel. A lot of work for one woman to do, you know?"

"You know the guy then?"

"Yes. He's not someone you need to worry about."

Max's voice was tense, but firm.

"I'm sorry, Max. You know I gotta ask. Things being the way they are..."

"I know. You can't be too careful. I guess that means you're no longer convinced they're runaways."

Casey didn't hear anything more for more than ten seconds. He worried they had gone out of range when the cop started talking again.

"I'm not about to discuss the specifics of the case, Max. You know that."

"Then why am I standing out here in the dark talking to you about it?"

The cop sighed.

"It was a bad segue. To be honest, I don't have a good segue for what I wanted to say. With everything that's been happening, I didn't think bringing up the sale of Sam's motel was a good idea."

"Sam's dead, Frank. Unless he managed to become a pharaoh up here, which I suppose given everything is a distinct possibility. It isn't his motel anymore. It belongs to me and Anne."

"I understand," Frank said. "I apologize and mean no disrespect. I'm just saying, you're going to dredge up a lot of old feelings doing that. Maybe it would be best to hold on to it for a while. Keep it shut down. Winter it. The guys could help you out with the property taxes and you could... forget it for a while. I'd keep an eye on it, make sure it wasn't vandalized."

"No," Max said. "I'm not gonna let that albatross follow us anymore. We need get away from here and make the best of the mess my dad left us. The only way to do that is to get rid of that place as fast as possible. Leave my dad's disaster in the rearview where it belongs."

"I think you're being a little harsh on Sam."

"I don't think I'm being harsh enough," Max said

There was another brief pause, long enough for Casey to risk peeking out across the row of carts. He couldn't make out Max's face, but from her posture he could see she was unhappy to be having the conversation.

"If I can't talk you out of it—"

"You can't," Max said.

"Fine. At least be careful. Get in before dark and all that. Make sure the doors are locked. Have a phone on you at all times."

"I think the people here know me and Anne well enough to understand that we had nothing to do with my dad's business. I'm not worried about them coming out to the Sunset and causing trouble."

"It wasn't the people of Manistee I was warning you against, Max."

"Why, Chief Campbell. If I didn't know better, I'd say some amateur detective got you riled up."

Casey heard a pair of feet start walking toward the parked cars.

"All right, Max. You take care now."

The curt way the officer left told Casey that Max had hit a nerve. He peeked around the carts again to check on Max. She glanced at the store, then out into the dark lot. She was looking for something; that much was clear to Casey. He ducked closer to the shadows when she gave up her brief search and headed to her truck. He waited until she'd left the lot to move from his spot.

Chewing his lip, he re-played the conversations in his head. The city of Manistee was small enough that calling it a city could be arguably questioned. From his research, Casey knew it was made up of only around six thousand people. The tourists that flocked there every summer likely doubled that population, if only temporarily. Two missing teenagers would be huge news for a place like Manistee. It would be an event everyone would have an opinion on.

He considered the wisdom of heading to a bar to find a woman to shack up with for the night. His movements could be easily traced, and any questions he might ask would cement him in the local's minds as someone of interest; that interest was unlikely to be the good kind. After a few minutes mulling it over, he started walking north. There wasn't anywhere else for him to go – not after how he'd treated Max.

The streets of Manistee were the same streets he'd walked for most of the last twenty years. Quaint houses lined them; most were small family homes, though a few were set back on large properties, wearing skirts of wrap-around wood porches for entertaining purposes, each standing at least two stories tall.

Well-lit, lushly draped windows at pleasantly spaced intervals completed the look.

He imagined George or Sarah living in one of those houses. Then, after a few seconds contemplating which of the houses they'd have lived in, he changed his mind. If George had lived in one of those types of houses, the locals wouldn't dare deface his flyers. People who lived in those kinds of houses in these kinds of towns held too much sway over the population for any of them to speak or act out so openly against them.

No, thought Casey, George didn't live in one of those. But Sarah – she probably did.

One of the windows on the largest house on the street was bracketed in light pink. A girl was sitting in the window, looking out onto the dark street expectantly. She was young and pretty – a contemporary, perhaps, of the missing girl, Sarah. Casey looked away from her before she spied him. He didn't need trouble, and that girl was definitely looking for it.

He felt her eyes on him as he passed by. He could almost taste her desire to call out to him. That sense came more from a place of intuition and familiarity than from anywhere else. It was the same in all of the places he'd visited – all it took to be interesting in these tiny towns was to be new, and Casey had the added benefit, or detriment as it sometimes went, of being handsome enough to turn heads.

It was easy to ignore her; Casey had long passed the age where teenaged girls were of any interest to him, even if they still insisted on being seen by him. Casey had the added incentive that in this girl's case, any attention she gave him would most certainly be a detriment, a fact that was borne out when a raucous SUV pulled up the street. He counted three male voices and one female. A bad ratio, especially for him. He already pegged the odds at fifty percent that after they picked up the girl waiting in her window, which he was sure was about to happen, that they'd be a problem for him. But with the men outnumbering the women in the car, the need to prove who was manlier upped those odds to eighty percent.

He checked the side roads, determining if taking one was more or less likely to draw their attention. It wouldn't matter much if the girl, who was now climbing out her window, decided to comment about him to her friends. Her words would light a fuse that would not burn out. She was not the kind of girl a young man would let become distracted.

The young men in the car were likely all vying for her attention, either openly or slyly, even if they already had a girl on their arm. It wasn't young people's predictability that informed Casey's thoughts, or that all small towns were the same – it was hormones that telegraphed their actions so clearly, the driver of most young men's ill-tempered deeds.

He decided that if it looked like he was running they were more likely to give chase, so he continued down the road, casually walking as if he was out for an evening stroll. When the SUV slowed down alongside him, he felt weariness seep in from all around. He kept his pace, but turned toward them and waved genially, an action borne from years of trial and error with this type of mid-western hooliganism. Wary or confrontational was an attitude they anticipated – and relished. Casey's neighborly approach was more often a success than a failure.

After the friendly gesture, he continued on his way. Saying anything was a mistake. They were looking for a reason to bother him. They could find some imaginary insult in anything Casey could think to say to de-escalate the confrontation. Unfortunately, it only took one asshole to decide to start something whether he spoke or not, and this SUV held three.

"Where'ya headed?"

The driver. The alpha of the pack. The one who very likely had a home to match the pink-window girl. It was probably his car and his girl. Casey silently cursed her for saying anything, almost sure her wanton words were what was driving the alpha. He could never tell with women whether they were simply too foolish to understand the power their attention could yield, or they knew too well and enjoyed it.

"Arnold's," Casey said. Then on a whim, added, "Anne said it's a solid joint."

Laughter erupted from the car.

"Anne?"

The young man was big for his age. If Casey felt bolder, he might have tried to engage him in more productive conversation. He looked like he could be a football player – someone who might've known George. Someone who might have something to say about his disappearance that didn't show up in flyers. Casey was not feeling bold. His searching was finally yielding results he could work with. Acting hastily would squander all the work he'd done to get to this point.

"Yeah. From the Sunset. Runs the place with her sister."

The laughter in the car started up again then quieted when the alpha started talking again.

"Yeah. We know Anne. Kind of a bitch."

"Kind of?" a girl's voice chimed in from the back before more laughter drowned her out.

Casey waited patiently for them to finish snickering before continuing.

"She's one of those people you have to let grow on you," Casey said.

"Yeah, her and that dyke sister of hers," Alpha said.

Alpha was clearly looking for a fight. His words bristled

with the need for it. If Alpha thought his words could rile Casey up, he was mistaken. Not only were Alpha's words ineffectual, they let Casey know his foe was intellectually incapable of saying anything truly hurtful – only small-minded folk still somehow felt it was an insult to call someone gay. He imagined having a good chuckle about the whole thing with Max before he remembered he'd walked out on her.

"You have a good evening," Casey said before moving on.

The car's tires inched forward; the sound of the slow rubber on the weary concrete far too intimate for Casey's liking. The number of peaceful options he had left were running out, and annoyance began to crowd out his patience.

"I'm not done yet," Alpha said, most of the upper half of his body now hanging out the window, one hand still on the wheel.

"I had a feeling," Casey muttered.

"I don't care who you know, asshole," Alpha said. "My good friend George is missing. And as long as that's true, no one I don't know gets to walk through town without checkin' in with me first."

"Sounds like a full-time job for you," Casey said. "But you can breathe a sigh of relief. Your backup, Chief Campbell, has already checked me into the city limits. I left all my papers with him."

This had the opposite effect than what Casey was hoping for. The vehicle stopped abruptly and Alpha exited, rushing to plant himself in front of Casey. Alpha was easily a couple inches taller than Casey, and a half dozen wider. His face was vaguely familiar as well.

"I don't care what my fucking dad said to you, bitch. We're the only ones looking for George's killer, and we say where you go, when you go."

"Killer?" Casey interrupted.

"Jay."

Pink-curtain girl was leaning across the driver's seat to get to the window. The look on her face was not one of excitement, but concern.

"Not now, Jessie," Alpha said.

"I thought he was just missing," Casey probed.

Alpha knew something – something real – and that was not information Casey could pass up, despite the risk of his questions getting back to the authorities.

Alpha stepped into Casey's personal space with abandon, his nose close but not touching. When he spoke, spittle flecked Casey's eyelashes.

"I think it's time you checked in with me," Alpha said.

The menace in his voice was real, but Casey wasn't budging. The time for questioning, however, was clearly over. He wouldn't get anything out of this group. His best bet was to turn this around before things snowballed into something that would require a statement in a police station.

"I get it," Casey said, his voice low and even – low enough that it carried only as far as he wanted it to. "This is a small town. You need to do small town shit to prove your worth. You could do that here. You can try your small-town shit on me. But fella, I'm not from a small town. You might find that small-town shit doesn't work with people like me. You might find that doing small-town shit to me comes at a price you can't afford. And the people who bought the tickets to your small-town shit show? They're watching. But they aren't watching to see you do your thing. They're watching, and waiting, for you to fuck up, so that the next time a small-town shit show comes round, they're the star player. Your fifteen minutes have expired."

Casey watched as Alpha's eyes shifted back toward the car. Casey had no doubt who would come out on top in a fight between them, and it was looking like Alpha was coming to that realization, too. He could tell that, as much as it hurt the big teenager's pride to head back to the car without a fight, the kid knew the damage would be far longer lasting if he was left bleeding on the sidewalk in front of his friends. He could call to his buddies – get backup to ensure his victory – but Alpha had made the fatal mistake of getting out of the car without them, and Casey had no intention of letting him bolster up before he struck.

"Jay! We're close to my house. I'm not supposed to be out. This is seriously not a good time for a dick swinging contest with some tourist."

Alpha looked between the car and Casey, before finally giving Casey a shove.

"See you around," Alpha said menacingly.

Casey didn't see any sense in responding. He let the young man scrape what little he could from the confrontation. Better that than force Alpha to come back to save face. He waited for them to leave and made note of the make and model of the car so he could avoid it in the future. Alpha gunned the engine, then pulled away, leaving Casey to walk the rest of the way to Arnold's in peace.

FOUR

The bar was clean, if well-worn. It was exactly the kind of place Casey was hoping for. A smattering of thirty-somethings like himself, and several who skewed even older occupied the local hangout. He wouldn't find anyone younger here. The twenty-somethings were still young enough to lurk in the trendier, tourist-trap pubs where they could buy any number of a hundred different microbrews priced high enough to keep the town of Manistee in business through the long winter without the tourists to prop them up.

Arnold's was a place for people without options. It was the perfect place for someone like Casey, looking for somewhere to stay for the night. The women at Arnold's would gladly trade lodging for the chance to end up in a bed with a man who was equal parts wish fulfillment and rose-colored memory – recollections of a time when they could still hang out at a dive named after an exotic fish or with "The" in its name, the kind of place where the only difference between it and any other rundown bar in town was a fresh coat of paint and the occasional piece of fruit in the mixed drinks. The women here didn't need to know Casey had just as few options as them, and they didn't want to know either. Casey was fine feeding their illusions, so long as he had a place to stay.

He made his way to a barstool and plunked down his duffle bag, knowing he didn't need to approach anyone. The hungriest would come to him first, and they would be the easiest to convince to take him home without many questions. It didn't take long for someone to sit next to him. He felt her warmth before he looked up.

Her age was hard to place. Her hair was colored and her face plastered with makeup. She wore a high-collared blouse with bare arms, a flattering look for a fit older woman who was trying to hide the sag under her chin. But boozing regularly aged a woman, and she might have been younger than her skin suggested. It didn't matter to Casey, either way. A woman's bed was a woman's bed, no matter her age.

"Buy you a drink?" she asked.

She had a nice voice, raspy and deep like a blues singer's. Casey smiled and nodded at her. She didn't act shocked he accepted the drink. She knew why he was there as much as he knew why she was. The silent negotiation between them lasted mere seconds.

She was interested in his non-verbal invitation, but she was also wise enough to feel him out first. Casey had met the kind of men he was sure this woman was trying to avoid – the kind who were looking to hurt a woman. Had the woman been careless, she wouldn't have even offered the drink. Less cautious women chose to rush him home before anyone more appealing might show up to steal their catch. This woman's caution was sadly familiar to Casey.

A bartender approached. He didn't look keen to serve

Casey – tourists probably didn't make their way to this end of town very often, and they were likely more trouble than they were worth when they did.

"Whatever's on tap is fine with me," Casey said.

The bartender begrudgingly filled a cup with cheap, brand-name beer and set it in front of Casey before moving off.

"Carl doesn't care for tourists much," the woman said. "I'm Janelle."

"Casey."

He sipped his beer while surreptitiously looking around for nuts or pretzels. It was too late to bemoan turning down Max's offer of a real dinner, but he needed something in his gut besides cheap beer if he was going to get anything done this evening.

"Looking for the pretzels?" Janelle asked.

Casey nodded and took another drink.

"Carl only puts 'em out during happy hour."

Casey waited for the invite. It was the perfect opportunity for Janelle to come up with a reason to ask him back to her place; she could offer him something to eat. Instead she took a sip of her own drink and eyed him.

"You're really good looking to be in a place like this," she said. "You a serial killer?"

Casey chuckled. He appreciated the directness. He leaned against the bar and gave Janelle his most charming smile.

"Would a serial killer have a smile like this?"

Janelle's laugh was more like a bark. It drew the eyes of everyone in the bar, which, when Casey thought about it, might have been the point. He leaned into the idea.

"Besides," he said, "this would be a real dumb place for a serial killer to work his mojo. Ain't a person comes in here Carl doesn't know, right?"

Janelle smiled knowingly.

"So," Casey continued, "that would mean anyone he, or any of these folks, saw who wasn't recognizable would be instantly recalled in case of trouble. Especially if that man went home with one of Manistee's charming women."

"Is that what you're gonna do, Casey? You gonna come home with me?"

"Only if you want me to."

Janelle tapped her long, fake nails on the bar as she mulled over her options. It was a show; he knew it from the way she looked at him like he was some kind of snack fresh from the oven. But he didn't say anything. He had no trouble with her pretending she might say no, now that she was sure he was safe enough to take home. If she wanted everyone in the bar to think she had someplace else to go, someone else to go with, then who was he to call her on it? She downed her drink and placed her hand on his arm.

"Let's go."

They left the bar together, driving to her place in a run-down car with threadbare seats. He never minded the lack of luxury in these endeavors. On the contrary, he felt more comfortable with people like himself than with people who lived in houses like the big one with the pink curtains. Still, he was glad to get out of the car when it finally stopped. Not being able to smell the air around him was confining.

Janelle lived in a duplex. Her half of the home was decorated with enough kitsch for six houses: tiny glass hummingbirds attached to spinning, colored metal, a cacophony of wind chimes and angels on every available surface. The inside wasn't much different from the outside. The home was cluttered with knickknacks of the sort one would find at a dollar store. There was so much of it, Casey almost felt as if he'd entered a modern art exhibit – Things We Buy When We're Bored.

Janelle closed the door behind him and, before Casey could even drop his bag, she approached, coming in for a kiss. Casey had expected it, and was usually quite good at sustaining a thin veneer of attraction for the women he went home with, but this time he felt awkward and uncomfortable even before their lips met. Once they had, things only got worse. Janelle pulled away almost immediately, turning on the overhead light to get a look at him.

Casey was afraid he'd hurt her feelings, but the look on her face wasn't pain, it was confusion.

"You don't want to do this," she said.

"I'm sorry," Casey said.

He was desperate to salvage the situation. He couldn't go back to the bar, not after he'd already left with someone. Carl wasn't likely to be more inviting the second time.

"It's not you, I—"

He was cut off midsentence with a wave of her hand.

"I know that, honey. I've been going to that bar long enough to know that when it comes to desperate men, any vagina will do. Doesn't much matter that this is all I've got to work with." She looked him over briefly. "You're as surprised as I am by this."

Casey was taken aback by the shrewd observation.

"I... I am."

Janelle sighed before motioning him to follow her.

"Come on, honey. Let's get you something to eat. Maybe you're just hungry."

"Maybe," Casey said, doubtful it was true.

He followed Janelle into her kitchen. Like the rest of the house, it looked like a garage sale had exploded in it. Clocks of every type painted the walls. Hundreds of colorful magnets clung to the fridge – so many that the handles looked like they were drowning in them. A collection of spoons had a central spot right over a kitchen table that seated two, each tiny spoon in its own slot.

"Sit down," she said. "I'll nuke something for ya. I think I have some leftover casserole from the church potluck."

Casey sat while Janelle busied herself at the microwave, peeling back tinfoil and scooping a cold chunk of formed food onto a plate. His stomach growled angrily as the smell of microwaved meat filled the air. She turned to look at him, an eyebrow arched.

"You're not gay. At least I think you aren't," she started. "Definitely not married."

"I could be either one of those things," Casey said defensively, not really sure why he said it.

"No. I've been with both. Gay men, the closeted type of course, try harder than you. They force it to happen to prove to some imaginary person they've been arguing with their whole life that they aren't what they are." She pursed her lips as she examined him. "And married men don't feel bad before. They feel bad after. You're covered head to toe in regret and we haven't done a thing. This is something else."

"What about being hungry? It could be that," Casey said.

"I just said that because I didn't want you to try kissing me again. The first time was pathetic enough. I'll give you what you want. You don't have to take me to bed to get it."

"I'm not sure what you're—"

The microwave beeped before he could finish his sentence. Janelle pulled out the plate and put it in front of him. Whatever it was, it looked a mess, but Casey took the offered fork and dug in nonetheless. While it wasn't going to win any contests, it was tasty enough that when he polished it off and Janelle started to heap a second helping onto the plate, he didn't protest.

She loaded the plate into the microwave and studied him. Casey began to feel less like he was on an impromptu date and more like he was being minded after by a nosey aunt.

"Arnold's isn't a place people find on accident," she said. "And I didn't notice any new cars out front. Who brought you?"

Casey was taken aback by this new line of questioning. He was unused to the women he picked up in bars challenging him. He was unused to them talking about much at all. Most of them understood the unspoken contract and had no interest in upsetting the chance they'd get to spend the night with him. It was why he chose the women he chose.

"I got a ride from... a friend."

Janelle grinned widely, showing off several silver caps on her teeth.

"Ah, there it is. You like someone."

The microwave beeped to indicate the food was ready, giving Casey a brief respite from Janelle's intense scrutiny. She slid the hot plate in front of him. He was ready to leave, but it felt too rude to walk out just then. He forked up a couple more mouthfuls of casserole while Janelle watched.

"Yeah. Must be someone from here, too. Lucky woman. Who is it?"

What had started as a one-night stand gone awry was turning into a gossip session. Casey wasn't interested in gossip, especially not when it was about him. He crammed the rest of the food down and stood up.

"Leaving?" she asked, a sly smile still on her face. "Might be a mistake. Seems to me you're out of your depth with this woman and need some help."

"I'm sure whatever you're talking about is something I'm perfectly capable of handling."

He started to leave and had gotten all the way to the entry way before he heard her respond.

"I'm sure you can handle it. And that's why you were in a dive bar in Manistee, Michigan, picking up the most used-up broad in the place just to get a bite to eat and a place to lay your head. Sounds exactly like a fella who's got everything under control."

His hand on the doorknob, he turned to glare at Janelle. Her straightforward manner was no longer charming. She examined her nails in a clumsy attempt to feign disinterest in his desire to leave.

"I don't bring men back to my place to feed 'em," she said.

"You need your pound of flesh?" he tossed back.

"If it's a pound, she really is a lucky woman."

He spun and opened the door.

"I don't need flesh," she said, "but I do a brisk trade in information."

Casey paused. It was all the encouragement Janelle needed to continue.

"It's all I got in this town. I'm not pretty enough to get attention. I'm not smart enough to get out. I'm not rich enough to not care. But people come to me to find things out. A guy who rolls through and meets a girl that ruins his game, well that's a fella who could use to know things, too."

Casey closed the door, sensing an opportunity he couldn't pass up.

"What do you want in return if not... my companionship."

Janelle sniggered.

"How very professional of you. But it would be no fun at all bedding a man who's barely interested. I know. I've done that, too. Come back to the kitchen. I'll fix you a drink."

Casey followed Janelle back into the kitchen and sat. She procured a couple of glasses and filled them with whiskey. Casey stared at his uneasily. He wasn't much of a drinker, and he was worried Janelle might be trying to loosen his tongue. But she didn't seem to care when he didn't pick up his drink and enjoyed hers without him. She downed it in one go then poured herself another.

"I saw at least three women peeking out their curtains when we got here," she started. "That's not including the women at the bar. A guy like you is gonna have a lot of eyes on you.

"Women trapped in hopeless marriages for the most part look down on me, except on the rare occasion I catch something interesting in my net. Then they'll part with all sorts of dirty little secrets just for a glimpse into my night with the tall, dark and handsome stranger they saw pass through town. They'll want details, and I'll deliver, and I'll never even have to have touched you. They'll believe it, because you were here most of the night."

Janelle downed another whiskey then looked at Casey pointedly.

"You want me to spend the night?"

"You wanted to anyway. I might not know how you got yourself desperate enough to go trawling at Arnold's just to find a place to crash, but I do know that's why you were there."

She tapped her glass as if waiting for him to deny it, but he didn't.

"Yeah, I knew it," Janelle said. "I've met your type, too. Guys looking to step away from things for a while. Guys needing a place to stay while their girl is mad. Men who booked a week's stay at the fancy hotel on the water, who said or did something wrong, and they don't want to spend the night on a public bench. I don't know your reason and I don't really care. But you wanted to spend the night, so don't act like it's a burden."

"I wasn't planning on it," Casey said. "So... that's all I have to do? Sleep here?"

Janelle poured herself another drink, then looked at Casey's glass.

"Maybe if you drank a little you'd get back in the mood," she suggested.

"That ship has sailed," Casey said.

Janelle downed her third glass and shrugged.

"Can't blame me for trying. I'm sure you've seen yourself in the mirror." She slid his glass toward herself and looked up at him, her cheeks flush from drinking. "I'll trade you info. You can ask me anything about your woman, if you tell me who she is. The room and board is payment for the gossip you'll send my way for months to come."

Casey crossed his arms. He didn't understand this woman's motivations, but he could guess well enough. He was an outsider. If any person in town had a liaison with him, it would be news. The value of the news would go up if said person was someone of note. Janelle was probably hoping for the latter – in the currency of gossip, the bigger the fish, the more power the rumor had. It was harmless enough, since he had no intentions of living in Manistee, even if everything was sorted and he'd found his prey – even then, in his most closely held fantasies where he was a hero who got the girl, even then, they never ended up at a place like Manistee. Still, he felt uneasy telling this woman about any of his feelings.

"Come on," she pleaded. "You can tell me tonight, or I'll

find out tomorrow. And tomorrow's news is likely to be less accurate. But I'll still know. People here see everything."

Casey remembered that the cop had seen him driving with Max. The cop was likely not the only one.

"I've been helping out at the Sunset," he said, trying his best to keep it vague.

"Max?"

Janelle looked genuinely surprised. Casey was annoyed that she'd guessed correctly so quickly. She laughed heartily, even slapping her knees.

"Holy shit, friend."

"Anne works there, too," Casey said. "And there are guests."

"Sure," Janelle said, downing Casey's shot of whiskey. "Anne is about as much your type as I am. And guests? No outsider would know about Arnold's. And no one from town would go anywhere near the Sunset. Not anymore. Not now that everybody knows—"

She stopped abruptly with a chuckle.

"Knows what?" Casey asked.

"No sir," Janelle said. "I like that girl. She's got spunk. Isn't afraid to talk back to the sheriff. And doesn't look down her nose at me. I don't talk dirt about those I like. So, that's not a story you'll get from me. But ask me something else about Max, something I can convince myself will be good for her, and I'll answer."

Janelle gave him a suggestive look.

Casey leaned back in his chair. He could waste this opportunity and ask about Max – about the kind of person he needed to be for her to take interest in him. Janelle would tell him all he needed to know, of that he was sure. To hear her tell it, she had the pulse of the city and was willing to trade her secrets. But he wasn't in Manistee for himself; there were more important things he needed to do. He hadn't thought he would be fortunate enough to stumble upon someone he could ask questions without worrying about it getting back to law enforcement. A part of him knew Janelle would keep what happened in her kitchen – the truth of it anyway – to herself.

"I'd like to know about those missing teenagers," he said.

Janelle's mouth hung open wide enough to catch flies. She closed it and poured another drink. Casey hoped she'd keep downing shots at that pace. That would increase the odds that their conversation would never leave her kitchen.

"That's not what I thought you'd ask," she said, downing her fifth drink.

"It's not what I really wanted to ask," Casey admitted. "Unfortunately, it's what I have to ask."

"All right," Janelle said. "Where do you want me to start? You want to know about George's family? Sarah's? Who was cheating on who?"

"I don't care about any of that," Casey said. "The people themselves don't matter."

"Then what do you want to know?" Janelle asked, confused.

"I ran into an idiot tonight. Jay, I think his name is."

"Jay Bingham. And idiot is too nice for him. I'm sure it's him, because I don't know any other Jay's. High school kid. Big black SUV. Drives around like he's already taken over his father's job as the chief of police."

"That would be him," Casey said. "He seemed to think those other two kids, George and Sarah, were dead."

"I wouldn't be surprised," Janelle said. She rubbed her chin thoughtfully. "He's been going around talking about how his dad is failing the city. Since his dad is convinced the kids are still alive. And Jay and George were real close. There were rumors."

"They were more than friends?" Casey guessed.

"No. They were sharing that girl of Jay's. Jessica Simms. The story was, Jay has a substandard... pound of flesh. He asked George to do the dirty work, as it were. I don't know the truth of it, but I will say Jay put on at least fifty pounds of muscle over the course of last year. What I hear, the kinds of drugs that do that also..." Janelle held up her pinky finger and wiggled it. "Anyway, that's what people say. If it's true, they would have to be pretty damn close."

"Close enough to know what George was doing out at Bear Track Campground late at night?"

"I'm guessing you're not buying they were camping," Janelle said with a wink.

"Small town like this," Casey said. "I doubt very much a teenaged girl's father is going to let his daughter go camping alone with her boyfriend."

"No," Janelle said. "He wouldn't. Certainly not Sarah Linkman's father. Mayor doesn't want his daughter getting a reputation."

Casey looked out the tiny kitchen window. It was dark enough outside he couldn't make out anything, yet it felt like he was being watched, and not by one of the women Janelle had mentioned. He turned back to her and tapped the table.

"There was a spot out there they went to," he said. "Some place they could hang out, drink beer and do the things teenagers do."

"Probably," Janelle said. "George's truck was found near the campground. But they couldn't find any sign of them nearby." She leaned in close to Casey, running her finger around the lip of her glass. "Not many know this, but they took dogs out there, the tracking kind, but the dogs were too spooked to leave the car. They tried another set, and the same thing. Never heard of dogs acting that way. Chief Campbell hasn't tried again, worried about what people might start saying, worried about how it might affect the tourism, maybe even his job. It also put Scott Linkman in a bit of a pickle, him being mayor and all. Can't press too much about his daughter, or he risks trouble for the city."

"What kind of man stifles an investigation into his daughter's disappearance to save his job?" Casey asked, horrified.

"You'd have to ask him," Janelle said. "My best guess is that it has to do with all his business dealings. He's got his hand in most of the pies in the city. A lot of money in the vacation industry. Hell, maybe the dog thing is a rumor they started. There's a new whisper going around that the mayor and the chief know exactly what happened, and neither one wants to deal with the fallout. Something about Sarah being pregnant, and sent off somewhere."

"You believe that?" Casey asked.

"No," Janelle said with certainty. "I grew up with Scott Linkman. Went to high school with him. He's a grasping little weasel. You asked what kind of man would care more about his job than his daughter? If I had to pick one, it would be Mayor Linkman. But whatever the real story is, it's probably juicy. I'd be willing to trade a lot more info if you happened to come by the answer."

Casey reached out and poured Janelle another drink. He smiled at her and slid it over.

"I don't suppose you know where this spot is where the kids hang out?"

Janelle took the glass and held it up. She looked over the top at Casey.

"If I knew that, I'd be telling the chief first. I'm a gossip, not

82

a criminal. I don't want kids to be dying. If there's evidence somewhere in those woods that could help find them, I wouldn't keep it to myself."

Casey waited until Janelle had downed the glass. He poured two more, sliding his cup back over to his side, and downed it, hoping Janelle would follow suit. She did, and he poured another for each of them.

"You trying to get me drunk?" she slurred.

He downed his drink and stood up, his mouth tingling from the alcohol.

"I'll sleep a little better with those is all. If you don't mind, I'll stick to the couch."

Janelle clucked her tongue before swallowing the last of her drink.

"I'll let you ask that question you wanted to, the one about Max, if you tell me why you're so interested in them kids."

Casey smiled ruefully before turning around.

"Good night, Janelle. I'll lock up when I leave."

"Fine. I'll go upstairs and dream about what could have been."

Casey sat down on the lumpy couch. He heard Janelle clumsily make her way to her bedroom. Thumps accompanied with grunts of pain as she banged into walls and doorways made it easy to track her progress. He stared at the ceiling as the house grew quiet.

"Eight shots in under an hour," he said to himself. "Is that enough for her to forget?"

A sound came from outside. A scream – two cats, Casey thought. It had to be two cats. He hoped it was two cats. He wasn't ready for them. Not yet.

FIVE

A sound woke Casey from an uneasy sleep. He sat up, taking care not to let the old couch make any noise. He waited a few tense seconds. When he heard the noise again, he relaxed. It was Janelle, snoring up a storm in her bedroom. Casey rubbed his face, his mouth sticky from hanging open while he slept. He found his way to the kitchen sink and drank deeply to clean his tongue of the awful taste. His gut grumbled to life as if to complain that water wasn't going to cut it.

He checked one of the numerous clocks on the wall. He'd managed a few hours of sleep; it was only two AM. Making his way back to the living room, he walked right by the lumpy couch, unwilling to subject himself to further suffering. He checked the door to make sure he could lock it before closing it. In small towns like this one, people often didn't bother. Janelle hadn't been concerned about it when he mentioned he would be gone before she woke, but Casey wasn't going to leave her door unlocked in the middle of the night, particularly not with his scent all over the place.

He pulled the door shut behind him, double checking it was secure. Satisfied, he headed out into the street. His dead reckoning was uncanny. It always had been, even when he was a child. He instinctively headed back toward the highway that led out of town back to the Sunset.

Cities like Manistee were eerier than most at night. People didn't leave their lights on. There was no crime which meant most people didn't feel the need to wire up their houses, so they could feel safer under the blast of a motion sensing security light. People opted to save money on electricity rather than worry about problems that didn't exist.

On top of that, night life was non-existent in the parts of town where local people lived, leaving the roads dark and untraveled. The headlights that would normally pop up to remind Casey he wasn't alone were few and far between in these quiet neighborhoods. The late-night drunks, booted from their cozy bar stools at closing time, wouldn't stray this far away from their second homes.

Casey had spent many late evenings lurking in towns just like Manistee, only to find the remnants of what he was looking for. This time was different – he could feel them here. Their scent was everywhere. It made him wonder if they were staying in town, too. He blasted that hopeful thought from his mind, lest it make him second guess what he had to do. There wouldn't be time for second guesses when he found them. They might not even give him time for a first guess.

He walked with purpose, his stride long and even. He figured walking the ten miles or so to the Sunset would get him there close to dawn, so long as he wasn't distracted from his task. He mused as he walked, about the way the mind played tricks on people. At night, sounds that would be innocent during the day took on a dangerous air. It was almost as if the darkness shrouded not only what you could see, but what you could hear, casting it in gloom and making the listener think the worst was out there.

He kept that thought with him as he walked, in part to warm the ice forming along his spine, and in part to quell the irrational fear taking hold in his mind, before it turned a raccoon rummaging through garbage into something far more dangerous. Far down the street, headlights flashed across the road, reminding Casey that the darkness wasn't the only thing he should be concerned about.

Being found walking through town after midnight would be more than a distraction. If Casey was unlucky, it would be the police that happened on him. They were unlikely, especially in a place like Manistee, to keep driving by if they saw an out-of-towner wandering around. With two missing teenagers, they'd be foolish not to investigate.

Casey could hardly hold it against them if they harassed him. They'd have little reason to keep him for long – he expected he'd merely have to mention Janelle for the cops to understand why he was out and about at two AM.

He was far more concerned with running into Jay and his cronies again. If that happened, he didn't think it likely he'd get away a second time without it coming to blows. Jay would not make the same mistake twice, and Casey would be forced to face down a trio of idiots.

But the car didn't turn in Casey's direction – it kept moving north. He took that as a sign he should take a different route back to the Sunset. He detoured around the house with the pink curtains. The chance of running into Jay would be greatest there, where he'd have to drop off his girl at some point.

As Casey got closer to the highway that cut through town, things started to get brighter. Gas stations and fast food joints still had their signs lit, proudly advertising their deals for anyone passing by. The faux signs of life did little to calm Casey's nerves. Light did not mean life; the neon signs were only an illusion of human activity at this late hour. He was still very much alone on the road.

At the city limits the lights faded, and all that was left was the occasional highway light to indicate a crossroads. The moon wasn't up, leaving the sky dusty with stars. As long as he could hear the wildlife around him, the lack of light didn't bother Casey. He continued along the road at a comfortable pace, more concerned with the chance of a vehicle coming so fast it wouldn't see him than anything prowling about in the woods bordering the road.

He was halfway to the Sunset when the smell of death stopped him cold. The trees nearby creaked as the wind moved through them. Casey looked up, startled to notice what he hadn't before – clouds had rolled in, covering the sky with uneasy movement. A storm was coming, and its winds carried the smell he'd been both searching for and dreading.

He veered off the highway, heading into the wind. The insects and small tree creatures whose sounds had accompanied him on his trek so far had ceased their chatter. It wasn't a sure sign; they'd behave in a similar manner prior to a storm, their sixth sense telling them to take shelter and wait the worst of it out. But paired with the smell, it caused every hair on Casey's body to stand up straight.

He followed his nose deep into the woods, stepping carefully to avoid making too much noise, though it hardly mattered. If they were there, they'd have smelled him by now. The stench grew by orders of magnitude as he got closer, all but confirming he was smelling more than rot. As he passed a tree, his hand brushed it, coming away with a thick, sticky substance.

His nose overloaded as he brought his hand close to inspect the gunk smeared across his palm. They'd marked the territory. The scent was special – different than the smell they emitted when on the hunt – stronger and more potent, but the potency came with a shorter lifespan. Unlike their natural smell, this one had to be refreshed after every rain. It was normally used to warn away the curious, liberally spread around the den to keep all creatures far away. But it was far from the strength it should be if Casey was close to the den. That meant they'd left it here for other purposes.

It was days old at the minimum, from before he'd arrived, but it was hard not to suspect they'd done it for him. They would know he'd take the main route into town. They'd know he would have smelled this had he been looking for it, which they'd know he would be.

Casey continued further into the woods. They wouldn't have simply marked the territory. They would have left him a gift. They always did.

It didn't take long for Casey to stumble upon the leavings. The remains of a black bear were spread out on the forest floor in a gap between several trees. Its fur was splayed open; the carnage, foul and rotting, consisted of scraps. Only the feet retained any substantial fleshy bits. The rest had been devoured – scraped away from the white bones, peeled back from the skin – leaving only the bloody hide behind. The head was hollowed out. Casey leaned over and peered through its empty eye-sockets. The still-attached fur made the empty head even more disturbing.

He sighed as he stood. Looking up, he saw his gifts. Two cubs, the size of retrievers, hung from the branches over the mother bear. They were untouched, other than the broken necks Casey assumed they had. They were bloated so badly, he wasn't sure how big they'd been to start.

He could never really understand the motivation of these offerings – what the purpose was. He had some guesses, but he was afraid to entertain them fully – afraid of what it might mean. Finding the "gifts" always made him uncomfortable. Perhaps that was the sole purpose, and nothing else. He was hunting them, after all. Putting him off his game would be in their best interest.

Lightning flashed in the sky, followed by a bolt of thunder seconds later. The sound shook Casey from his thoughts as the scene was briefly lit to reveal all the gruesome details. He turned away from it, heading back toward the highway. They weren't there, so there was no point in investigating further. They wouldn't have left anything they didn't want him to find; he'd scoured enough similar scenes to know that.

The rain crashed down on him just as he reached the road. He silently thanked its arrival. No one else would find the horror in the forest now. The storm would wash away that part of the scent that had kept carrion creatures from cleaning up the monsters' leftovers. The insects, birds, rodents and assorted other opportunists that smelled the invisible warning that accompanied that scent would be free to finish the feast after the rain dried up.

There was never any hope he'd catch them unawares, but Casey wished they hadn't anticipated how quickly he'd catch up to them. Maybe they weren't making mistakes, as he'd originally thought. Maybe they were as tired of the game they were playing as he was. The thought was a small comfort to Casey. If it was true, it meant, one way or the other, he was done with the hunt.

By the time he reached the Sunset, the rain had stopped and

the clouds had continued their travels east. The sky had cleared up and was brightening with the coming sun. It was just warm enough for Casey to feel even more awful about being soaked.

The humidity surrounded him like a cloak, steam rising from the black asphalt of the still wet highway. The muggy Midwest air had never been to his liking, but late August was especially bad. He'd expected, being as far north as he was, it wouldn't be as much of a bother. He'd been wrong on that front.

When he reached the parking lot, he headed straight back to the pool. The idea of taking a shower before covering himself in mold and dust again was dropped as soon as he thought of it. A morning swim was an in-between option, cooling him down and refreshing him without making him feel like he was scrubbing himself down just to go roll in a dumpster. It didn't even occur to him that he no longer had a choice in any case, since he'd returned the key the day before. He'd come back to the motel on automatic, never once considering what his reception might be.

Casey heard splashing before he saw the pool. His curiosity aroused, he trundled over to the gate and let himself into the pool area. Someone was swimming laps. He ran through the options in his head – Anne didn't strike him as a swimmer. Something told Casey she was the type of woman who would try to skate by on good genetics and trendy diets to stay looking thin. He hadn't seen any extra vehicles about, so he doubted it was a new guest. That only left the one option.

She must have noticed him, because she stopped at the end of a lap and climbed out of the pool. Upon seeing her, Casey simultaneously remembered why he'd checked out the night before and forgot why he'd wanted to come back. He'd had a reason, he was sure of it – a good solid reason for why he should risk something so selfish as coming back to the Sunset. He just couldn't remember what it was. He began to doubt if he ever had a reason, or if his drive to see her again was so deep in his gut it didn't need permission from his brain to take over his legs and walk him right back to the Sunset.

As Max pulled herself from the pool, Casey braced himself for a deservedly cold greeting. Maybe she'd be happy to see him. It was a longshot – an impossible shot if he wasn't deluding himself – but, maybe he was lucky and whatever drew him back to the Sunset without thinking wasn't one-sided. The realist in him prepared for the worst, however.

She was wearing a swim cap made up to look like a gaping maw was swallowing her face, albeit in a cartoonish way meant to engender a laugh rather than a scream. She peeled it off, letting her light brown hair free. She didn't look surprised to see him, though she did look troubled as she plucked at his soaked shirt.

"You get caught in that storm we had this morning?"

"Uh... yes."

Her reaction was as disorienting as it was unexpected. No shouting, no angry looks, just casual conversation; the incongruity chased all the pre-planned conversations he'd been imagining away in an instant. In an effort to disguise his discomfort he went to get a towel, then handed it to her.

"If you'd have called," she said, wiping down her arms, "I'd have picked you up."

The phone. He'd forgotten he had it. He pulled it out of his wet jeans with some effort before trying to hand it back to her.

"No. It's yours. I told you, paid up for the month."

He had trouble meeting her eyes.

"I didn't think you'd be coming back," she said.

"I know," he said. "I was stupid."

"Which part?" She walked over to pick up another towel and then tossed it to him. "The leaving or the coming back?"

He twisted the towel in his hands.

"I'll let you know when I figure that out."

Max's smile was all Casey needed to know that she wasn't going to hold any of his actions against him. If she was angry, it was obviously something she was willing to get over.

"You going for a swim?" she asked jokingly.

"Actually, I was thinking about it. This heat is the worst. Showering just feels pointless before tearing up carpeting."

"I gotcha," she said. "You gonna…"

She indicated his wet clothes with a wave of her hand. Casey looked down at himself, then slapped his forehead.

"God dammit."

"You left your bag somewhere?" Max asked.

Not just somewhere, Casey thought, Janelle's.

He had no idea how to explain it to Max. What he did know was that he didn't want to tell her. It wouldn't matter much if he kept it from her. She'd hear about it eventually. Janelle would be rolling around town telling anyone who would listen. Maybe she'd even make an event of it. He didn't think Max would ask around about him to try and find out where he'd been – she seemed the type who minded her own business. But the next time she was grocery shopping, someone would probably ask her about him.

He scratched his head and grimaced.

"Janelle's… I think."

For a second, Casey was afraid of what Max might be thinking. Her face was blank. And then she started laughing.

"Oh, boy. Okay, tell you what. I'll give her a call after noon. She won't be up until then. When I go for lunch, I'll take you with me. We'll run by there and pick up your stuff. It should still be mostly intact." Max paused, then repeated, with a grin, "Mostly."

Casey shared her grin, but more out of relief than at the situation. It looked like Max wasn't too bothered by the fact that he'd been to Janelle's. Then doubt started to creep in. Why didn't she care if he'd slept at Janelle's? An unfamiliar ache began to build inside of him.

"Sounds good," he said without much enthusiasm.

Max must have misunderstood where his mood swing originated, because she patted him on the shoulder and gestured to his clothes again.

"Swim trunks, shorts, underwear. It's all mostly the same. One just dries faster. Just wear something when you swim. I'll catch an earful from Anne if she sees you in the skinny out here. And I know I already have one earful coming my way when she finds out you're back."

"Thanks," Casey said.

He forced a smile on his face, upset he couldn't shake the Janelle thing from his head. He started to take off his shirt, then halted. He looked up to see Max still standing there, watching him as if she was anticipating something. She blushed and turned around quickly before heading out the gate.

"I'll get your key. And something to eat. Be back in thirty minutes or so."

He stood still for several minutes, basking in the moment. He knew that look. He hadn't seen it on Max before, but he knew it. Women all over had given him that look for years. He'd never enjoyed it as much before. The unease he'd felt vanished as quickly as it started. Heat crept up his neck as he luxuriated in the feeling.

He stripped off his wet shirt and placed it over the back of a chair in the hopes it might dry out by the time he was done. He pulled off his jeans and did the same with them. He dove into the water and began his laps, taking each stroke methodically, enjoying the feeling of the cool water flowing over his shoulders as each arm surfaced. He wasn't sure how long he swam and hadn't kept track of his lap count. He stopped when he was out of breath. Max hadn't returned yet, but he was done with his swim. He pulled himself out of the water and sat on the edge of the pool, letting his feet prune up.

The sun was just starting to crest the trees beyond the swing set, casting long shadows across the pool. Casey allowed his mind to drift, imagining a place where he could finally relax, where shadows were just shadows and dead things were just a part of the natural cycle, and not a message he dreaded finding. When he heard the noise behind him, he panicked, suddenly aware he still wasn't wearing a shirt. He leapt up and spun about to see Max approaching with a tray of food. She wasn't blushing now, instead her eyebrows were tightly knitted together and her eyes were guarded.

Casey snatched up his shirt, which had dried quite nicely. He pulled it on hastily, not even bothering to turn it right side out.

"That's some tattoo," Max said, breaking the awkward silence.

She placed the tray on a table and began sorting out the paper plates and cups.

"I got it in Mexico," Casey said. He was doing his level best to remain calm. "I was a lot younger. A lot. I don't even remember doing it. Just woke up with my back covered in gauze and this monstrosity on it. You know what it means? I've asked around, and no one does."

"Nope," Max said.

He couldn't tell if she was lying or not. Whatever she'd been thinking when she saw his back, she was keeping to herself.

"Huh. I've always been worried it's a recipe for tamales or

something. You know those stories where people get Japanese writing tattooed on themselves, only to find it says something ridiculous, like, 'Eat at Joe's.' It's why I don't like people to see it. I don't want them to think I'm an idiot. At least, not right off the bat."

He waited for Max to laugh, or even smile at his joke, but she just eyed him as she poured some juice.

"It wasn't what I expected," she said suddenly. "Anne said you had prison tats. I thought maybe a topless mermaid."

Casey glanced away to hide his amusement. Good old Anne, he thought. While Max continued to set out the food, he touched his jeans. They were still damp.

"Want me to toss 'em in the dryer for you?" Max asked.

"If you tell me where, I'd be happy to do it for myself."

She pointed to a gap on the opposite side of the building from where his room was. He nodded and jogged away, relieved to have a minute to think.

The laundry area was small but modern. Max must have updated it as well, because all the machines were new and shiny. He picked one of the two dryers and dropped his pants in them. They hadn't been fitted with coin ops, which surprised Casey. The room was set up to be used by guests – no special locks on the doors. Free laundry wasn't common, even at upscale places. There was a small window above the dryers. Casey peered out at Max from the relative secrecy of the laundry room. She wasn't acting scared, or wary. She was still setting out the food, as if nothing had changed.

He wasn't exactly sure why he worried save that he always took pains to keep his tattoo covered when out and about. Even the women he went home with didn't often see it as over the years he'd established a long list of excuses for why the lights needed to be dimmed or positioned himself in such a way that his back was always away from them.

Most people who saw it just thought it was odd and nothing more. The few who could read Spanish had told him it was gibberish. No one, to his knowledge, had ever understood it – he'd told her the truth about that. Perhaps she could read Spanish, but was confused by what the words crudely inked on his back said. That might explain the look on her face after she'd seen it.

The funny feeling in his gut wasn't enough to bother him too much. If it was a problem, it was too late to fix it now. Plastering on a cheery, carefree look, he headed back out to the poolside. He padded over to Max in his bare feet and sat in a chair near where she had set out his plate. He noticed there were only two plates but decided against bringing it up. Guessing why Anne had decided to eat elsewhere wasn't difficult.

"When I first got here, this was a mystery to me," he said, pointing at the pool. "Olympic sized, right?"

Max nodded.

"I thought so. Salt water, too. I thought it was a strange investment. It seems like it would be a money sink to me. This far north, there's not much of a season for an outdoor pool."

"It's heated," Max said. "You can swim in it year-round."

Casey chuckled at the very idea of someone trudging through two feet of snow to take a swim, even if the pool was heated. But, when he looked across at Max, he didn't doubt for a second that she'd be the one to do it.

"You swim every day, don't you?" he asked.

"Yup. I was on the team in high school. Not here," she clarified. "This was my dad's thing, this motel. His baby. In the winter he was a teacher at a community college near where we lived. In the summers, he came here to personally run the Sunset."

Casey chewed on a bagel while Max talked. He noted a distinct downward curl of her mouth when she mentioned her father, a curl that only deepened when she mentioned his relationship to the motel. Something Janelle had revealed swirled back up to the surface of his thoughts.

"He was the big man here," Max said. "When he ran this place, he was his own boss. I always knew when summer was closing in, because my dad was practically floating around the house." She tossed the remainder of a croissant she'd been working on down and wiped her hands of it. "My mom, Anne and I lived in Rochester all year round. We never came here." She glanced up and noticed Casey watching her. She cleared her throat. "Sorry. I don't know why I keep doing that with you."

"Talking?" Casey asked teasingly. "Do you not normally talk to people?"

Max tossed a balled-up napkin at him and hit him squarely in the nose with it.

"Telling you personal stories no one wants to hear. I'm probably boring you out of your mind."

"You're not. I promise," he said. He cleared his throat nervously when she eyed him. "I... What did you swim?"

She leaned forward, cupping her chin in her hand, a hint of a smile teasing the corner of her lips.

"Butterfly was my specialty. I was decent enough to get on the team in college, too."

"Scholarship?" Casey asked.

"Didn't need it. I had one through the softball team."

"You're a jock!"

Casey enjoyed the sound of her laugh, but he enjoyed even

more that he was the one who elicited it.

"Please," she said. "I'm a faded jock at best."

"You can't call yourself faded if you swim every day."

"That's a reacquired habit. I stopped for a long while after college. Picked it back up about..." She paused, picking her croissant back up and tearing off a piece. "A year ago."

"Oh," Casey said, realizing the significance of what she was saying. "Keep your head occupied."

"Exactly. It helped. Something to do. Something where you can't smell or hear, and everywhere you look is blue. A good, calming color."

She popped the bread into her mouth before sighing. Casey suddenly felt irrationally angry at a complete stranger.

"I hope your ex is miserable with his new wife," he blurted out.

He blushed hotly before gulping down more juice in a vain attempt to look like it was a perfectly normal thing to say to someone you'd only known a couple days – just another casual breakfast conversation.

Max, chin still in her hand, looked at him quietly for a while. Casey recognized a gentle appreciation in her eyes, and it only made him feel warmer. She took a drink of her own juice before responding.

"I don't," she said.

He was surprised to hear it. It was rare to find someone who'd been tossed aside by their partner so cavalierly without any anger remaining, but Max looked as calm is if she was discussing the weather.

"Why not?" he asked.

Max looked like she wasn't sure she should answer. Casey was about to take back the question, to say it had been too personal, when Max changed her mind.

"If all I had was that last year we were together, I might feel that way. But we were married for fifteen years. Fourteen of those years were lovely. That's a long time to love someone and then wish them ill. Maybe it's stupid to think so, but I feel like if I wished he was miserable, it would cast doubt on what I thought I felt all those years. If it was so easy to hate him, did I ever really love him? And wishing this new wife is awful to him? Well it would really suck for him if he made a mistake loving her, because he can't come back now."

The dryer buzzed loudly enough that they both jumped when it happened.

"Your jeans are dry," she said, standing up. "I'll clear this up. I think today is a painting day for me, since you cleared all those rooms."

She collected all the leftovers and garbage without any more conversation. Casey felt reluctant to leave the table. He wasn't sure what he wanted to say to her but he knew he wanted to say something. He decided to wing it.

"I'm baffled there are men out there who would leave someone like you. No one he finds will ever measure up."

He walked away without waiting for a response, his ears burning with embarrassment. He felt brave and stupid all at once. Everything inside him felt unfamiliar – not bad, but not entirely good either. How he had managed to get through his early teenage years without ever feeling this way for anyone, he'd never know.

There was a suite of different fears coursing through him – fears he'd never had to contend with before. Despite all that, he couldn't deny the joy he felt when he looked back and she was still there, her motion halted by his words, looking after him. Despite his clumsiness and inexperience, he'd said the right thing after all.

SIX

The morning was waning when Casey dropped the last moldy cushion in the dumpster. He'd filled the rusty metal container right to the top. It was an industrial-sized unit, something Max must have ordered special for the remodeling. The dumpster was stored on the same side of the motel as the laundry facilities. Several cargo containers full of mid-grade motel furniture in the same neutral colors Max had chosen for the remodeled rooms sat behind the dumpster.

He'd been in and out of those containers all day, hauling all the components required for kitting out a motel into rooms that had finished construction. He thought he'd get used to the strong smell of plastic that filled each of the metal boxes, but every time he entered one of the containers, with the sun beating down on the un-insulated metal, he felt like he was working in a shower curtain factory.

All the motel rooms were now empty of old furniture. Casey liked the idea of having an entire part of the project done. If he went out on his hunt and fortune didn't favor him, he wouldn't be coming back to the Sunset. The possibility he might not come out of his scrape on top troubled him in ways he wasn't used to having to think about. Since he'd taken up the hunt, he'd never had anyone but himself to worry about if he disappeared. Having finished cleaning out the rooms eased those concerns. It was a small, but significant, comfort to know that at least Max wouldn't have to haul mattresses with a thousand different genetic samples deposited on them.

"You do work fast, don't you," Max said, joining him around the side of the motel. "I think I need to give you a raise."

"Please don't," Casey said. He wiped his brow and walked over to her. "I mean it. You've done too much for me as it is. It would feel weird to take more money from you."

Max wiped her face, leaving a smear of eggshell paint behind.

"Okay. I won't bother you about it again." She looked a little uncomfortable, and Casey realized it was the longest conversation they'd had since breakfast. "But I do want you to know, I really appreciate how hard you're working."

"Thank you," he said.

She pursed her lips, and Casey wondered if she had lost her train of thought as she rocked back and forth on her feet a few seconds. His nerves – on edge from making an obvious overture during breakfast – calmed when he realized he wasn't the only one who felt awkward about it. He still wasn't sure it was a wise idea, considering everything going on. But telling her how he felt, even if it was spur of the moment, helped him feel more level headed than he had since he'd met her.

He'd always gone into the small towns his tracking took him through with a fatalistic notion – he might never leave them. For the first time since he could remember, he wanted to make it out. He wanted to see what would happen on the other side of this mess he was in. Even the possibility of there being another side was exhilarating. He'd lived this way for so long, he'd forgotten what is was like to feel like a normal person. He couldn't imagine anything more normal than falling for someone; that included all the normal feelings of anxiety, the rushes of adrenaline and the softness of the glow that came with mutual appreciation.

He wanted to get her back on track, not make her feel like she was bothering him, and she was still standing there as if caught in a loop in her head.

"Is that... it?" he asked as gently as possible.

His words brought her back to the present. She snapped her fingers and pulled out her phone.

"I called Janelle," Max said. "She has your bag."

Casey inhaled sharply. He'd forgotten Max was planning to call Janelle around lunch. He blushed a little as he thought about seeing her with Max in tow.

"Oh. Um. I could just..."

"Come on," Max said. "I know I'm tired of fast food and there's a place in town that serves homecooked meals. It'll be good. I'm gonna wash my hands and then I'll meet you at the truck."

She walked off before Casey could protest further. If she was bothered by the Janelle thing, he couldn't tell. He went into the nearest room to clean up, washing his hands and face thoroughly before heading out to the truck.

"You want anything from Two Day's?" he heard Max shouting.

He rounded the corner and saw Anne standing outside the office. Anne shared a cool glare with him before turning back to her sister.

"Mashed potatoes."

"Mashed potatoes aren't lunch, Anne," Max said.

"Mashed potatoes and gravy then," Anne said.

Max put her hand on her hip while Casey got in the passenger side of the truck.

"Fine," Anne said. "If Sue has fresh corn on the cob, I'll take that, too."

Satisfied, Max got in the truck and started it up. Anne stared daggers into Casey as they pulled away. He wondered if she would stand there glaring after him the whole time they were gone – she looked mad enough to do it.

"She doesn't like me much," he joked.

"No," Max said. "But she really is a terrible judge of character. So she doesn't get a say in whether or not you stay."

"What makes you so sure about me?" he asked.

It was a question he'd had since the very beginning. More accurately, it was a variation of the question that had been burning inside him – "Why are you helping me?" He couldn't imagine trusting someone so immediately.

"Because you trust me," she said.

The answer was surprising. He wasn't sure where she'd gotten that idea.

"You don't know that."

"Sure I do," she said. "You came back. You knew I'd let you back in. You trusted me to be here when you needed something. You took the phone. You took the room. You weren't worried I'd hurt you, or call the cops on you. You ate the food I gave you. You slept in the bed I made. You trust me."

Casey scoffed, but only halfheartedly. He could see some sense in what she said, but it still sounded a touch dubious.

"I'm a man. You're a woman. It's easy for a man to trust a woman."

Max looked away from the road a second to toss him a questioning look.

"Men aren't usually afraid of women hurting them... physically," he clarified.

"You don't think I could take you?" Max asked.

She was half-joking; he could tell that much.

"I..." he looked over at her and she grinned at him. "Yes. But I don't think you would."

"Because you trust me."

"A lion trusts that a gazelle won't hurt it either," Casey said. "Doesn't stop the lion from eating the gazelle."

"Ah," Max said. "A lion is aware it means to harm the gazelle. It's always aware of that. It knows that when it does, that gazelle will fight for its life. It might break the lion's jaw with a kick, or gore it. Or simply outrun it. A lion doesn't trust the gazelle not to hurt it. The lion behaves like a lion does because it knows the gazelle will try to hurt it. It stalks. It sneaks. It waits for the right moment. Then it attacks. A lion doesn't waltz right up and give its name to the gazelle, then relax like its on holiday poolside. A lion behaves like a lion."

Casey folded his hands in his lap. What a difference a day made, he thought. He was glad he'd decided to come back to the Sunset.

"You're still not convinced," Max said when he didn't reply.

"Not exactly," Casey said. "I think it probably works most of the time to think that way. Because most people aren't lions, so it doesn't matter if you're wrong. But I think there are lions that have learned to pass as gazelles. And those are the lions that worry me."

"Fair enough," Max said. "But I have a failsafe for that, too."

"What's that?"

"I'm not a gazelle. I'm Max. And I can handle myself."

There was no arguing with that.

They passed by the supermarket she'd dropped him at the night before. During the day, it was much busier – the lot was packed with people coming and going from the building with such regularity that the stack of grocery carts he'd hidden behind was a quarter the size. That's when he remembered her conversation with the police chief.

"Max?"

"Yes?"

Now was as good a time as any to test whether he really trusted her or not.

"I might have overheard you talking to that cop yesterday."

She chuckled.

"I had a feeling. I saw you lurking outside Bob's office. Were you worried what I'd say about you?"

"No." It was the truth, he realized. He hadn't worried at all, now that he thought about it. "I saw those missing kids posters. I heard you talking about it. I guess I was curious."

Max was quiet as she made several turns. Casey recognized the streets they were going down. The pink-curtained window on the large house was still open. A flash of concern swept through him before he realized if something had happened to that girl – if she hadn't made it home – there'd be cop cars all around the house.

"Why these kids?" Max asked.

"Excuse me?"

Max stopped at a sign and turned to look at Casey. Her look was inquisitive, but her eyes were guarded once again.

"These kids. Why were you curious about them? They're teenagers. Almost eighteen, in fact. Maybe they eloped."

Casey searched her face for a sign of what he could say that would satisfy her. There were no clues there. He looked at the street corner. Not far from where they were stopped was where Jay had threatened him. The memory provoked an idea.

"Not them. You." Before she could respond, he continued. "You said something about amateur detectives finding something that bothered the police. I got the feeling you were talking about yourself. If those kids were murdered—"

"Are you trying to say you're worried about me?" Max asked, disbelief tingeing her voice.

"Yes," Casey said. He turned and faced her, his expression deadly serious. "I've been trying to say that since I met you."

He couldn't tell at first if he'd managed to deflect her suspicion. Telling her some of the truth felt like the best approach – he really was worried about her, but not because he thought she was out sleuthing and would stumble upon something she couldn't handle.

While Max obviously cared about some of the people of Manistee, Casey had been around her long enough to deduce that she was practical. So practical, she was unlikely to think hiking out into the woods to search for clues was going to work any better for her than it had the police. It wasn't armchair detecting Casey was worried about; he was worried the danger would come to her.

The truck sat at the corner for half a minute before Max finally moved on.

"I'm not investigating them," Max said. "You don't have to worry." She glanced over at Casey and offered him a small smile. "I do, however, appreciate your concern."

She turned down a street close to where Janelle lived.

"But I was a little pissed Frank didn't listen to me at all."

Casey wondered if she was baiting him – waiting for him to ask about what she'd told Frank. It would prove to her his curiosity extended further than her welfare. But she kept talking without any prompting.

"I told Frank there were at least two other disappearances from the area over the summer that might be related. He wasn't appreciative of the tip."

"Why do you think they were related?"

If the question concerned Max, she didn't let it show. She pulled into Janelle's driveway and turned off the engine.

"Maybe it's nothing. Frank could be right, it could be coincidence. But I have a cousin who runs a campground south of here. Down by Big Rapids. A couple who was camping there went missing. Same as George and Sarah. The missing couple's car was still there. The camp site was still set up. Everything was there."

Casey tensed up. He rubbed his sweaty palms on his jeans casually.

"That does sound suspicious. The cops didn't even check it out?"

"No."

Now it was Max's turn to look tense, though Casey suspected it was for different reasons than him. She sighed and leaned on the steering wheel.

"I'm not being entirely fair to Frank. He did call the Big Rapids' police department. That was something, at least."

"I'm guessing that was the end of the investigation, though."

Max made a disgusted sound.

"Conflicting reports," she said. "A neighboring camper said they saw the couple go off on one of the hiking trails. Didn't see them come back. Another said they saw them sneak out onto the water after dark. Search and rescue found some clothes in the water that they confirmed belonged to the couple. Case closed, I guess."

Casey leaned back in his seat. He was surprised Max had made the connection between the two disappearances with such contradictory information.

"Clothes in the water," he said. "That sounds an awful lot like a drowning."

"I know what you're thinking," Max said. "It's a stretch to say that's related at all to what happened here. But, they haven't found the bodies yet. And the couple was in their sixties. Sound like the skinny-dipping type to you?"

"No," Casey admitted. "But if someone saw them... maybe it's a bucket list thing."

"Could be," Max said. "I don't really trust what the witnesses had to say about it, though."

"You think they lied for some reason?"

"No, but... How much do you know about camping culture?"

"It's a culture now?" Casey asked with a grin.

Max's mood lightened visibly. She laughed and twisted in her seat a little so she could look at him directly.

"Culture is a highfalutin word for drinking beer." She looked at him in a new way, or, at least, Casey hadn't seen the look before. It was more open – more comfortable. "Lots of little campgrounds out here thrive on the roving drunkard. I like to think of that kind of camper as someone who went to Spring Break once and thought, 'I never want to leave this feeling.' But when they get older, Acapulco isn't in their budget anymore. And they get weird looks from all the college students at Fort Lauderdale. Camping is where the eternal Spring Breaker retires."

"I wouldn't have pegged camping as party central," Casey said.

"Yeah. It really depends on the campground. If they don't

want that element, they work hard to keep it away. Lifetime bans, rules on alcohol, those kinds of things. But a lot of these places are run by people who just happen to have land in a pretty spot. Land that isn't close to anything except a mile of water and a hundred acres of forest. Some will set up campsites and invite all comers. Others will buy a fleet of used school busses and a metric ton of rubber rafts and start up a float trip company. And the campers and floaters will show up with more beer than sense or water, and spend their days and nights hammered, dehydrated, beet red from the sun, and more bleary eyed than a naked mole rat.

"My cousin's campsite draws serious campers, because it's a good location, but she doesn't keep out the partiers. Every time I call her she thanks god Michigan is a deposit state so even when she does spend half her days fishing beer cans out of the water and the brush, she gets something for it."

"The people who saw the couple go into the water?" Casey asked, beginning to connect the dots.

"She said they were regulars. They come every year, with a boat and a truck bed full of coolers and not much else." Max paused for a beat before adding, "And then there were the dogs."

Casey didn't get the chance to ask a follow-up. Janelle tapped on the window of the truck just then, a smirk on her face. Max jumped a little in surprise. For his part, Casey groaned inwardly. He had almost forgotten why they'd made this trip. The conversation, if not pleasant in content, certainly friendly in tone, had lulled him into a welcome, warm fuzzy feeling. He almost reached out to stop Max as she opened her window. Sense won out, and he kept his composure.

"Janelle," Max said in greeting.

"You guys been sitting out here a while," she said. "Neighbors gonna talk if you don't come in soon."

"We're here to pick up your last gentleman caller's duffle bag, Janelle. I think the neighbors are already talking."

Janelle winked, or tried to, in Casey's direction. It ended up looking more like a face spasm than a wink, which, Casey noted, was probably true with most winks. Winking was a kind of art, and he hadn't managed to master it, either.

"Come in for a drink," Janelle said. As if anticipating the polite decline, she added, "Smoothies, I should say. I got carried away at the farmer's market and bought way too much fruit. Come help me eat some of it so it doesn't go to waste."

She headed off without waiting for a response. Max and Casey exchanged a look before she opened her door to get out of the truck. This time, Casey's arm did dart out, his hand touching her shoulder and halting her progress.

"I didn't... I mean to say..." Casey tried to swallow but it felt like his tongue had dried into a husk. "I didn't sleep with her."

Max simply stared at him. When she didn't respond, he decided he hadn't been clear enough.

"We didn't have sex."

"Yes," Max said. "I got that the first time."

"I just... you were..." Casey closed his mouth. It was being its most traitorous self at the moment, and he needed to cut it off before more nonsense escaped it. He took a breath and started again. "I came here with that intention. Then I realized I'd made a mistake. Not because there's anything wrong with Janelle. I came here because I was afraid, and I thought by coming here, it would give me enough distance from my fears that I could deal with them and move on."

He looked up at her, willing her to understand. It had been incredibly difficult to say, and he didn't want to have to say it again, particularly since he'd been as clear as he was emotionally capable of being. If he had to spell it out, he didn't think his nerves would let him.

"I wanted... you... to know."

With these words, it looked like his message, vague as it was, finally hit home. Max sucked in a breath of air, then let it out in a slow sigh.

"I see," Max said. She looked awkwardly at her hands. "We shouldn't keep Janelle waiting."

She left him sitting in the truck, dumbfounded. Casey buried his face in his hands. If someone had told him before that moment that he was bad with women, he'd have laughed it off. He was good. He could walk into a bar and leave with anyone he wanted to, even the ones who'd come with someone, should he want a challenge and the inevitable fight. His looks helped him out, but it was more than that. He'd learned from trial and error how to talk to women, how to charm them. Not even Anne, who despised him, was beyond his reach. He wasn't prideful about it; it was a survival mechanism.

Occasionally, when he'd come into a bar and snag a date, men would marvel at the ease with which he did it. They'd say something along the lines of, "you just landed the coldest fish in the lake." He never thought of it as a gift or a talent. If a man needed to learn which berries were poison and which were okay to eat or he'd starve, he'd learn. Casey had learned; that's all there was to it.

Now, he was beginning to wonder if not caring was also part of his ease with women. He didn't want just one night with Max, a warm meal and a place to sleep. He wanted all the nights with her. He wanted to wake up in the mornings and swim in the pool, side by side, even if he had to trek through two feet of snow to do it. He became angry with himself for messing all that up. If he could only have been forthcoming, instead of double speaking and obfuscating, things would have gone better. In the seconds he sat there, he continued to upbraid himself until it was all blown away by one word.

"You coming, Casey?" Max shouted from Janelle's doorway.

The fog of self loathing lifted in an instant. He hopped out of the truck and jogged jauntily over to her. She looked at him bemusedly when he reached the stoop, a silly grin plastered on his face.

"What?" she asked.

"You called me Casey."

"You asked me to."

Casey's grin widened. Despite his brain actively shouting at him to remain chill, he couldn't stop himself from acting like a fool. It didn't look like it was hurting his chances, either. Max's blush was all the confirmation he needed.

"Come on," Max said, shaking her head. "Let's get this over with. I'd still like to get some things done back at the Sunset."

The house was just as Casey remembered it, save his bag was sitting near the stairs. That wasn't where he'd left it, but like Max, he'd assumed Janelle had rifled through it. He wasn't angry about it – the only shocking thing she would have found in his duffle bag would be the rolled-up socks he'd yet to clean. Otherwise, it was clothing, mostly from secondhand stores. Even the bag came from a thrift shop; it wasn't uncommon for him to leave his bag behind somewhere. Sometimes it was more hassle to track it down than to simply start over. This bag was only a year old.

Janelle was in the kitchen, waiting with a pitcher of something thick that was the color of a fresh bruise. Casey filed in after Max and took a glass when it was offered. The strong scent of blueberries filled his nose as Janelle poured.

"Kent had some out for people to try," Janelle said. "I bought two pounds without thinking about it."

"Blueberries?" Max asked.

"Yes," Janelle said. "There's a couple bananas in here, too."

Max and Casey sipped while Janelle looked pointedly between the two of them. The smoothie was delicious.

"Wow," Casey said.

It was a little strange for Casey to be in someone's house, casually drinking a homemade smoothie. It was so mundane, so normal, it made him feel uneasy – not because he didn't enjoy it, but because he did. The event was nothing: a regular day in a regular town. Realizing that made him feel worse. It hit him that, in all his adult life, he'd never had a regular day. He was thirty-five years old and had never had a regular day.

His feelings must have leaked through to his face, because Max set her drink down and looked concerned.

"I've never seen anyone have a life changing smoothie before," she said. "Everything okay?"

"What?"

Casey could barely comprehend the question; his mind was still in shock from the revelation. The two women sounded like the adults in a Peanuts cartoon.

"You look like you've seen a ghost," Janelle said. "You aren't allergic to blueberry, are you?"

"No," Casey said. Their sounds were forming words again. "It's very good. Thank you."

Janelle was the first to dismiss Casey's strange behavior. She turned to Max, who still looked concerned, and clinked glasses.

"To new beginnings," she said.

"New beginnings?" Max asked.

"I don't know," Janelle said. "That's a thing people say when they toast, right?"

Casey was pretty sure Janelle knew exactly what she meant when she made the toast, but he didn't say anything. Whatever game Janelle was playing, he wasn't worried she'd catch Max up in her net. He polished off his smoothie and set down the glass in a not so subtle attempt to indicate he was ready to go. Janelle foiled his plans by refilling his cup almost as soon as it hit the table.

"Have another, big guy."

"Janelle..."

Max's voice was full of exasperation, but Janelle either didn't notice, or purposefully ignored it.

"I heard some interesting news this morning about George and Sarah," she said.

Casey tensed. Eight shots were clearly not enough to make Janelle forget. He could tell from the look in her eye she was relaying this information for his sake, not Max's. He hoped she wasn't about to tip off Max about his interest in the case, especially not after he'd taken such pains to convince her he wasn't concerned about it.

"Have they found something?" Max asked.

"No," Janelle said. "But I guess Travis is coming down from his hunting shack early this year just for this. If it's bears that got them police tracking dogs in a tizzy, he says his hounds'll do better. That's what he uses them for. They're heading up to the campground tomorrow."

Max finished her drink and set down her cup. She anticipated Janelle's move and held off the refill just in time, blueberry smoothie sloshing in Janelle's pitcher as Max waved it away.

"We had a lot of rain this morning," Max said. "First since the disappearance. Wonder if that hurts the dog's chances at finding anything."

No, thought Casey, it will only help – especially in this case.

"No idea," Janelle said. "Travis didn't seem too worried about it. He was at the Farmer's Market telling anyone who'd listen that his hounds would find 'em and bring 'em home."

Casey finished off his second smoothie in silence, trying his best to remain passive. He held his glass, prepared to deposit it the second Max looked ready to leave, keeping it away from Janelle's hovering pitcher.

"He shouldn't do that," Max said.

"What? Lend his dogs?" Janelle asked.

"No. Talk about finding them. Miriam is a mess. Travis comes in talking big, she might see an end to her suffering, only to feel worse when he doesn't find them alive."

"You think they're dead, too, then," Janelle said.

Casey bit his lip to keep his face still.

"Who else thinks they're dead?" Max asked.

Casey looked anywhere but at Janelle. His eyes landed on a cuckoo clock shaped like a skyscraper.

"Uh," Janelle stammered, "I heard Jay was saying they were dead."

"Jay?" Max asked. Casey risked looking over at Max only to see her look of surprise. "Does he know something? Has he told his father? When I talked to Frank, he was still nurturing the idea it was a runaway case."

"It could be nothing," Janelle said. She set the pitcher down. "Jay's upset, you know. George was his friend. He's probably just blowing off steam."

Max looked unconvinced, which only heightened Casey's stress. If she went back to the police with this info, they might find the trace evidence before he did. If that happened, his search would start all over again as his prey ran for safer hunting grounds.

He set his cup down again – he was unconcerned that Janelle would try to delay them any further. A good gossip knew they couldn't out their sources, and Janelle had almost outed him. She looked genuinely apologetic about it.

"Your bag is by the stairs," she said. "You'll want to clean your things, by the way. Something in there stinks something awful."

Janelle had given him the diversionary topic he needed. He put on his most shamed face and picked up his bag.

"Yeah. I'm sorry. I meant to ask yesterday about laundry." He turned to Max. "I'll make sure it doesn't stink up the room you gave me."

Max looked more than a little baffled by the sudden change in topic. Casey went to the door, taking the opportunity to lead her back outside where she couldn't probe Janelle with more questions. She followed almost automatically, waving when Janelle said good-bye and heading mutely to her truck. Once they were both in, she turned the key, but before she pulled out of the driveway she turned to Casey.

"Did that seem weird to you?"

He shrugged.

"I can't really say. I don't know her all that well."

He put on his best innocent look. It must have been enough for Max, because she clucked her tongue and put the truck in gear. For the first time since he'd met her, Casey was glad she wasn't in a talkative mood on the short trip to the restaurant.

SEVEN

The paint cans clattered together as Casey tipped them into the dumpster. He sipped from a bottle of water as he looked over the evidence of his work. Old carpet, mattresses and empty paint cans filled the dumpster to the point of bursting. It was a monument to his two days of hard labor, and it felt good to have done it. In all the years he'd done odd jobs, he'd never felt as accomplished before. It was certainly the best paying job he'd ever secured, but that wasn't why he felt so good about it. He had his suspicions it had something to do with his employer.

He heard footsteps in the gravel behind him and turned around with a welcome smile on his face, only to have it fall immediately.

"Anne," he said. "Were the mashed potatoes cold?"

She crossed her arms. Over the last couple days, whenever he'd encountered her she'd had an almost cartoonish look of disdain for him on her face. Something had changed, and her look was far chillier and vaguely dangerous.

"I've been patient with Max," Anne said. "She's my sister,

and she's been through a lot in the last year. But she's wrong about you."

"I'm doing my best to stay out of your hair, Anne." He gestured at the dumpster full of old furniture. "I don't know what else I can do to prove I'm just looking for work and a place to stay."

Anne took a few steps closer. She was at least eight inches shorter than him, but that didn't make her any less imposing just then, not when she was armored in anger.

"I thought I was done with you," she said. "I thought you'd gotten your cash and would get with whatever floozy was easiest. Then you'd be gone. Now, you're back. And she's smiling when she thinks no one is looking."

Casey couldn't stop a smile from showing. It was only a flash, but she'd seen it.

"No!"

She shoved him backward into the dumpster, causing several of the empty cans of paint to spill out onto the ground.

"You're a liar," Anne said through tightly clenched teeth. "Yesterday, I told her she was lucky you left. She gave me some sad story about how you were starving, how you were hungry all the time, how worried she was about you."

Anne looked him up and down with a sneer. Casey felt it best to weather the storm and kept quiet until he thought Anne was finished.

"I had a boyfriend who looked like you. Went to the gym three days a week. Had to cook him a pound of chicken every night. You haven't gone hungry recently. Probably not ever."

There was nothing Casey could say to assuage Anne's fears about him. She wouldn't hear anything he told her when she was so enraged, and the truth was not an option. He kept his mouth shut.

"I thought so," she said. "I'll let you stay and help Max fix this shithole up. I want out as much as she does and, I'll admit, you're moving things along. But you're going to stop this thing you started with her. You're going to stop it now. You're going to be nice about it, too. Tell her you've decided to go back to your ex. Something. Anything. Just be nice about it."

Anne got up in his face. Her whole body seethed with contempt.

"If I find out you slept with her, I'm calling the cops. I know people in this town. They won't need a reason. All I'll have to tell them is I don't like you. They'll come down here and haul your ass off. It won't matter if you're innocent, they'll make sure you go down for something."

Anne backed away. She gave him one last hard look before she turned around and left the way she came. Casey took a breath, realizing he'd been holding it while she'd backed him into a corner. His hands shook as he wiped his brow.

All the way back to his room, he wondered if she'd actually do it. Something told him she could – her words had the weight of truth to them – but being able to do something and going through with the deed were two different things, something he knew all too well. He closed the door behind him with a shuddering breath.

It had been a long time since he'd felt such hatred directed toward him. People who felt that way were capable of a lot of things. A woman like Anne was far more formidable than someone like Jay. Jay was a bully who used physical force to get his way. Casey could deal with that. But Anne – she was coming at him sideways, using methods he couldn't easily deflect. The danger in her threat was real, and would have terrible consequences in ways he'd never be able to convey to Anne.

His eyes fell on a laundry basket on his freshly made bed. He approached it slowly, still feeling jittery. Inside, his clothes were clean and folded neatly. He inhaled, a warm lemon scent filling his nostrils. Max had washed his clothes for him. He had no idea when she'd have had the time to do it. She'd been working in the same rooms as him most of the afternoon.

With a heavy heart, he stepped away from the basket and headed into the bathroom. He flipped the shower on, making it so hot steam filled the tiled room from top to bottom. Anne's threat was as present in the room as the sound of the shower. Casey stood under the water, the temperature close enough to scalding that pain coursed through his skin. He pressed his forehead against the cool tiles.

He couldn't stay. He wasn't sure if Max would understand his leaving a second time, but he couldn't risk it. Had Anne threatened to hurt him in almost any other way, he knew it would be unlikely to come to pass, but this blow was only a phone call away. It was such a small hurdle for her to overcome, it might as well not exist. Casey was too close to his goal to risk that. Staying at the Sunset would be playing with fire – a fire that was already blazing around him and out of control, a fire that licked his flesh, trying to catch hold.

After soaking for nearly an hour, he washed up and got out, his whole body pink from the heat. He felt sick to his stomach. It had been a long time since the pains he felt were anything but hunger. He sat on the toilet, wrapped in his towel, and put his head in his hands while plotting a course of action.

He could leave Max a note – something as honest as he could make it – in the hopes she'd be understanding. He'd leave late, after everyone had gone to bed, taking to the road and making his way to the campsite. He might make it there before dawn, giving him enough time to investigate before the dogs got there. He'd be the better tracker and find wherever they were hiding before anyone else. Then all he'd have to do was clean up this mess.

He let that last part of the plan remain blurry in his mind, as always. Everything else up to that point, he visualized with perfect clarity. He'd have to be fast, so as not to be beaten by the officials. He'd have to be unseen, so as not to draw attention. He'd have to be strong, so as not to lose his nerve.

His thoughts so concentrated on the task at hand, when the knock at the door came, he got up to answer it on autopilot, not even bothering to dress. He opened it to Max standing there with an envelope in one hand and a plastic bag in the other.

"Oh!" She blushed and turned away from him. "I'm sorry. I hope I didn't drag you from your shower."

She held out the envelope without turning back toward him. Casey took it dumbly. It took several seconds for his brain to switch gears and notice that he was still in his towel. Max's appearance wasn't helping his concentration, either. She looked different in a way he couldn't pin down. Her hair wasn't tied up in a pony-tail, and she wasn't wearing the cargo shorts or the tank top. Instead, she had on a pair of jeans that fit snugly around her hips and a pink top. The top was made from something that fluffed up in a cloud of fibers, swathing her in softness.

"Are you going out?" he asked without thinking.

He immediately regretted it as he suddenly realized she'd dressed this way for him.

"What? No. I'm... I don't really know."

She backed away, and Casey could sense she was losing her nerve. This was probably the closest she'd ever get to asking him out on a date. The idea she was changing her mind and walking away from his door dispelled all his careful planning, leaving only one thought behind: he wanted her to stay.

"Is that dinner?" he asked.

Max stopped in her tracks and turned. She gave him an apologetic look.

"Sorry. Yes. Chinese. I ordered a bunch of different things. American sugar chicken, too, since I wasn't sure you liked Chinese and from what I can tell, people who don't like Chinese still like American sugar chicken."

"American sugar chicken?"

"General Tsao's. Orange. I think it's all the same, just variations on how much sugar. This one is Orange. I think."

She held out the bag. Casey glanced at it for a split second before stepping back from his door to invite her in. Max stared at the gap he'd made as if it were a toothy mouth yawning to devour her.

"Come on," he said. "I promise I won't bite. I'll even put some clothes on."

"You don't have to do that," Max said.

Casey raised his eyebrows. Max closed her eyes and shook her head.

"I mean, you don't have to invite me in."

She couldn't have looked more awkward if she'd tried. Casey found the whole situation incredibly endearing. He hefted the bag in his hand and looked at her quizzically.

"This feels like five pounds of food. Is there anything left for you?"

A pained expression passed over her face. Casey tried not to smile. His guess had been right – she had planned to eat dinner with him but chickened out at the last second.

"You can just, uh, you know what? I'm fine. Whatever you don't eat, I'll come by and pick up later."

She started to leave again. Casey panicked at the possibility he was letting yet another opportunity slip by him. The need to keep Max safe still lurked just under his baser desires, but the surge of endorphins running through him temporarily blinded him to his sense of duty.

"Max," he called out. "Please stay. I'd like it very much if you ate with me."

He wasn't sure if he heard her mutter an expletive or not, but it didn't matter. She turned around, and, with a smile, accepted his invitation.

He set the food down while Max maneuvered her way into a chair as close to the door as possible, as if already planning her rapid escape. Casey grabbed a shirt and some jeans from the laundry basket on the bed.

"I'll just be a minute," he said.

"Sure," Max said.

She looked wound up. There was enough nervous energy in the room for four people, so Casey hurried into the bathroom and rushed through dressing, concerned he'd come out to an empty room. He was glad that when he opened the door, Max was still sitting there.

"I... I want us to be—" He stopped, choosing his words carefully. He sat on the bed so he wasn't looming over her. "I feel like there's something here. Something good that could be something amazing. And I'd like us to be more than just friends. But I also don't want you to feel weird around me."

"That makes two of us," Max said.

She laughed nervously. Casey mentally flew through the things he might say to calm her down. None of them felt right.

"You know, it's funny," he said. "I'm scared out of my mind right now. It's funny because of all the things to be scared of, this, sitting alone in a room with a lovely woman, shouldn't be on the list."

Max ran her fingers through her hair before clasping her hands in her lap. She looked thoughtful as she met Casey's eyes.

"We're scared of pain, really. Getting into a relationship is like exposing your belly to someone. Few things hurt as much as having your trust broken by that person. If you need—" Max paused. She smoothed her fluffy shirt then looked back at him. "I don't know how you ended up on my doorstep. I don't want to ask about it if you don't want to talk about it. And maybe that's the problem. Maybe all of this is too fast. If you're feeling scared, it's because I'm pushing, I think. Overenthusiasm. I shouldn't have come to your door. Not like this."

She stood. Casey jumped up, suddenly anxious she was going to leave.

"It isn't just that, though," Max said, continuing her thought. "The fact you're working for me. I know that's a problem, too. It's wrong of me to pressure you like that. I don't want you to think you have to do anything you aren't ready for. I'm sorry I've made you uncomfortable."

She started for the door. Casey opened his mouth, but nothing came out. He was unable to fully process what she was saying quickly enough. He went to her and grabbed her hand.

"I'm not—" he started.

"It's okay, Casey. I'm not saying we can't explore whatever this is," Max said. "I'm just saying, we can put this on pause until it isn't scary. For either of us."

Casey pulled her around to face him. He took her other hand in his, and made his case.

"I am not scared about what might happen between us. I know what I want and how I feel and nothing has ever felt as right to me before. I'm scared because I'm afraid I'll fuck it up.

Because I've never done this before. I've never exposed my belly. I'm not scared of what will happen if I do. I'm not scared of what you might do. You wouldn't hurt me. I'm scared that I won't know what to say or do to make and keep you happy. It's all I want to do right now, and I'm afraid... what if I don't know how?"

Casey waited, barely bothering to breathe. His hands still held hers. She hadn't yet tried to pull away. She just looked at him, as if unable to move. He leaned in, slowly and deliberately. When his lips met hers, the fire that had been threatening to consume him finally caught hold. It blazed through him like an inferno, catching Max up in its eddies.

He couldn't remember getting her to the bed. He couldn't remember pulling off his clothes, or how hers ended up on the floor. He did remember every second of how she felt, how her skin smelled, how warm she was against him, how her fingers entwined with his while he moved atop her. He remembered the way her hair tickled his nose when he wrapped himself around her, the softness of her kiss and the sound of her deepest sighs. He held these memories close as the sheets tangled and twisted into knots around them, tying them together in a heap of moist air and quiet promises.

Casey set a plate of food on top of the microwave. It was so hot; the steam made a sound as it escaped the caramelized bits of meat.

"You sure you don't want any?" he asked Max, who was admiring him from the bed.

At some point during their tumble, he'd gotten up and turned the AC all the way down, chilling the room to almost uncomfortable levels to avoid having to stop to take a break. Max was bundled up in a cocoon of all the blankets. He grinned at her.

"I think you're taking your life into your own hands if you eat that," she said, shaking her head. "It's been sitting out for hours."

"I nuked it good," he said. He forked a piece of meat and sniffed it before popping it in his mouth. "And I have a cast-iron stomach. I can eat almost anything."

"Hmm," Max said.

A look crossed her face that Casey had trouble deciphering, but it was followed by her opening her cocoon to invite him back to the bed, so he forgot it almost as quickly as it faded from view. He held his plate aloft as he crawled into bed, allowing Max to wrap him in her blankets and hold him close. While he ate, she leaned into him, placing her cheek against his shoulder.

"I probably don't have to tell you," she said softly, "but let's not mention this to Anne."

The food caught in Casey's throat. He had to swallow several times to get it to go down, and, even then, the feeling something was sitting there just below his neck, wouldn't go away.

"I wouldn't dream of it," he said.

He felt Max snuggle in, then her breathing slowed. He looked down to see that her eyes were closed. After a few more bites, he set his plate down and carefully leaned back against the headboard, pulling Max close. She mumbled a little as he moved, but didn't wake up enough to open her eyes.

The deed was done. He'd pulled the trigger without a thought for the consequences. Even now, with Max curled up around him, he still had difficulty accepting any downside. He knew he might not feel that way if Anne found out and went through with her threat but, just then, he didn't care.

He still had other things to do though; things he couldn't easily explain to Max – not just yet. After twenty minutes, when it was clear Max was deeply asleep, he slipped out from bed, carefully bundled her up, and went to the dresser. He picked up a motel branded pad of paper and looked around for the pen. It had rolled off into the garbage. When he reached down to fish it out, he saw a gum wrapper in the bin with it. He pulled it out, inspecting it with a puzzled look. He brought it close to his nose and inhaled, catching the scent of spearmint.

Anne.

He looked at Max in his bed. This was something he hadn't thought about when he'd made his plans. If Anne came into his room and saw Max there, it might redline her. He briefly considered carrying Max back to her room, but aside from the fact that he'd have to do it without Anne seeing him, he didn't know how he'd explain it to Max when she asked, and he knew she would.

He didn't see any way to deal with it that wouldn't cause more trouble. Starting a fight between the two sisters was the last thing he wanted and telling Max about Anne's threat was a sure-fire way to do just that. He went ahead with his plan, and hastily scrawled a note to Max.

You were right. The food was inedible. I was going to wake you up to ask about borrowing your truck, but you were too beautiful to disturb. I'm running into town to grab something to eat. If you want to place an order, I've still got that crazy diamond phone with me. I'll pick up some donuts for the morning, too.

I'll be back soon,

Casey

He put the note under her phone on the bedside stand. Hopefully, he'd be back before Max woke and she'd never see it – it would be easier to explain to her after the fact that he'd borrowed her truck after he'd returned, and no one could worry if he'd stolen it. He was positive that would be Anne's first conclusion.

He dressed, then found the keys to the truck. He started to pick up the envelope Max had brought but decided to leave it. He had the money she'd given him yesterday. Leaving the second day's pay behind in an easy-to-see spot would lessen concerns he'd run off with her vehicle. After cleaning up all the Chinese food, he peeked out the door. Anne wasn't anywhere in sight, so he was good to go.

He moved to the truck with purpose. Anne's room was adjacent to the office, likely because staffing it was her main contribution to running the motel. Her car was there, and the lights in her room were off. He hoped she was asleep, soundly, thinking of how well she'd cowed him with her threat, and not waiting in her darkened room watching for any sign hanky-panky was going on. He unlocked the truck, slipped in, turned the key and pulled through the lot at an achingly slow speed, all the lights off.

By the time he turned onto the highway, his palms were coated in sweat. He picked up speed slowly, then turned on the lights when he felt comfortable. Now, he just hoped he was lucky enough that the sisters were sound sleepers.

He remembered the route into town well enough. It was creeping up on midnight, so most of the places that catered to locals were closed. He kept driving until he hit the tourist area, still lit up with restaurants, trendy bars and a few high-profile fast food chains. He hit up the convenient store first, hoping to limit the number of stops he had to make to one.

The cashier didn't even look up when he entered, likely used to a steady flow of unknowns passing through. Two young women near the snacks gave him more attention than the clerk behind the counter. He smiled politely at them, then he picked up several packages of mini donuts, some beef jerky and a bag of chips and started toward the counter. Just as he finished paying, a large, black SUV rolled up to one of the gas pumps outside. The clerk groaned audibly.

"Everything okay?" Casey asked.

The clerk just waved his hand noncommittally and handed Casey his change. He looked exactly like the kind of kid you'd see grumpily manning a cash register at a gas station – young, greasy hair and a permanently drippy nose. Casey had a feeling who was in the SUV based on the clerk's reaction to its arrival at the pumps.

He made his way to the door cautiously. Jay was standing at the pump, filling his car. Max's truck was just past that. Casey bit his lip as he thought. Jay could set him back significantly if he decided to start trouble. He hoped the local bully would only pay as much attention to Casey as any of the other tourists.

The girls, still eyeing him intently, finished paying for their things, and were making a beeline for him with a look in their eyes that said they were determined to corner him and flirt aggressively until he paid them the attention they merited. For a few seconds, Casey thought he might be screwed – the girls would delay him long enough for Jay to see him – then he realized he might be able to use them to his advantage.

"Ladies," he said, flashing a sparkling smile.

"Hi," they both said together, giggling.

"Where are you staying?" one of them asked.

Casey nodded across the street to where a large lodge dominated the skyline.

"That's where we are, too!"

The girl's interest rose a few notches while Casey looked furtively outside. He'd need to work fast.

"Oh yeah?" he asked, "You going out on the water tomorrow? The day should be amazing. I've been out there all week with my buddies."

"You have a boat?"

The girls looked duly impressed.

"Forty-footer. 'Ain't she a peach.' That's the name."

Their eyes lit up like kids in a candy store.

"I'd love to go out on a boat like that," one of the girls said.

The other girl nodded enthusiastically.

"Really? Well, maybe we can work something out." He pointed outside the store at Jay, then raised his voice enough that the cashier would hear him. "I'd like to get back to my truck without that guy seeing me. He was a real asshole to me yesterday."

"That guy?" one of the girls asked.

"Yeah. I don't get it. He just tried to pick a fight with me. Maybe because he's a local? This guy knows."

Casey looked over at the cashier, who was now paying attention to him. The girls followed his gaze and looked at the attendant with real interest for the first time. The gangly teen stood up straight, unconsciously tucking his shirt into his jeans.

"Yeah. He's a real asshole."

"See what I mean," Casey said.

The girls shook their heads sympathetically.

"What can we do?"

"I bet he'd turn your way if such lovely women said hello,"

Casey said. "You two could attract the sun on a cloudy day." The girls both blushed and giggled. "I only need a few seconds. Think you could do that for me?"

"Sure!" one of the girls said. "Then we get a ride on your boat?"

"Absolutely. I'll be here tomorrow morning around eight picking up supplies for the day. You can meet me here, and we'll all go out on the water."

The girls nodded and started out the door.

"Give us about thirty seconds. He won't be looking anywhere else!"

Casey smiled at them in his most dashing way. As soon as they turned around and headed toward Jay's truck, he walked up to the cashier.

"You working tomorrow morning?" Casey asked.

"Uh, why?"

"Well, come tomorrow morning, two young women are going to come in here looking for a good time. They won't find it. An enterprising fellow might find that situation to his advantage. He could offer condolences, call the guy who ditched them an asshole. Maybe rent a jet ski with them to make up for the bad start to the day."

"Oh, I can't really afford to rent a jet—"

"What is it? About a hundred bucks an hour?" Casey placed five twenties on the counter. He patted the teenager on his arm enthusiastically. "You have to be bold, kid, or they'll never look at you."

As Casey left the store, he saw the cashier pick up the money and put it in his pocket, a determined look on his face. He smiled to himself as he strolled past the now-occupied Jay. The girls were doing a bang-up job of keeping his attention, all smiles and twirling hair. Casey risked a look into the SUV and didn't see anyone in the passenger seat – a small favor. If Jay was planning to head out to his regular spot, it would interfere with Casey's plans to scope the place out, but odds were Jay was unlikely to do go out without his girlfriend. Casey would have a short head start.

Casey got into the truck, happy that things had gone as well as they had. He gave the girls a thumbs up as he pulled away, leaving Jay none the wiser.

He had a rough idea of where the campground was situated from his research into the area. There were only so many roads in this part of the state – the campground he was looking for was to the east. He got on the only highway leading east and headed out.

It took him thirty minutes to find the lonely road the campground was on. The sign advertising the place was near the entrance, and Casey could see how easy it would be to park just behind it, out of sight, without actually entering the campground.

He started to pull in behind the sign. As his tires settled into ruts hidden in the long grass, Casey furrowed his brow. He shifted the truck into reverse and pulled back out onto the shoulder, staring at the dark spot behind the sign. He hopped out of the truck, leaving the engine running.

The gravel crunched under his shoes as he crept up to the sign. Elephant grass was planted decoratively around the huge posts holding it up. Beyond the planned landscaping, the native grasses had been allowed to grow unfettered. Behind the sign, the grass had been trampled down by numerous feet. Amid the trampling, he found a set of tire ruts that had been refreshed within the last week, the depressions damp and deep, as if someone still used this spot.

Casey peered into the campground warily as he puzzled out

what it meant. The multiple sets of shoeprints were likely from the investigation into George and Sarah's disappearance. If this was where the missing teenager's truck had been found, officials would have been all over the place. Local rangers wouldn't have thought foul play at first – missing hikers maybe, but not foul play. They wouldn't have thought to preserve the scene for signs of George and Sarah. Local cops wouldn't have been much better coming from a small town like Manistee – unused to investigating homicides.

If Jay's friends parked behind the sign, it didn't take a huge leap to think Jay would choose the same location. Casey got back into the truck and reluctantly put it in drive. He drove further into the campground and parked close to the bathrooms. If he was going to be questioned about his activities, he preferred the questioning come from a park official, rather than Jay.

The air was still when he got out of the truck – still and muggy. He couldn't smell any sign of the creatures he was hunting in the area, which didn't surprise him. They rarely ever returned to a spot they had hunted before – it was too dangerous. This was the latest disappearance he could reliably trace to them, however, and Casey knew that meant it was his best chance to pick up their trail. When he found it, he suspected the trail would lead back west, somewhere between where he'd found the bears and where George and Sarah had disappeared.

He headed into the woods, looking for any signs of frequent travel. The police likely looked as well, but they weren't trackers by trade. Finding a local hideaway that probably moved with each new generation of high school students wasn't something they were trained for.

Casey had little trouble, though. In the years of lurking

around forests, looking for small signs that something clumsier than a deer had passed through, he'd developed a keen sense when tracking. Specifically, he'd become an expert in finding the traces of a prey so adept at hiding he doubted there was another person in the world who would even begin to know where to look. Finding the lightly traveled path a group of teenagers took to their favorite drinking spot was a simple matter comparatively. It only took him a moment to find the path the kids had used.

He followed the low-key trail back to a clearing the size of a small living room. A stream, only about six inches wide, ran through the middle of it. A huge tree, fallen years ago and now covered in moss and lichen, looked like it had been sat on frequently enough to change its shape. Crushed beer cans were piled at one end of the log, and someone had meticulously taken hundreds of pull tabs off the cans and created a metal mosaic in front of the log.

Casey was used to finding such oddities in his searching: bottlecaps pressed into the ground to form tiny mazes, notches in trees listing dates and names, and once he'd even found a panty collection hanging from the branches of a dead sycamore. It amused him to think that one day, these things would fossilize and be pondered over by scientists so far removed from the present day they'd have no clue what they meant. It certainly made cave drawings seem a lot less mysterious to Casey. He imagined those as the getaways of lusty teens from long ago, wiling away their time by creating art with whatever they had handy.

He crouched near the log and sniffed. There was no sign of them, only a strong smell of the humans who'd spent considerable time in the area after the disappearance; Jay and his friends had come back to the spot a lot. There were signs of the teens everywhere – urine soaked earth and fresh bottles, the labels still easy to read. He approached an area where it looked as if something had clawed the tree. He pressed his fingers into the wound and brought them out, passing them under his nose. It was there – faint, but there. It would have smelled particularly foul before the rain, even to Jay and his friends. He wondered if they were at all curious about the stench.

Casey could see signs of a hasty retreat heading in the general direction of the campground entrance. He followed it for several feet. Whoever had come this way had been panicky. They'd missed their normal path by a good six feet and had been heading more east than south. When he found the spot where the first of the missing had been killed, he bent down. Though the rain had washed away most of the signs, Casey could still smell the strong iron scent in the ground. A lot of blood had been spilled there. Most of it would have been licked up, but more than enough had been absorbed by the earth for Casey to sniff it out.

The dogs, when they came, would find this spot too, now that the rains had washed away the warning scent that was specifically left behind to throw them off. The police would have to test the earth to know what the dog's baying meant. There was no visible sign of blood.

Whoever had died there had died quickly. The first meal after a long fast always went quickly. They would have eaten the person completely, stripping the flesh from the bones like a dog, leaving only the pale, white leftovers. They'd have collected those, too, Casey thought. They'd started clearing up the gristle and bone shortly after the first time Casey had found them. Their change in habits had made it a lot harder to track where they'd been.

The other victim would have been brought back to their

lair, alive or dead. Casey had no illusions that someone was still alive – they would only have been able to wait a day or two before their hunger drove them to finish off the remaining teenager. He continued tracking until he found the second location. It took longer than the first, because there was so much less blood. Casey touched the ground. Whoever had been caught had been close to getting to their car. He could see the trees thinning around him and the lit-up sign just beyond that. He wondered if they would have risked going after the runner under the lights of the campground. Even getting this close was a risk. They were growing bolder.

He found their trail again and followed it across the road the campground intersected with. He started to cross the road, then stopped in the middle. Any vehicle coming down the long straight would be able to see for more than a mile. With their lights on, they'd spot the crossing figures without any trouble. Carrying a body across the road, even at night, would have been extremely dangerous.

Another risk, he thought.

At almost all the other kills sites he'd discovered and investigated, they hadn't crossed any open patches of land so close to humans. They were normally as cautious with their kills as they were in choosing their dens. Only once had they ever hunted so brazenly, and then he'd been sure it was because the winter had been unusually long. This was not like that time. They'd been feeding regularly as far as Casey could tell, so it wasn't extreme hunger driving them to take more risks.

He continued into the woods, where the trail grew fresher. More scratches, these much newer, marked the trees. Their scent was all over the place, growing stronger with each step Casey took. Some of the marks had been placed after the storm from the morning before.

He paused, his foot half-way to touching down as he realized something. They'd been keeping an eye on the location of their last kill. It was the only explanation for all the fresh marks. They'd been coming back and checking, maybe even keeping tabs on the investigation. It was even possible they were using their scent to continue to keep the dogs at bay, refreshing it after every downpour. It was unusual behavior for any location that wasn't a den. And, once again, it was risky. Part of the reason they were so hard to find is they never stayed in one place too long. The signs Casey was finding told a different story – they looked more like a couple of creatures that had settled in than a pair passing through.

A noise interrupted Casey's thoughts. He ducked behind a tree just as a beam of light pierced through the woods.

"Turn that off, you idiot!"

The light went out. Casey realized who the voice belonged to; Jay had finally arrived. He moved along a parallel line to them, darting from one tree to another as quickly as he thought was safe. He needed to get to the truck and out of the area before he was seen. An outsider found so close to the crime scene, with little in the way of an alibi, would be too enticing for the cops if he was caught. Nothing he could say would keep him out of jail. Even if he was kept only for a night, he didn't have the time to spare.

"Jay."

That was the voice of pink curtain girl. They'd picked her up after all.

"I don't like this," she continued. "We should call the police. Tell them what we know."

"My dad couldn't find shit in a shit shack, Jess. He's in the fucking mayor's pocket. And Sarah's dad is an asshole. You don't know—"

Jay's voice stopped suddenly which caused Casey to stop. He was afraid they'd spotted him.

"I'm just saying," Jay resumed, "the guy's an asshole. I'm sure as shit not gonna tip off the main suspect that we're conducting our own investigation."

"I don't know man," one of Jay's minions piped up. "Why would the mayor wanna kill his own daughter?"

"Why does anybody wanna kill anybody, shit for brains? Everyone says, ninety-nine percent of the time, it's family that does a person in. My dad isn't even looking into Scott Linkman."

Casey made it to the road. He could see the black SUV tucked behind the campground sign. Whoever parked it had been in a hurry; it wasn't as hidden as it could be.

"Are you sure you saw something out here, Terry?" Jay asked.

"I think so. Coulda been a deer."

"Why do these woods stink so much?" Jess asked. "It smells like something died. Why does it always smell like something died?"

Casey left the group behind, scurrying across the road. He paused at the sign for the campground, in case they'd seen him.

"We're gonna get in trouble when they bring them dogs out here, Jay," Jess said.

"Why? Can the dogs talk?"

"What does that have to do with anything?" Jess asked.

"Because if the dogs can't talk, they can't tell the cops who was here. They'll find a trail. Nothing more. Ain't no one gonna give them dogs a pair of your panties to sniff to compare. Stop worrying about stupid shit."

Casey continued toward the truck. He wondered if the teenagers were already drunk. They were loud enough he could hear them all the way to the bathrooms. He got in Max's truck quietly, closing the door softly. He turned over the engine and pulled up to the road at three miles an hour. Jay's group was still searching the woods; he could hear them bickering, but he couldn't make out what they were saying. He turned onto the road and drove away, keeping his lights off until he felt safe to turn them on.

All the way back to the Sunset, he couldn't stop thinking about the fact that the kill site was being watched. That was not like them at all.

EIGHT

He pulled into the Sunset as quietly as he'd pulled out. Before he even got out of the truck, he checked to make sure everything was as he'd left it – Anne's car was still outside her room, and the lone light he'd left on in his own room still cast a gentle glow against his window. He hopped out of the truck, and started toward the door when he heard a noise. It sounded like splashing in the pool. He hung the sack of donuts on the doorknob of his room before heading toward the noise.

He crept toward the pass through between the motel's wings that led to the pool. The sound was intermittent, dying out completely between bursts of splashing. It was not the sound of someone swimming. His nerves were still on edge from his tracking through the woods, so his mind conjured up all sorts of disturbing images. When he finally peeked around the corner, he saw nothing in the pool, though it was lit up for the night.

The water's surface was disturbed, ripples emanating from a corner. The sound came again, causing him to start. He looked around the courtyard, in case whatever was in the pool was a distraction – it was a tactic he was wary of. Luring was one of their favorite methods of hunting. He'd found that out the hard way, and nearly paid for the lesson with his life. He sniffed the air and could sense no sign of the creatures he'd been tracking.

He kept an eye on the woods as he approached the fence enclosing the pool. The swing set was quiet – the wind was unnaturally still, and nothing moved. The only sound was coming from the pool. He opened the gate and stepped inside, his entire body ready for a fight. The splashing ceased again. Casey waited a few seconds for it to start up again, only to be confronted with more silence. He quietly stepped up to the edge of the pool and peered over.

"Casey?"

He almost fell into the pool in surprise. He twisted just enough to land on the edge of the pool rather than in it. Max, wrapped in a blanket, came running towards the pool.

"I'm so sorry," she said. "I didn't mean to scare you."

"It's fine," Casey said. He rubbed absently at his ankle. "It's my own damn fault for creeping around the pool this late."

"Did you twist it?" Max asked.

She pulled up his jeans to look, carefully probing the skin with her fingers.

"Ah," Casey said, wincing. "Maybe a bit. It'll be fine."

"It doesn't seem fine," Max said. "I'm really sorry."

She helped him up and into a chair. She turned when the splashing in the pool started again.

"What's that?"

"That's what I wanted to know," Casey said. He glanced out at the forest, now even more aware of his surroundings. Max's presence was extra worrying. "I heard it when I got back from the store and was checking on it."

Max headed toward the pool while Casey massaged his ankle. It was already swelling. He didn't pay it much attention; his eyes were glued to Max as she bent over the edge, his whole body tensed, ready to lunge.

"Oh," she said. "It's a bat."

"A bat?"

"Yeah. I've been having this problem since I put the pool in. I've tried keeping the lights off, but they still end up in here. I even put in a saltwater-chlorine generator. I thought maybe the fumes of the chlorine I had to use to shock the pool was making them pass out or something." She grimaced as she looked down at the tiny bat. "It didn't help."

Max got up and grabbed the pool skimmer attached to the fence.

"Are you going to pull it out?" Casey asked.

Max dipped the skimmer into the pool near the bat. Concerned, Casey stood and hobbled over to Max.

"Don't touch it," he said.

"You don't have to worry about that," she said. "I've done this a bunch. I'll feel really stupid if, in the end, I find out it's the same bat getting stuck over and over."

Casey looked over the lip of the pool to see the creature. It clung to the net, its eyes wide with fear. It was soaked, but otherwise looked okay.

Casey bent over to get a closer look, not really sure why. If the thing had rabies, he wasn't qualified to know. Other than being in the pool, he couldn't tell if it was acting erratically or not. As quietly as he could, he sniffed the air. There was a whiff of chlorine, but the rest was all wet bat. He couldn't smell any decay or blood.

"Are you trying to smell the bat?" Max asked.

Casey pulled his face back from the skimmer, embarrassed she'd noticed.

"Yes?"

After looking between Casey and the bat, she moved the skimmer over the water, causing the tiny creature to shift nervously.

"Well?"

Casey looked up at her. If he didn't know better, he'd have thought she was ready to dunk the bat under the water at his say so. It was a bizarre thing to think. She probably just thought he was crazy or weird, sniffing small rodents whenever he got the chance. He decided she was teasing him, and went with that.

"Smells like wet bat, I guess. I don't know why I did that."

Max gave him another of her incomprehensible looks before moving the net, bat included, to the fence. She leaned the long pole up against it, putting the bat high in the air. After checking to make sure the pole was secure and wouldn't fall over easily, she re-tucked the blanket around her chest.

"He'll be fine. He'll dry off, then fly off. At least I assume that's what's happening. There's never a bat there in the morning." She sidled up close to Casey and offered her shoulder. "You can lean against me. I can handle it."

"What?" he asked, still thirty seconds behind, busy staring at the bat crawling around the net.

"Your ankle."

"Oh." Casey took a few steps, gingerly pressing down. "I'm fine now."

"You sure? You were limping just a minute ago."

He took a full step comfortably to prove it to her.

"Yeah," he said. "I was just afraid to step on it. I'm good now." He offered his arm to her. "You can hold my arm if you like. I can handle it."

Max tucked her arm into his with a grin. They walked together to the truck and stopped outside the room.

"You sure about your ankle?" Max asked. "I have an ice machine. It's one of the few perks living in a motel. More ice than you know what to do with."

Casey shook his head.

"It's good. I swear. Just felt a little twinge right after I fell. Nothing else." He paused, leaning against the truck. He fished the keys out of his pocket and handed them over to her. "I'm sorry if I worried you, leaving like that."

"I saw the note," Max said. "It wasn't the leaving that worried me. I was afraid Anne had caught up with you and was threatening to castrate you somewhere."

"Not yet, anyway."

Max smiled. She pulled the blanket tighter around herself as a light breeze kicked up.

"I should probably get dressed," she said. She gave him a rueful look. "And probably get back to my room."

"I get it," Casey said. "You want some privacy, then?"

"No," Max said with a soft chuckle. "But you shouldn't come in there. If you did, we'd end up right back in that bed. I don't know that we should push our luck."

Casey leaned over the hood of the truck and rested his chin in his hands while he looked appreciatively at Max. The thought of going back into the room with her brought an uncontrollable smile to his face.

"No. Don't look at me like that," she said playfully. "I am resolved not to give Anne any more reasons to hate you."

"Okay," Casey said after a brief pause. "I'll be here if you need me."

He gave her his flirtiest look.

"Not helping," she said as she backed into the room.

When the door closed behind her, Casey sighed. After a few more pleasant minutes thinking about Max, he glanced toward Anne's window. It remained dark. He saw the curtains flutter, but hoped that was just the AC kicking on, and not Anne looking out.

The door opened back up and Max came out, dressed as she'd been when she'd brought dinner by. Casey had forgotten the fluffy pink sweater. As soon as she came into sight, he had the urge to wrap her up again in his arms. The strength and insistence of his feelings were going to get him in trouble – he could already see it coming.

"Get some sleep," she said. "Let me know if that ankle gets any worse. We can spend the day lounging poolside while you rest."

"I'm sure Anne would love that," Casey said.

After a final good night, she headed to bed. Casey returned to his room, noticing Max had moved the sack of donuts to the table, and flopped onto the bed. He fell asleep almost as soon as his head hit the pillow.

It wasn't the light that woke him, as he'd expected. It was the sound of people arguing outside his door. He sat upright, still in his clothes from the night before. His shoes still had mud caked in the grooves from his forest exploration. He kicked them off and tucked them close to the wall, out of instinct. He quickly changed his shirt and then padded to the door, leaning his cheek against it.

He could hear Max clearly. The tension in her voice made the hackles on the back of his neck stand up. It took effort not to swing the door open to stand with her against whatever was upsetting her. He caught Anne's voice, too, but it wasn't Anne that Max was angry with. There was another voice, a vaguely familiar man's, that was the target of Max's ire.

Casey closed his eyes and took several breaths, settling his testosterone-fueled anger. He opened the door and looked out to be greeted by four sets of eyes, only one friendly. Along with Max and Anne, Chief Campbell and another officer Casey didn't recognize stood in a circle just feet outside his door.

"Is something wrong?" he asked.

"Mr. Pierson," Chief Campbell said. "We have some questions for you. If we could come in and—"

"No," Max said. "Not without a warrant, Frank. You can ask him your questions here. And then you can go."

Casey would have to thank Max for that later. She was within her rights to allow the police access. He wasn't paying for the room, merely staying there as a guest. It was a point Anne looked like she might bring up, until Max shot her a glare so fierce it would have stunned a grizzly.

"Max, we don't need to make this difficult," Frank said.

"We aren't. Here he is. Ask your questions."

"This isn't how we do it, Max," the other officer chimed in.

Frank held up his hand to silence the man.

"It's okay, Mike. Max and Anne are our people. They won't cause trouble."

Max nodded in agreement.

"We'll stand over here," she said, gesturing to Anne for her to follow. "And be quick about it. I need to get started on the next rooms. I'm running out of summer."

Max and Anne moved closer to Max's room. A quiet argument broke out between them, but Casey couldn't spare any attention for that. The police were there, and he had no idea why. The reasons could be many, but Anne's threat loomed large at the top of the list.

"Where were you last night, Mr. Pierson?" Frank asked.

It was a hell of a first question. There was no way Casey could answer it honestly without causing more issues.

"What time?"

The two officers exchanged looks. Casey knew it wasn't wise to try to stall when being questioned by the police. They always saw it as an indication of guilt, no matter your reasoning – but he had to have a few more seconds to think.

"Let's start with around eight o'clock," Campbell said.

"I'm pretty sure that was right around the time I finished showering up after work. Max came by with dinner and my day's pay. We ate together and chatted. She fell asleep. I was still hungry and I tried to reheat some of the food. It didn't turn out too well, so I borrowed the truck and went into town to get something else."

"And what time was that?"

"Uh... Wait. I might have the receipt."

He pointed to his jeans pocket, and waited until Chief Campbell nodded his assent. He reached inside and fished out a wad of ones, a receipt curled up in the center. Peeling it off the ones, he handed the receipt over to Campbell. He glanced over to see Max biting her fingernail and watching closely.

"Eleven thirty-seven?"

"Sounds right, I guess. I wasn't paying a lot of attention at the time," Casey said.

Campbell handed the receipt to the other officer, who took it back to the squad car in the lot.

"We'll be checking with the Stop n Go to confirm that, Mr. Pierson."

"Of course."

The cashier would remember Casey well.

"And after that?" Campbell asked.

"I came back. Got turned around trying to find a place that was open that late. Ended up on the wrong highway going east. But came back after that. I'd guess I got back close to one-ish."

"You came straight back? Didn't stop anywhere else in Manistee?"

"No. Unless Free Soil is still part of Manistee. I stopped somewhere out there to look up where I was, but there was nothing there but forest. Free Soil is the road I ended up taking back here when I figured out where I was."

Campbell looked Casey over before walking up to the truck. He checked the bed, then the cabin, before turning back to Casey.

"Anyone who can confirm you came back here around one AM?"

"Max."

"Max?"

The look on Campbell's face told Casey the cop had already questioned Max and was looking for discrepancies. He hoped she hadn't tried to cover for him. He wouldn't want her to get into trouble for him.

"Yeah. I got back, heard something in the pool. It must have woken her up, because she came out to look. There was a bat in there. She fished it out, then we both went to bed in our rooms. I slept until about ten minutes ago."

Campbell waited while his partner came up and whispered in his ear. He nodded, then gestured to Casey's jeans.

"Would you empty your pockets for me, Mr. Pierson?"

Casey was now convinced this had nothing to do with Anne. The questions were too specific. Campbell was looking for something, and he couldn't be sure what. He pulled the wad of ones out and set it on the hood of the truck. He had several pennies and a quarter that he added to the pile. He placed a Minnesota driver's license, scuffed and well-worn but still legible, next to the money. The only thing left in his pocket was the yellow diamond-studded phone. He put that down with a clunk, officer Campbell eyeing it in surprise. He pulled the cloth out of both pockets and let them hang in the air to show he had nothing else on him.

Campbell picked up the license, examined it, then handed it to his partner, who again shuffled off toward the police car. He looked at the phone, turning it on before replacing it on the hood of the truck.

"Max," Campbell said. "Would you come over here please?"

Max left Anne by the door to her room and joined Casey and Campbell.

"What do you need?"

"Anne, you too," Campbell said. "Max, where are the keys to your truck?"

Max pulled them out of her pocket to show Campbell. He turned to Anne. Without having to be asked, Anne fished the keys to her sedan out of her pocket.

"Does Mr. Pierson have a key to either of your rooms?"

"Absolutely not," Anne said.

"There's no need for Mr. Pierson to have any keys except to his own room," Max added. "Any of the rooms he's worked on, I've unlocked for him."

Campbell's partner came back with Casey's ID and handed it over to Campbell. Campbell held it out to Casey, but as Casey went to grab it, he pulled it away.

"I don't have any more questions for you right now, Mr. Pierson. But if you suddenly up and leave, we'll come find you. I won't be as accommodating then."

He brought Casey's ID back within reach. Casey took it and stuffed it back into his pocket. Campbell tipped his hat at Max and Anne before both policemen returned to their vehicle and drove away. It wasn't until they were out of the lot that Casey turned to Max with fifty questions on the tip of his tongue.

"Janelle's gone," Max said.

Casey's gut tied into knots in an instant. The air felt too cold and thin as he struggled to breathe regularly.

"She left Arnold's last night," Max continued. "Around three AM, so you're safe. For now, at least. Until they find some way to blame you if they can."

"It's not that big a stretch, Max," Anne said.

"He was here, Anne." Max sounded like she was on the verge of telling Anne off. "Ten miles away. Without a vehicle. It's not possible. And if you could get over whatever grudge you're holding against him for one second, you'd see that."

"She's gone?" Casey asked, daring to speak up.

"Yes," Max said. "Fortunately for you, she has very nosy neighbors. They know her habits and watch for her to come home every night, because the people in this town have nothing better to do than gossip and cause trouble. They like to see who she manages to bring home, if she manages it. Apparently last night she hadn't. She came home alone."

Max looked overcome by emotions. She chewed her lip and Anne reached out to comfort her. The sisters embraced for a while in silence. Casey felt out of place and loathe to interrupt, but he had to know for sure.

"They see anything else?" he asked, earning a nasty look from Anne.

"Not exactly," Max said. "When they realized she didn't have anyone in her car, both Shannon, she lives across the street, and Monica, she lives next door, started to go to bed. Monica says she heard a terrible scream. She got up and looked, and saw Janelle's car door was still open, but no Janelle. She opened her window and called out, but Janelle didn't answer. Then she said she heard a child crying. At three AM, she heard a child crying outside. It freaked her out so bad she called the police. They were all over the place before dawn, but couldn't find anything. I think they're bringing dogs in now."

Dogs who wouldn't be able to track a thing, Casey thought. He knew it for sure now – they had taken Janelle. The baby's cry was a favorite of theirs. He was almost as sure they had done it because of him as he was that they had done it. He blamed himself for all of it. He'd walked through town, stopping at a location they'd eaten at – where they'd left him a message; he'd left a scent trail right to Janelle's without thinking. His odor would be all over her house; that was all the evidence they'd need that she was someone worth hunting down to get to him.

He pressed his fingers into the knot between his eyes. He'd also walked back to the Sunset. He'd left them a map straight to Max. It was sheer chance they'd chosen to follow his path into town instead of out of it. The next place they'd check would undoubtedly be the motel. He couldn't wait any longer; he had to find them tonight and deal with them once and for all.

"Under the circumstances," Max said, looking at Casey with concern, "maybe we should take the day off. You, too, Anne. Put up the 'No Vacancy' for the day."

"You sure?" Anne asked.

"Yeah," Max said. "I think we can put off the flood of customers until tomorrow."

Anne headed off toward the office. Casey gathered up his belongings from the hood of the truck. He felt Max's arms snake around him from behind and he leaned into her embrace.

"You okay?" she asked, her chin resting on his shoulder.

"I'm fine. Just... if you want to sneak into my room tonight, call first. I don't want you walking around outside alone. And lock your doors. Even poolside. Anne should, too."

"You think whatever did this will come here next?" Max asked.

The casual way she said "whatever" and not "whoever" was not lost on Casey. Chief Campbell would have done well to listen to Max, he thought. It was too late for that now. They were hunting in town – not in an isolated camping spot, not even on the fringes, but in town. They wouldn't stop now until they'd dealt with him.

He picked up one of her hands and kissed the palm before resting his cheek against it.

"You'll lock your doors?"

"I promise," she said.

NINE

I t was late afternoon. They'd done their best to try and relax, sitting by the pool and letting the sun bake them. Anne was constantly on her phone, updating Max and Casey with any news people in town had sent her. She was almost cordial, though Casey couldn't figure out why. His best guess was that she had something else to distract her from her dislike of him. Whatever it was, he welcomed it. Anne's preoccupied state allowed Casey and Max to squeeze in some sneaky hand holding by the pool, and, once, when Max needed sunscreen applied, he dared offer to do it himself. Anne seemed oblivious to the whole exchange.

Despite the attempt to remain calm, the undercurrent of the morning was still one of dread. By the time the afternoon rolled around, none of them were willing to play pretend anymore. Max finally broke up their group when she declared she wanted to head into town to pick up some things from the hardware store. Before Casey could offer to join her, Anne volunteered.

Casey was left alone. He seized the opportunity to check

the motel grounds for any sign his prey had been there. It was the perfect time to do so; with Max and Anne gone, he wouldn't have to worry about them questioning what he was doing. There was no need to upset the sisters if he was wrong, and his quarry hadn't been to the motel yet.

He circled the motel repeatedly, each time going wider, eyes on the ground as he walked, checking even the smallest of disturbances – bent grass, trampled soil, rocks that looked out of place. After an hour he decided they hadn't been there, and he went back to the pool. He sat beside it uneasily, checking the yellow-jeweled phone every ten minutes, wondering how much longer Max would be.

The sun baked into his skin and his breathing slowed. He concentrated on the swing set in front of the trees. He was just about to call Max when he heard it. A distinct sound echoed out of the woods just on the other side of the swings – a baby's cry.

He got up slowly. The sound didn't stop when he moved. Pushing past the unease, he left the pool area and approached the playground. The swings were still. He moved closer to the trees and the cries stopped.

"Hey."

Casey bolted around. The sound came from behind him, but he couldn't see anything there except the motel.

"Hey."

Casey turned again, this time toward the woods. He was sure the second voice had come from there. Then he heard a scream followed by a splash. Disregarding the voices, he ran back to the motel, leaping over the fence. He skidded to a stop at the edge of the pool. The splashing noise continued, but he couldn't see the source. The surface of the water was all turbulence and foam, so much foam it was hard to make out anything beneath it. But something was there at the bottom of the pool – a pale figure looking up at him.

"Casey! We're back. Everything all right?"

Casey gasped as he woke. He'd fallen asleep again. Rushing to the side of the pool, he looked down into it, only to see the blue-tiled lane lines. He backed away from the edge slowly, gathering his wits. He didn't want Max to worry, so he tucked away his fear and headed out to the parking lot to help them unload the truck. It wasn't until he saw them both unharmed that some of the tension faded.

There were a lot of bags in the truck. Casey joined them unloading the supplies into one of the rooms.

"If I were you," Anne said as she dropped a large bag of copper wire onto a bed, "I wouldn't go into town anymore."

"Why's that?" Casey asked.

"Officer Jay," she said with a laugh. "He's out for blood. Pissed as hell his dad didn't arrest you. Better hope he doesn't come out here tonight to do some amateur police work."

Whistling as she left the room, Casey wondered if Anne's good mood was from the idea he might get pummeled by a local, or some other terrible thing she had yet to inform him of.

"She's chipper," he said.

"We had a long talk on the way to the hardware store," Max said. "I told her to knock it off."

She unspooled a foot's worth of copper wire, bending it as if testing its flexibility.

"And she listened?"

Anne listening to anything Max said would've been a surprise. She didn't seem like the type that took orders or advice.

"I told her you were important to me." Max was still fiddling with the wire, so Casey couldn't see her face. "I told her if she wanted to keep causing trouble, that was fine, but she'd have to do it without me here. I told her that, as much as I loved and cared for her, if she pulled anything stupid, anything that would put your life in danger, anything that would hurt you, I would choose you over her."

The sound of the AC kicking on was the only noise in the room. Casey didn't even notice he'd sat down; when he came to his senses, he was on the bed, staring at the back of Max's head.

"I can't imagine she liked hearing that."

He couldn't think of anything else to say. No one had ever cared for him that much before. Max had gotten to that point after only three days. He wondered what he'd done to deserve it – there was nothing he could think of, and there was no way his performance in the bedroom was good enough to spin someone like Max so easily.

"She didn't." Max looked up at him finally. It wasn't the look of a love-sick woman, or someone who'd come to her decision without a great deal of thought. She looked at him with the confidence of someone who knew her mind and her heart. "But she understood."

Max rose and tucked a loose strand of Casey's hair behind his ear. He pulled her close.

"I bet she said had some other choice words, too," Casey said, his voice muffled by Max's shirt. "Something like, 'If he ever hurts you I'll crush his balls into jelly.' Sound about right?"

"Uncanny," Max said.

He pulled her down until she was sitting on his lap. Minutes ticked by without a word between them. Casey was afraid to speak, both afraid he'd tell her everything and fearful he'd never get the chance. His eyes roved the room and fell on the copper wire.

"You adding electrician to your list of accomplishments?" he asked jokingly, doing his best to lighten the mood.

"Yep," she said. "That's what I was about to do. A nice safe thing. Playing with electricity. Want to help me out?"

A shadow passed by the door and they both looked up. Anne opened it and lugged a dusty box into the room. She plunked it down on the table and wiped her hands on her jeans.

"I found it," she announced. "He gonna help with this project of yours?"

"I better not," Casey said. "I can't install a fresh battery without shocking myself. I'd just get in the way. Plus, I was thinking of going for a walk."

"A walk?" Anne exclaimed. "Are you mad? It's about to get dark. And with Janelle—"

"And Jay," Max added, standing up.

"And Jay," Anne said.

"You shouldn't worry about me," Casey said. "I've been walking roads like this for years. At all hours of the night. I'll be fine."

Neither of them looked like they agreed. It couldn't be helped. He needed to get out into the woods before what was in the woods came to him.

"I'll be back soon. If I run into trouble, I'll call," he lied.

He was surprised that even Anne looked unhappy about his leaving. Maybe she really had changed her tune when Max laid out the facts.

He left the room wondering if he was making a mistake. It felt insane to even think about telling Max the truth but, for a second, he almost turned around and did. Sense came thundering back in instead as he turned to see her in the doorway. The wave died in his hand as soon as he saw her face.

Casey didn't want the last thing she remembered of him to

be a wave goodbye. He realized his hand was still hanging in the air awkwardly. He quickly covered by bringing it to his lips to blow her a kiss, hoping she wouldn't notice. Dredging up every shred of happiness he'd felt in the last three days, Casey let a smile spread across his face.

"See you soon," she called after him.

His voice caught in his throat. If he spoke just then, he knew the waver in his voice, fueled by the fear he might never see her again, would scare her if she heard it. The raw energy of his feelings as well as why he was heading into the forest – she couldn't know any of it. He couldn't let her stop him from going. He turned away from her and didn't look back.

Casey was several miles down the road when he veered into the woods. He was close to the area he'd found the bears the morning before. He didn't head in that direction, however. He turned east, taking a line he'd calculated was in the direction of the campground some twenty miles away. By his reckoning, the lair would be somewhere in between the two kill sites. As long as they hadn't changed their patterns, it fit with everything he'd learned in his years hunting them.

His head held a detailed map of every kill site and den he'd ever found over the years. He'd spent much of the spring roving around Ontario, following traces as they killed. Twice he'd found out where they'd been too late. They'd moved on weeks before he got close enough to track them. The second kill had been further south, and Casey guessed they'd move into Michigan for the prime camping season.

He'd been right. The first kill of the summer had been in June. He'd been practically living in local libraries, keeping tabs on all the newspapers in a two-hundred-mile radius, when he'd read about Cindy Jones. Cindy had been hiking with friends in the UP. One night, she left the group's tent around two AM to use the restroom. She never came back. Just feet from the campsite, her friends found a friendship bracelet she always wore covered in blood. Dogs were brought to the site, but they were uncontrollable, barking in every direction.

Casey had scoured all their social media feeds, looking for any clues, and found one. In one of the many pictures they had posted, they were all marveling at what they thought, based on the caption, was bear claw marks in a tree. Casey could see instantly see that they were terribly wrong, and it had likely cost Cindy her life.

They'd never taken anyone so brazenly before. They'd never snatched someone away from a large party. It wasn't fear of being harmed by their prey that kept them from doing so; it was fear of doing something that might get them caught.

It was only one aberration, not a pattern. It wasn't until he found out about the couple at Max's cousin's campground that he realized the erratic behavior was not an isolated incident.

Max had been right about her cousin's campground. The older couple hadn't drowned. They'd taken the campers. He'd found their den within ten miles of the campground. It was a foolish move, and one Casey hadn't expected. Prior to this summer, they'd stuck to loners – hitchhikers, runaways – people on the fringes who wouldn't be missed.

In the past, hiding their kill was their primary objective when choosing prey. It had made it incredibly difficult for Casey to track them. Up until this year, he'd been months behind them at best. The only times he had ever gotten even remotely close to them, were the few times when he had guessed their next stop. Anticipating where they'd be had been his only hope of catching them.

When mid-July rolled around, Casey had gone back up north, predicting they'd move. They rarely hunted twice in one location and the north was more likely than the more populous regions in the east of the state. He was almost a hundred miles away, near Traverse City, when he first read about another missing person in the Big Rapids area. The missing man had been a Vietnam vet who suffered from severe PTSD. His family said he often disappeared for days on end, but this time he'd been gone for more than a week. If it hadn't been for the older camping couple going missing, Casey would never have connected the dots.

Despite all his investigating, his closest calls with catching them usually came from gut instinct. Missing persons were everywhere. It was only from years of finding old dens and kill sites that Casey developed any sense of where they'd be next. Even though they had just hunted in the Big Rapids area, Casey had a feeling the vet had also been one of their kills.

He'd packed up and travelled back down to investigate. The timing was too coincidental, the details too unusual to ignore. He knew he was right on top of them – if only he could catch up in time.

When he'd found their lair, he knew his hunch had been correct. They'd only recently left. Fresh feces, a day old at most, buried near the entrance, revealed they were close. It was slow going, but their trail was new enough to follow north, this time with certainty that was the direction they'd gone. They were moving fast, and he lost the trail more than once. They doubled back several times, making him wonder if they knew how close he was. They'd even managed to trick him into going south. He was nearly at Muskegon when they took the teenagers from

Manistee. It took Casey several days of hard backtracking before he'd stepped off the bed of a pickup truck into the parking lot of the Sunset. He'd hoped he hadn't missed a crucial part in the trail by rushing, but he couldn't waste time checking to see if they'd already moved on. They were getting bolder, and he thought they might hunt the area again before leaving.

As he walked through the woods, he couldn't get over the feeling they were waiting for him. For reasons he hadn't yet discerned, they were reluctant to move too far. They'd hunted twice in Big Rapids. Now they'd hunted twice in Manistee. The thought that they were as tired of running as he was of chasing was a tempting one. It felt too simple, though – too easy.

Casey started finding their marks on the trees just as the last light left the sky. Crickets and frogs began their singing, creating a blanket of sound it was impossible to hear any details through. It hardly mattered. The marks were practically leading him along. He never spent more than five minutes looking before he found another.

He crossed several winding dirt roads, their sand a rusty red color, making them easy to see even by the dim light of the moon. Each time he stepped deeper into the woods, he thought it might be the end of his search.

It wasn't until he'd been walking for more than an hour when the song of the night went still. Then he caught their scent. The smell they left behind in their territorial marks was bad enough. Smelling them in the flesh was another thing altogether. The scent struck him like a hammer. He felt the urge to transform as soon as it hit him. His insides twisted and curled, demanding him to give in. His back burned as if a hot iron had been pressed into it. He doubled over from the effort of maintaining control.

He held on to his sanity, calling forth the image of Max

standing in the doorway of the motel, waiting for him to return. He couldn't let the hunger take him over. If he allowed the hunger to call the shots, even once, he'd be lost forever to its control. Casey had to be the one to bring it out, leashed to his will. He closed his eyes and pictured Max, tall and lean, strong and good. When he opened them again, he had mastered the beast within.

He continued forward, following the smell as it thickened into a fog of scent. It led him to an old hunter's shack, long abandoned. The wood was weathered, grey and rotting. So much leaf litter had fallen on the roof over the years, it had created a suitable habitat for seedlings, and a thick blanket of young plants covered it.

Their scratches were obvious, gouging the wood in regular intervals, but something wasn't right. The shack was covered in graffiti and surrounded by garbage. It wasn't hidden enough or private enough. He could see a dirt road roughly eighty feet away. It wouldn't be heavily travelled, but that wouldn't matter to them. They'd never sleep so close to a place where humans could find them by accident, and never in a place that showed as much evidence of ongoing human use.

"Hey."

He looked up. She was standing on the top of the shack looking down at him. Tears sprung to his eyes as soon as he saw her. She was worse than the last time he'd found them, nearly eight years ago. Her skin was pulled so far back from her face, he could almost make out her skull. Her teeth were stained yellow, the gums pulled back from them creating a garish smile. Saliva dripped from her cracked lips – lips that looked torn and tattered, barely holding on to her face.

She'd grown some sort of horns from her head since he'd seen her last. They looked to be jagged bone, piercing through the skin in such a way they'd created permanent wounds, easily visible through her stringy hair. She was taller than he'd remembered, too, as if she'd been stretched to the point of snapping, her abdomen concave and distended all at once. Her long arms swayed at her side, looking fragile and delicate, belying their true strength – enough power to snap a man in half. They ended in dirty claws, made of the same thing the horns were, jagged and suppurating at their base.

She hopped down, surprisingly agile considering she looked like an old scarecrow that might fall apart at any second.

"Hey," she said again.

It was disconcerting to hear her voice coming from this creature's mouth – disconcerting and disarming. It made him feel as if she was still in there somewhere, trying to get out.

"Hey," Casey said in reply.

He reached up and she leaned in, allowing him to touch her face. It was slick with death, but he hardly noticed. He couldn't stop the tears from falling.

"Luca," he said. "I've missed you."

"Hey."

He turned when he heard the second voice. Looming right behind him, easily several feet taller than Casey, was the second creature. Like Luca, he was gaunt and horrifying. The only true difference between them was that his horns were slightly larger, as if they'd sprouted earlier than hers and been allowed more time to grow.

"Noah," Casey said.

He reached out and, again, the beast leaned in, allowing him to touch it. For a moment, they were together again – a family. He could see in their eyes; they felt it, too.

"Hey."

Luca's voice drew his eyes, and he turned back to see

something in her hand. She stretched it out toward him, the bones in her body grinding as she did, the sound not unlike that of a gnarled tree in the wind. She opened her claws to reveal a lump of flesh, the skin still attached.

Casey's jaw clenched when he caught the scent of Janelle's perfume still clinging to the skin. He looked up at Luca, and there was pleading in her eyes.

"This is what you want?" Casey asked.

He looked between Luca and Noah. There was no malice there. His tracking, his attempts to bring them down, even his failure to help them – all would be forgiven.

In that instant, he knew what the offerings were for – all the bear cubs, deer and assorted other dead things left for him to find. They were gifts, messages that he'd be welcome should he return to them. He almost broke in that moment. He almost fell to his knees and let them take him. The fact that there was still enough of them inside those husks to recognize him – worse yet, to forgive him – tore him to pieces.

"I can't," he said. "It's not right. Don't you see? Don't you see what you've become? Don't you see what you're asking me to be?"

He looked back and forth, but they didn't see. They took a step back from him. Their eyes became closed off, no longer family.

"Luca. Noah. I'm so sorry. I love you so much, but I'm sorry. I have to do this."

A growling noise started with Luca and moved to Noah. The sound grew until it was all around him. Casey reached out, bringing forth the hunger he now controlled. His skin felt like molten lava, burning to a crisp, then flaking away from his muscles and sinew. The dried pieces floated away into the air like ash, all while his body was pulled up from his middle like a piece of clay being stretched. His sense of smell changed. The odor they emitted no longer turned his stomach. It was familiar and comforting. His lips pulled back from his mouth, splitting and bleeding as they stretched. His bones crackled as they reformed beneath skin that oozed a substance so foul it could knock a person out.

His pants lay in a heap beneath his feet, having fallen away as he grew. He tore at his shirt with his claws, tossing it to the ground so it wouldn't impede his movement. They took another step back from him, a sense of alarm showing in their oversized, red eyes. His growl joined theirs, and the attack began.

He lunged at Noah first, the stronger of the two. Casey's teeth tore into bitter skin, grinding bone as he bit down hard enough to snap a femur in half. Noah howled in pain, attempting to push him off, but failing. Luca tackled Casey from the side, her strength surprising him. He clawed her arms as she tried to grapple with him, scraping flesh away from bone in large strips. She knocked him sideways and to the ground with a blow to the head so hard he saw double.

He rolled away, narrowly avoiding Noah's clawed foot as it smashed into the earth where his head had been. He rose to his feet and attacked immediately, this time choosing Luca. He crashed into her, throwing her to the ground. They rolled several feet, clawing and biting as they went, neither managing to make any real headway. When they came to a stop, Luca tucked her feet close to her body, then kicked, sending Casey flying into a tree.

The blow knocked the wind out of him. He shook his head to clear the buzzing, but it wouldn't relent. His head had hit the tree too hard. He couldn't see straight or hear properly. He had to rely on his sense of smell, dodging blindly as one of them got close. It was the end of the fight. Without his eyes or ears, it was only a matter of time. They knew it; he knew it. His only hope was to take one of them down with him.

He let down his guard, panting as if he was out of breath. Noah took the bait, Luca growling at him when he did. She was always the smarter of the two, thought Casey, as Noah came within biting range. He ducked, and aimed low, catching Noah in the groin. He felt the vein he was looking for catch in a tooth. He clamped his jaws shut and pulled back hard, desperate to sever the artery. Noah howled in anguish as the vein was pulled from his body, refusing to break through some mystical intervention. Casey cursed, but it came out as an ungodly scream. The femoral artery looped outside Noah's body, like some grotesque noodle, but was still intact, purple, engorged and pulsing with blood that had backed up inside.

That's when Luca hit Casey, knocking him to the ground. He felt his head crack into a stone buried halfway in the dirt. His eyes watered, and he smelled something strange. Something was dripping down the back of his neck.

Luca drug her claws across his belly, peeling back the skin as she went. Viscera erupted from the wound, wet and steaming. Casey howled as his vision blurred from the pain. He saw a flash of white, and thought it was the end for him. There was nothing more he could do. He fell back into the dirt, waiting for the finishing blow as he clutched his stomach, each gulp of air causing it to bulge.

The sound of an engine gunning brought him back to consciousness. He lifted his head to see Luca turning toward the truck. It was coming fast, and in between it and a sizable tree crouched Noah.

"Max," Casey breathed.

The word came out garbled, but the fear in it was clear as

day. He watched helplessly, unable to get up, his head still pounding from absorbing two concussions in rapid succession.

The truck slammed into Noah, then crushed him between the tree and the grill. A scream tore from the beast as he clawed desperately at the hood of the vehicle. Max backed up, and gunned the engine again, this time aiming for Luca. She leapt, high and away. Max stopped, idling for a few seconds before she got out of the truck.

"No," Casey said, his voice barely above a whisper. "Get back in."

Max was stepping toward him, her face a mask of concern, when Luca landed with a heavy thud on the hood of the truck. Max raised the bat she had been holding.

"There you are," she said. "I know you understand me."

Luca screamed, the sound reverberating through the woods, silencing everything in range with fear.

"Yeah," Max said. "I figured as much."

Luca started toward her and Max flipped a switch on the handle of the bat. That's when Casey noticed the heavy rubber gloves she was wearing.

"Right," Max said. "So here's the thing. I played ball in college. They called me the clean up lady. I batted fourth. Didn't matter if the ball came at fifty, sixty, even seventy miles an hour. I always found it with my bat."

She planted her feet and stared down Luca.

"This bat has three tasers wired up to it. Your head is a lot bigger than a softball. And I'm willing to bet, a lot slower, too. You wanna take that chance? I'm game."

Luca screamed again. Max didn't move. Then the creature charged. Casey felt his heart stop as Luca bolted toward Max. He wanted to close his eyes, not willing to see her die, but a part of him wouldn't let him. This was his fault – he needed to see the full cost of his foolishness.

But Luca never touched Max. As soon as Luca came within range of the bat, Max swung. She was in perfect form. As soon as the charged weapon came into contact with Luca's outstretched arms, she was blasted backward by the force. A burning smell joined the various stenches in the air. Her body slid across the ground before resting in a heap, motionless.

Casey swallowed hopefully, but Luca pulled herself back onto her feet with the help of a tree. She shook her head and took a step toward Max.

"Really?" Max said. She flipped the other two switches on the bat. "Have it your way. But that was only one taser. Now I've turned on all three."

Luca looked like she might have taken the chance, until Noah made a pained sound on the other side of the truck. The cry stopped the creature in her tracks. Luca turned toward Noah and mewled in his direction; it was almost tender. She took one last look at Max standing over Casey's prone body, hissed, then hopped away, gathering up Noah and disappearing into the woods.

Max remained in position for a couple minutes before lowering her bat. She flipped the switches, deactivating it, and took off the gloves. She looked over her shoulder before bending down to inspect Casey's wounds.

"No," Casey said. His voice was hoarse, but still recognizable. "Please, no."

"Are they coming back you think?" Max asked.

"No. Don't come near me. Not now."

Max sat back on her heels and sighed at him.

"Too late. I've seen ya. I know how you smell. I know how you look. And yeah, it's ugly. But if I can clean up the toilet after my ex has been to an all-you-can-eat Mexican buffet, I can handle this."

Casey was in too much pain to laugh; he wasn't to cry. He let the tears fall from his sunken eyes as Max stood up and looked around. She pulled the handkerchief out of her hair and considered it, before tossing it to the ground.

"That won't do," she said. "I need something bigger to bind your stomach. I expect you to do your part and whistle, or grunt, just something, if they come back."

She disappeared before he could tell her to stay. He was slowly regaining his full vision and looked around at the carnage. Max's truck was a mess. She'd hit the tree hard. It was still running, so he assumed that meant it wasn't totaled. When she came back with the remains of his clothes, he grunted. Why had she bothered? It wasn't until she started wrapping his middle with his jeans that he realized why she'd gone back for them.

"Can you stand?" she asked.

"Maybe," he said.

She reached down and gripped his clawed hand. He was amazed she wasn't more repulsed by him, or even in any kind of shock. Not only did she pull him up, she hoisted him onto her shoulder to help him walk.

He could see her discomfort with every step. Just before they reached her truck, she had to stop to retch. He watched in awe and sorrow. She shouldn't have to see this, let alone get close to something so repulsive as him. Once she'd emptied her stomach, she stood up and took a shaky breath.

"I think we'll drive with the windows open. Okay with you?"

She didn't wait for an answer, just helped him inside. Once he was sitting, he saw that the airbags had deployed. They draped limply over the dashboard and the steering wheel. Max got in the truck and turned the air on full while opening the windows. She backed up, and made her way to the dirt road, using turn signals and all. It was so normal, Casey started to think he'd gone unconscious and it was all a dream.

"How'd you find me?" he asked.

Max pulled the yellow-jeweled phone out of her pocket and placed it on the seat between them.

"Another thing you do with your little sister's phone when she has the decision-making abilities of a fifteen-year-old? You put a tracking app on it."

Casey leaned back against the headrest and smiled. He hoped Max didn't see it, because he was sure it would be a fright.

"Thank you, Max."

"You're welcome." She turned on the radio and an upbeat tune filled the cab. "Next time, take me with you."

TEN

"So," Max said. "Do you change back? Or is this... you... now?"

It was taking longer to get back home than Casey had expected. It took him a few minutes to realize why – Max was using back roads to avoid being seen.

"You worried how this will affect our sex life?" Casey joked.

"Nah. But the wedding will be awkward."

Forgetting for just a moment what he looked like, he reached over and took Max's hand in his claw. She didn't pull away in disgust. She didn't even flinch.

"You make me feel ordinary," he said.

"I hope that's a good thing."

She glanced over at him, giving his deformed hand a squeeze.

"When you're a monster," he said, "it's the best thing."

He reached past his knees and sliced off the deflated airbag with one claw. The material gave easily, falling to the floor in a heap. He then clawed at the glove box, trying his best to open it without mangling the catch.

"What's in there?" Max asked.

"Jerky. I stashed some in here last night. In case..."

He finally got his nail under the latch and clicked open the glove box. After some more fumbling, he pulled out a bag and sliced it open with his finger tip.

"I just need to feed the hunger," he said. "Then I'll be back to normal."

There was more fumbling as Casey attempted to spear a piece of dried meat and get it into his mouth. As soon as he started chewing, he felt the hunger begin to retreat. His teeth ground together from the pain of changing back.

"You alright over there?" Max asked.

"I'll be... fine," Casey gasped. "It's an unpleasant experience."

Sinew pulled him back together, crushing bones back into place, shifting organs around rapidly. His skin burned, the tough wendigo hide sloughing off in ashen flakes, burned by an invisible heat source, leaving the surface of his body as raw as a fresh wound. His human skin grew over it, stinging as it spread across his arms and legs. The hair that burst from the freshly healed pores felt like ten thousand pin pricks. The jeans that Max had used to bind his stomach became so tight as Casey returned to his human body, it was difficult to breathe. He loosened the makeshift bandages, releasing a fresh rush of blood which soaked through them in seconds.

"Shit," he said. "I'm sorry. Your truck is going to look like a murder scene."

Max pulled the truck over as soon as she saw the renewed flow of blood. She turned and hurriedly started applying pressure on his stomach.

"Doctor?"

"No," Casey said. "Too many questions. Too dangerous. I'll be alright. I just need to sew it up. Then, it'll heal quick. I promise. I was hurt worse than this the last time."

"The last time?"

The alarm in Max's voice was hard to miss.

"We should get back," Casey said. "Anne is alone at the Sunset."

"Right," Max said.

She turned to the wheel and put the truck in gear, launching a spray of gravel as she pulled out. They didn't stop again.

By the time they got to the Sunset, Casey had managed to staunch the bleeding. He hadn't, however, managed to keep the blood from making a mess of the truck's upholstery. The whole cab looked like a crime scene. Anne came running over to the truck, a horrified look on her face.

"Oh my god!"

She stopped Max, who was coming around to Casey's side of the truck to help him out. Anne patted her down, looking for injuries.

"Are you okay? Are you bleeding? Where is all this blood coming from?"

"Me," Casey said. He leaned against the door, unable to open it without releasing pressure on his abdomen. "Does she know?"

The question was aimed at Max. She didn't answer. Instead, she gently pushed Anne away from her.

"Can you get us some clean towels, hot water and the big first aid kit?"

"The big one? Okay."

Casey was astonished Anne ran off without further

questions, complaints or instruction. The change in her was almost as dramatic as his own – hers was just less visible.

Max opened the door to the truck slowly, not just out of caution for Casey, but because the crash had deformed the body of the truck badly enough to make the door ill fitting. The sound of angry metal being bent in ways it wasn't designed for filled the air.

"That can't be good," Casey said.

"You should see the other guy."

As Max helped Casey out of the truck, he remembered the sound Noah made after being hit.

"Did you?" he asked quietly.

Max was hoisting him up carefully, trying not to bump his midsection.

"What?"

"See him," he said. "The one you hit with the truck."

"That was a 'he?' How could you tell?"

"I know them really well." He paused. "How did you know which one was me?"

Max stopped, her hand on the doorknob to Casey's room.

"I... don't know. I just knew. You did look less like them, but I didn't really notice that until after I'd hit the one with my truck. They had horns, right? Almost looked like antlers, if antlers were demonic."

"That's new," Casey said. "They didn't have those the last time I saw them."

"You don't have them," Max said. She opened the door to Casey's room and helped him to the bed. "Did yours get knocked off?"

Casey lay back against the pillows. Everything in him hurt; so much so, that it took him several seconds to process what Max had asked.

"No. I've never had horns."

Max didn't respond. Casey watched her blearily while she busied herself about the room, gathering things he couldn't quite see. She went into the bathroom for a couple minutes, leaving him alone. He stared at the mirror across from the bed. He was quite the sight – naked, bloody and dirty. Tonight, his luck should have run out – would have run out, save for Max. He should have died.

Max bustled back into the room with a bundle of steaming, white terry cloth. She pulled a chair up next to the bed and began the process of slowly cleaning his skin. Once a cloth became too dirty or bloody, she dropped it in the waste bin.

"You could wash those, you know," he said.

He tried to smile, but it hurt too much. Max didn't notice, as concentrated on her task as she was.

"I don't know how all this works," she said. "If it's like an STD or something. I figured better safe than sorry. Treat everything like it's a biohazard."

A thought occurred to Casey just then. As Max's hand passed across his chest, he took it gently in his own.

"How long have you known?"

Max looked into his eyes. She picked up a fresh cloth and started wiping his face.

"Since I saw your tattoo."

"It's gibberish," he said. "Spanish gibberish on top of that."

"It looks like gibberish because it's not all Spanish." She finished wiping his face and dropped the cloth into the bin. "I read a little Spanish. Took it in high school. My friend took Latin. We'd help each other study sometimes with flashcards. I don't really know Latin, just picked up a few things, but I know there's at least one Latin word on your back. Pretty sure most of what's on your back is legible, if you knew all the languages. But the word wendigo is wendigo, in Spanish, English, Latin... And whatever other languages are on your back."

"Wendigo could have been a word in another language," Casey said. "You made a pretty good guess based on that one thing."

Max wiped a smudge of something off his cheek. Her fingers lingered against the side of his face as she smiled at him.

"I told you my dad spent his summers away from us, right?" she asked. Casey nodded. "I spent a lot of time alone over the summers. My mom worked, so I was left to do all the things teenage girls who feel like the world is against them do. I wore black, lots of eye liner and listened to the Cure."

"The Cure?" Casey asked with a smile.

"Emo wasn't really a thing yet. The Cure was the closest I could get."

"You were a nineties goth?"

"I was a nineties teenager. Black eyeliner or not, we all thought our lives were the worst ever and no one could understand. Besides, flannel and Nirvana just didn't do it for me."

Casey chuckled, then winced.

"Are you about to tell me you dated a wendigo in an act of teenage rebellion?" Casey asked.

"Not quite."

Max continued cleaning as she spoke. The warm, damp cloth against his skin was more than a physical comfort. Her touch felt like it was washing away something deeper inside of him – the years of isolation and pain that had calcified around his heart.

"But I did get into horror stories. Not just into them, I obsessed over them. Everything from Stephen King, to Clive Barker, even back to Lovecraft and Poe. When I ran out of those, I started reading stuff by Grimm, and that led me to other tales of horror. Native Americans have a ton of really good horror legends."

"The wendigo," Casey said.

"Yes. I always find the ones where humans are the source of horror to be the scariest. They feel the most true to me."

Casey took her hand and held it against his chest. He couldn't help but feel there was a more personal reason Max was obsessed with horror stories.

"You still reading those kinds of things?" he asked.

"No. Not anymore. Actually, the Native American stories helped me grow out of the goth-obsessed days of my youth. I read a Coyote story, and from then on it was tricksters that held me in their sway."

Max smiled at the memory before continuing.

"Anyway, I didn't guess what you are just because I knew the story." She rubbed her arm absently. "I was out there at the campground helping people search for those two kids. I smelled... I'm sure I don't have to tell you what I smelled."

Casey nodded. He knew all too well.

"My cousin told me the same thing," Max continued. "She smelled death out there on the lake. It's why she called me about the missing couple. It scared her. That stuck in my head. Then when I saw the word 'wendigo' on your back, and the timing of your arrival... Everything clicked. I honestly felt kind of stupid thinking it. Every time I'd look at you..." Max gave him a brief, lusty look. "I thought it was just my wild imagination playing tricks on me, trying to ruin my mood."

"Your mood?" Casey asked with faux innocence.

Max blushed a light pink and clucked her tongue.

"You weren't supposed to ask that."

"I'm sorry," Casey said with a grin. "But now I've asked..."

Max narrowed her eyes, but Casey could tell she wasn't really upset.

"I liked you. A little too much." She broke eye contact and the blush deepened. After a few seconds, she recomposed herself. "I wonder exactly how many languages are on your back. Do you know why it's like that?"

"I do," Casey said. "The only person I ever found who could help me, the one who tattooed me... They were afraid making the warding too obvious would lead the spirit that cursed me to him. It was a way to trick the spirit, so it couldn't follow him home. I've never known what was written there or in which language. He just told me he mixed up the languages."

"He didn't tell you what he wrote?" Max asked.

"Nope. In fact, I hardly got a chance to talk to him," Casey said. "I didn't find him directly. A woman took me to him. Blindfolded. I never even saw him. I'm pretty sure I heard the woman say his name, but I won't say that out loud. The guy risked a lot to help me."

"You think saying his name out loud will endanger him?" Max asked.

"I'm a wendigo," Casey said. "When you know that's a thing that can happen, you start to believe anything is possible."

Max didn't say anything for a bit.

"And you're sure it's the tattoo that fixed you?" she finally asked.

Casey sighed, but not at the question. He'd wondered the same thing himself, thousands of times.

"One of the people I talked to when I was looking for a cure said there was no cure. He said it as if he knew it for a fact. He said the only way to really be rid of the curse was to have the will to control it. That the spirit would leave if it couldn't have its way. Who knows? Maybe the tattoo is gibberish. Maybe it's got nothing to do with why I can control it. Maybe it's like the feather Dumbo carried. But I'm not taking any chances with anything. If it's the tattoo, great. If I can't ever say the tattooist's name aloud, fine. It's a small price to pay."

Max took his hand and held it quietly for a while. He wasn't sure if she believed him. He wasn't sure he believed it himself. Whether or not he believed what the tattooist had told him as he was inking Casey's back, it was an insignificant quibble – the hunger had abated, and Casey maintained control. Whether it was all in the mind or if the words of power on his back were what helped, the result was the same.

"You knew," he said. The words tumbled out of his mouth without warning. "Last night. When we... you knew."

Max nodded. She entwined her fingers with his.

"Yeah," she said. "Just for the record, it isn't a fetish thing."

Casey couldn't help himself. He laughed, causing pain to shoot through him. Max looked at him apologetically as he winced.

"I wasn't thinking that." He fidgeted with the jeans binding him together. "Just, you know. You weren't afraid of catching... it?"

"Oh. Well, you wore protection."

"Yeah, but... I'm a wendigo."

"Do condoms not protect against wendigoism?"

"You need to stop that," Casey said, doing his best not to laugh again. "You're going to kill me with charm."

Max bent over and gave him a light kiss. Before pulling away, she looked into his eyes steadily.

"If I turned, I'd be one of the good ones. Like you."

Anne came in then. It was a good thing, too, because Casey wasn't sure his injuries would keep him from pulling Max down into the bed and making a mess. But Anne, she could dampen a desert – his mood was no match for that. He watched her as she bustled over to the bed, her arms full of the things Max had asked her to gather. While Anne arranged them on the nightstand, Max partially covered Casey up with a clean towel so he wasn't completely naked. Anne handed Max a red plastic case.

"Let's see," Max said, opening it up.

She pulled out gauze, alcohol and a suture kit. She sorted through the kit until she found a tiny aerosol can as well. Anne was leaning over the kit, watching with interest.

"Does he need stitches?" she asked.

The suture kit trembled in Max's hands. Casey touched her arm to ease her concerns.

"I can do it," he said.

"Don't be stupid," Anne said. "You look like shit and you're paler than a fish belly. I'll help. You... just lie down and try not to move."

Anne grabbed a pair of scissors from the kit and moved to the other side of the bed. She had to climb onto it to reach Casey. Max grabbed one of the clean towels and waited while Anne cut the jeans away from Casey's middle. With the pressure released, blood started welling up from the wound almost immediately.

"Jesus," Anne said. "I hope you have extra mattresses out there in those containers, because this one is gonna be toast after this."

Casey began to feel dizzy as soon as the jeans were removed. He closed his eyes, on the verge of blacking out.

"I don't even know what I'm doing," Max said. "What if I sew it shut, and he just keeps bleeding inside."

Without opening his eyes, Casey patted Max on the shoulder.

"Sew it up. I promise it will be okay. I don't break promises."

Then he blacked out completely.

The first thing that alerted Casey to the fact he hadn't died was a heinous pounding sensation in his head. It was almost as if he could feel every pump of blood coursing through the veins that snaked through his brain. He tried opening his eyes, only to have the pain bunch together just behind the sockets.

"Ouch."

Someone took his hand and touched his forehead.

"Max?"

"That's the one," she said. "You don't feel hot, but you're pretty sweaty."

Teeth gritted, Casey tried to open his eyes. This time, he succeeded. The room was dimly lit – a single lamp near the bathroom the only source of light. Max was still perched on the chair beside the bed, a book in her lap. The bedding had been changed at some point while he was out. The sheets were clean and crisp.

"Is it morning yet?" he asked.

"Not quite. Four-thirty. You should get some more rest."

"I can't," he said.

Something was itching across his stomach. The feeling, so insistent and intense, had woken him up from his slumber. He pulled at the gauze taped there, peeling it back.

"I don't know if that's a good idea," Max said in protest.

Casey kept pulling. His stomach was a mass of bruises, ranging in color from deep purple to light brown. Max's stitching was neat and tidy, impressive for someone who he assumed had never done it before. The itching was emanating from the thread weaving in and out of his skin.

"Scissors," Casey said.

"To cut the stitches?"

He nodded. Max didn't ask any more questions – just got up and retrieved the scissors from the far side of the room as Casey scratched around the edge of his wounds, trying not to tear the stiches out. The itching was maddening.

"Cut them," he said when Max returned. "Like a seam ripper. Quick. It feels like there are ants under my skin."

Max leaned over him and made quick work of the stitches, cutting them right down the middle.

"You might want to look away," Casey said.

"No. I can help. You just want them pulled out?"

Casey nodded again as he tugged a nylon thread. He pulled it free, and it was one of the most remarkable feelings he'd ever had.

"Oh my god," he said. "It's like scratching an itch inside my body."

Max smiled as she helped him pull the rest of the string from his rapidly healing skin. When they were done, the two perfect rows of holes on either side of the three claw wounds looked clean and pink. Max walked away again, this time returning with a bottle of alcohol and a bag of cotton balls.

"I'll probably be okay, Max."

"Humor me."

He allowed her to clean the wounds without fuss, enjoying the sensation of the alcohol rapidly evaporating off his skin. When she was done, she cleaned up and sat back down beside him.

"How are you feeling?"

Hiding a grin, Casey shivered.

"A little cold. I think if you got in bed next to me, I'd feel warmer."

"That so?"

"Yeah."

Max got up with a smirk and rounded the bed, shutting off the light before crawling in next to him.

"Better?" she asked.

He put his arm around her and pulled her in close.

"You don't even know."

They stayed like that for twenty minutes or so, enjoying the comfort of just being together. Casey had begun to wonder if Max had fallen asleep when she spoke up.

"You really do heal fast."

"Yup," he said. "There are only two perks to having a cannibal demon entombed in your body. The healing thing is pretty nice."

"What's the other?"

"Acute sense of smell."

"That's a perk?" Max asked. "It would drive me nuts. Any time I walked past a bathroom, or hell, a perfume counter, it would be agony."

"I'd have thought so, too, before I had it. But once you do, smells become... different. There are still bad and good ones, but they're more complex. Undertones and overtones, with practice you can focus on the parts that are pleasant. And of course, without it, I would miss how wonderful you smell."

"I've never been more aware of how long it's been since I've taken a shower than I am right now," Max said.

"You smell like lemons to me," he said. "Always like lemons."

"Oh. That's not me. It's the clothes. I put lemongrass oil on the dryer balls."

"No," he said. He touched her neck with his nose and inhaled. "Even when you aren't wearing anything, it lingers. A mixture of you and lemons. It makes it so hard to concentrate when I'm around you."

She kissed him. In the dark, he didn't see it coming. He felt the relief in her lips, as if the anxiety that had built up over the last several hours poured out of her with one quiet gesture. He held her close with a sincere hope he'd never have to worry her like he had. He was glad he'd made it back.

"How did it happen?" she asked.

He'd been waiting for this. Not with a sense of foreboding or dread, just with certainty that it would come up. He'd even planned how he'd tell her but, somehow, he couldn't remember anything he'd wanted to say or how he wanted to say it.

"My parents," he began. "Or, my father, I should say. He was the first. I don't know how, exactly. I've read up on wendigos. I've seen legends that say it's spontaneous, others that you have to invite it in. Some say all it takes is an act of cannibalism. Only the spontaneous theory makes any sense to me.

"My dad worked in New York City. We lived in a big house. A really big house. I had a vague sense my dad did something on Wall Street, but I never really knew. I called him an investment banker, because that's what all my friends called their dads and I didn't want to stick out. But I didn't know. It didn't seem to matter. No one asked for details. I lived my life oblivious to how my family was so well off, just like every other kid in my private school. The money was just there. Didn't matter how or why.

"Then, one night, when I was thirteen, he didn't come home. I know it wasn't planned, a usual business thing, because of the way my mom freaked out about it. She was all set to call the cops when he showed up at dawn. He was a mess. Dirty, smelled something horrendous, and he had blood stains on his shirt. Mom was convinced he'd been mugged, but Dad wouldn't say what it was. He just told us to pack our bags. We were going to the cabin.

"We all packed and got into the car without asking. I can still remember being terrified of the way my father said it. He was scared. I'd never seen him scared. I think that's why we all went without question. My younger brother and sister, twins, had just turned ten, so for them it was an adventure. But for Mom and me, it was something else.

"We got there after driving all day. Dad said everything would be fine now that we were out of the city. And then we just started living new lives, as if we'd never been to New York City before. I thought it was strange, but I never brought it up. No, that's not right. Once. Once I did. Then I never did after that. My father's eyes the one time I asked," Casey paused at the memory. "Only once. If you know anything about rich teenage boys, you'll be wondering why I didn't pitch a fit. I can't tell you, except to say the one time I asked, the look he gave me was so horrifying, complaining wasn't even an option.

"Two years went by. It was just normal then that we'd left New York, everything, behind. We never spoke about it. I think Mom acting as if everything was fine helped. Especially with the twins. I was less convinced, but too afraid to say anything. During most of that time, Dad isolated himself from us. He was either in his office or in his bedroom. Every time he caught sight of us, a ravenous expression would cross his face. Then he'd flee in terror.

"Mom put on a brave face, but I could tell she was scared every single minute of every single day.

"Some nights, I'd see dad leave the cabin. I'd watch him go outside, naked, even in the winter. He'd head out into the woods. A few times, I waited up. He'd be gone most of the night, and when he came back, he was always covered in blood from his chin to his groin. I didn't tell my family. I didn't think they'd want to know.

"Then one night, a family came to the door. The Locke's. It was winter. We had so much snow. They were on their way to a ski lodge. A mom, a dad and two little boys. They got off the main road and ended up in our dead-end neck of the woods. They'd seen the lights and were looking for help. I thought my dad would tell them to go. I wish he'd told them to go. Maybe he was tired of fighting it. Maybe he was afraid if he didn't sate it with the Locke's, he'd be forced to turn on us."

"The hunger?" Max asked.

"Yes," Casey said. "When you're infected with whatever this is, it never goes away. It constantly gnaws at your insides, whispering that it feels so right. The flavors. The textures. Eat, and sate this hunger. Sate it and find peace."

Casey felt the beast churn inside of him, as if woken by his words. He held Max closer and it quieted.

"It lies. It lies all the time. And you can't tell truth from lies. I know the madness my father must have been feeling. I know, when the Locke's came to the door, the hunger would have seen a chance to break my father's will. And it did. That night was the last time I saw my father in his human form.

"When I woke up, Mom said the Locke's had gone. They might as well have taken my mother with them. She was a hollow person after that night. We weren't allowed anywhere near my father's study. Only my mother could enter. The door was always kept closed. It wasn't long after that when something new moved into the shell of my mother's body. It moved quicker in her than in my father, I think because her will had been broken the night the Locke's disappeared.

"I started seeing them go out together into the woods, hand in hand. My mother, and the thing that had been my father. The less it looked like my father, the longer it would stay out.

"Around my sixteenth birthday, they vanished for three days. That wasn't the worst thing, though. The worst thing was I was starting to hear it. I'd eat, and couldn't fill up. I'd sleep, and dream of blood. I'd wake, and want to bite.

"Luca and Noah. I took care of them those three days. I would have done anything to protect them. But it was too late. It didn't matter what I fed them. They couldn't eat enough. I'd fed them every scrap of food in the house in those three days, trying to fight it. Nothing helped. The voice got louder than any noise I'd ever heard.

"Then our parents came home. I thought if I saw them up close, I'd be scared. But I wasn't. Their smell was overpowering but comforting. I knew, despite their appearance, that they belonged to us and we to them. They were dragging something behind them when they came. They dropped it in front of us."

Casey choked on bile just remembering the night. He swallowed it back, determined to continue.

"I wanted to eat the woman more than anything I'd ever wanted. I'd never known desire so strong. When I looked at Luca and Noah, I knew they wanted it, too. I did the only thing I could. I changed.

"I'd never done it before. I just knew that I could. No one looked surprised when it happened, not my father, not my mother, not even Luca or Noah. Their calm is the only reason I was able to do what I did.

"I killed my dad first. I tore out his throat with my teeth. When I turned on my mother, she didn't even struggle. When I looked in her eyes, I saw a sliver of the woman she had been. I know she came back just long enough to help me. She bared her neck and held my hand while I did it. Sometimes, in my worst nightmares, I still taste her blood."

Casey felt Max's hold on him tighten. He was nearly done. He pushed through the pain to finish.

"I buried the dead woman. I buried her deeper than I thought possible, digging until I hit stone. I couldn't let Luca and Noah eat her. It was wrong, and the idea that they were feeling what I was feeling was terrifying to me. I thought she'd be safe so deep in the ground.

"I spent weeks calling anyone I thought might have answers, fearful for our lives. Eventually, someone put the name to what we were. Wendigo.

"Most stories about wendigo end with their death. I could only find one mention of a ritual to reverse the effects. I knew asking around was dangerous. That it might bring someone to our door who'd rightfully end our lives, for the safety of others. But I got lucky. A woman agreed to meet me to take me to someone she thought could help. But it would be a long trip. I had to leave Noah and Luca behind. They were thirteen. Still children, but capable so I thought it was okay and I definitely couldn't risk them around people. They were much worse off than I was, having trouble controlling the change. Any time I brought them meat, the only thing that would give us a moment's peace from the hunger, they'd contort into the horror you've seen.

"Before I left, I hunted for a whole week. Mostly deer and elk, but even a couple bears. I thought it was enough. I thought it was safe to leave. I took the car and drove to Ohio.

"The man who saved me, I will never be able to thank him enough. I asked him about my brother and sister, and when he asked how long they'd been alone, he said there was nothing he could do. He said all it would take was one bite of human flesh, and they'd be lost forever. I swore they were alone and isolated with no way to find anyone. He told me I should be ready to kill them, and informed me he wouldn't risk coming back with me.

"When I got back, I found the grave I'd made had been dug up. The body was missing. There weren't even any bones left. And Luca and Noah were gone."

The light from the new day crept under the curtains. Casey had finally told his story. He thought he'd feel relief from having told it; he'd kept it with him for so long. But all he felt was sorrow. He'd spent every day since the night he'd killed his parents dedicated to one task – save Luca and Noah. Eventually, after he'd given up all hope that saving them was an option, that mission morphed into the one that plagued him now – kill Luca and Noah. He'd never had time to grieve.

He let the feelings come, buffeting him. Shielded in the arms of the woman he loved, he let them take hold of him. He felt them all, the sorrow, the anger, the guilt, the hurt, the betrayal. He let them come and wash over him. He let them come until the sun rose, consuming him completely.

Then he let them go.

ELEVEN

The truck was a wreck, but still drivable. Max circled it, inspecting it closely while Casey watched. He felt better than he had in years, even though he still had to find his siblings and deal with them. It was strange to feel so blasé about the whole thing. Saying what he had to do out loud made it easier somehow – more acceptable. Max's support and understanding made it that much simpler.

She came back around to the front of the truck and crossed her arms.

"Let's hope no one else disappeared last night," Max said. "Because if Frank comes out here now, and sees this, he won't need a warrant to haul us all off to a cell for questioning."

Casey leaned in close to the grill. Bits of flesh and hair were lodged deep inside. He didn't even need to sniff it to tell it belonged to Noah.

"You think you crushed him?" he asked.

"I do. He dropped to the ground when I reversed and didn't move. I thought he might have been dead, until the other one...

195

your sister went over and picked him up." She looked over at Casey and touched his stomach. "Will he heal like you?"

"I don't think so. We're not invincible." Casey pulled up his shirt and ran his hand over the light pink scars. "I know it looked bad, but this wasn't going to kill me. Her slamming my head into the ground would have, though. Like I said, the first time I caught up with them, it was so much worse. A week before I could walk. And I wasn't crushed by a two-ton pick-up."

"Will she leave?" Max asked. "Find somewhere else to do what wendigos do?"

Casey was surprised he hadn't considered that. It was the obvious thing to ask. If Noah was dead, would Luca move on? He touched a tuft of hair caught between the hood and the body of the vehicle, then looked sideways at Max. If someone had killed Max, he'd track them to the ends of the Earth. What he'd do when he found them was so dark, he didn't even want to imagine it.

"I don't think she will," he answered.

Max sighed. She went to the bed of the truck and pulled the bat out of it before coming back to him. She placed it on the hood. Casey hadn't gotten a good look at it, unsurprisingly, since he'd been barely conscious when she'd used it on Luca. For something so lethal, it looked surprisingly elegant.

It was an aluminum bat, a large one, the barrel thickness tapering far closer to the base of the bat than Casey was used to seeing. The grip had been wrapped with thick layers of rubbery tape. Just above the grip were what appeared to be three tasers that had been deconstructed, then pieced back together. Copper wires led out of the rigged tasers, up and around the bat, connected to copper spikes that had been welded around the top in two circular rows.

"Wow," Casey said. "Where did you learn how to build something like this?"

"I had a crazy uncle," Max said. "Literally. At least I think so. I never got any real confirmation on his level of sanity. I suspect my mom never wanted to inquire too deeply about it. He built booby traps all around his house. He was convinced people were out to get him."

"And your parents let you over there?"

"Not exactly. It was one of those, this is an adult who lets you do dangerous things so you visit a lot when your parents aren't looking, kind of things. Like if you have a grandfather who lets you play with fireworks. Or an older brother who let's you take a hit off his joint."

Casey picked up the bat and twisted it around, admiring the ingenuity.

"He taught you how to make this then?"

"No. He did teach me about tasers, stun guns, cattle prods, pretty much anything that could harm without killing."

Max deepened her voice and straightened her back.

"'Men are animals, Maxie. You need to teach them how to behave.' That's what he told me on my thirteenth birthday when I opened the first taser he gave me. I got one every year after that, too."

"I'm surprised you ever even dated, let alone got married."

"That uncle was my mother's brother," Max said by way of explanation.

It didn't illuminate anything for Casey, but he didn't want to press it, either.

"Will I have to meet this uncle at that wedding you talked about having?" he asked jokingly.

"Yes, but don't worry. I'll let him know I've already tamed you."

Casey laughed while investigating the tasers attached to the bat.

"How does it work?"

Max pointed to the tasers.

"I installed switches on these, instead of triggers. It'll turn on, each one pulsing fifty thousand volts per second. Normally, these would have about five hundred shots each. Each shot would be five seconds of power drain on the battery. The way I've got it set up, you get about a half hour of power before the battery on each one dies. You can turn on one, or all three. I hit Luca with one on. It threw her back quite a ways, and probably hurt like hell, but I don't think she ever lost consciousness. I'm pretty sure I could knock a horse out cold with three turned on. Once it's on, you just need to make contact."

Max went back to the truck bed and hauled out the rubber gloves Casey had seen the night before. She pulled them on before toggling one of the switches to 'on.' Electricity arced between the copper points at the end of the bat, snapping as it moved. She turned the bat off before setting it back down again.

"Aluminum isn't a great conductor for electricity, so it'll prefer the copper and move more fluidly through that, but I wouldn't touch the bat without the gloves. I've taped it like crazy down on the handle but, even so, I wouldn't trust it."

Impressed wasn't the right word for what Casey felt. Awe was more fitting.

"You want me to make you one?" Max asked. "I have a bunch more tasers."

"No. I'm sure I'd stun myself and just end up on the ground, covered in urine, everybody laughing. Which might work as a distraction, now that I think about it," Casey said. "That stuff about being the cleanup lady true, too?"

"Absolutely," Max said. "I wasn't much good at anything

else in softball. But you'd be surprised how much use they made out of someone whose only real talent on the field was connecting a ball and a bat."

Anne ambled up as Max spoke. The whole morning had gone by without Casey seeing her. He was more than a little curious what she'd been up to. She noticed the bat and frowned.

"Are you going back out there again?" she asked.

"I don't have much of a choice," Max said. "I'm thinking this creature will come to us, if we don't go to it."

Max looked at Casey for confirmation, and he nodded. Luca would be afraid, perhaps even desperate. She'd want to eliminate the threat Max posed to her. However, if Noah was hanging on out there somewhere, Casey didn't think his sister would leave her twin behind. Either way, Luca would eventually be back for them.

Casey wasn't crazy about the idea of Max going against Luca again, either. He'd have much rather gone after her on his own, but he knew well enough not to argue with Max about it. She'd saved his life, after all. He couldn't very well tell her he was better equipped to take Luca out when she'd dragged him to safety, batting away two wendigos to do it.

"I figured as much," Anne said. "If you're going to insist on being stupid, I think I have an idea."

"Is that what you've been working on all morning long?" Max asked.

"Yes. I made some calls."

Just then a black SUV pulled into the parking lot of the Sunset. Max moved between the car and Casey protectively.

"Anne? Please tell me that isn't Jay Campbell."

"If you're gonna be stupid, might as well go all in on it," Anne said.

"Anne," Max started.

"No." Anne leaned in close. Casey assumed it was because Jay had parked. "You're my sister. I don't want you fucking killed, okay? There's a monster out there and you want to fight it, fine. But I'm not letting you do this shit alone. Suzie has been texting me updates all morning about Jay getting ready to 'bust shit up.' He thinks you're harboring a fugitive or some dumbass shit. He wants to get the monster who killed his best friend. Why not tell him the truth, and point him in the right direction?"

"You're going to get them killed," Casey said.

"The only one who's gonna die is you, you piece of shit."

Jay stalked toward them with menace in his eyes. He remembered to bring all his friends when he exited his SUV this time, Casey noted. He'd also brought a shot gun. Casey started to move in front of Max, but she pushed him back.

"Stay behind me. He won't shoot me," she said.

"Wanna bet?"

Jay's taunt had little effect on Max.

"Knock it off, Jay." Anne marched up to Jay and his gang, getting right in his face. "I didn't call you here to start shit."

"You don't get to tell me what to do, Anne." Jay said Anne's name with such scorn, the words took on physical form. "You're not one of us. Your dad tried to destroy this town with this garbage motel. Guilt by association."

"I guess that makes you guilty, too, Jay," Max said. "Your father helped ours hide everything that went down here."

Jay's face went scarlet with rage.

"I'm not my father!"

"And we aren't ours."

Max's words echoed around the lot, facing only silence in reply. Their effect wasn't immediate. There were several tense seconds where Casey was sure Jay would level the shotgun at them and blow them all away.

"Jay," one of the teens behind Jay spoke up.

He had black hair, cropped short in a conservative cut Casey was used to seeing on men in uniform, though this boy was too young for that. He was maybe sixteen, his skin brown, his cheek bones high and prominent. Before Casey could get a better look at him, the young man turned toward Jay, taking position not quite in between Jay and Casey, but very close.

"Come on, man," he said. "Remember what we said before we got into the car to come out here? We'd be cool, right? We'd be like George."

At the mention of the missing teenager, Jay's demeanor changed dramatically. Guilt clouded his face and his shoulders drooped.

"Yeah, alright. Alright." Jay lowered the gun before turning to Anne. "Why did you call me here?"

Casey couldn't hide his shock.

"I wouldn't have bet on that outcome in a million years," he muttered under his breath.

Max, who was the only one close enough to hear him, took his hand.

"It can be hard to get over bad first impressions," she said. She squeezed his hand. "I'm glad when people surprise me for the better. Come on. I think the danger's passed."

He let her lead him over to Jay and his cronies, still not confident the whole encounter wouldn't end with someone severely hurt. But he trusted Max. She looked confident enough for the both of them.

With a few good whiffs of the air, Casey determined that the tagalongs with Jay were the same two guys Jay had been out with a couple nights ago. Casey knew their scent profiles by heart, ready to go in the other direction whenever he smelled them around. In the daylight and out of the SUV, Casey understood why they hadn't come out to help when Jay had confronted him before. They were far from the beefcake Jay was – very far.

One of the them was a little over five feet tall, and of Asian descent. He wore thick glasses, the kind teenaged guys tried desperately to get away from when they entered high school, begging their parents for contacts.

The other teenager, the one who'd intervened, was taller. Upon closer inspection, Casey strongly suspected the young man was Native American. He was a handsome boy but, in Casey's experience, that wouldn't matter.

In tiny towns like Manistee, anyone not falling somewhere on the WASP spectrum was an outsider; it didn't matter if they could trace their lineage back a thousand years across these lands, they weren't welcomed as part of the community. While that was probably also true of the other boy – it wouldn't have surprised Casey if his family was the only one in town of Asian descent – it would be even worse for a Native American teenager. Casey had never quite understood why there was a special level of contempt for Native Americans among a certain type of rural white American, but he'd run into it enough to make note of it.

Casey looked between the two boys accompanying Jay with wonder. His first impression of the brash teenager was shattered as he realized Jay's crew included two minorities. Jay wasn't the leader of a pack of bullies; in a place that only tolerated the other if they were leaving town at the end of the week or season, Jay's friends would have been the misfits in town.

"Tell me why I shouldn't shoot this guy dead right now," Jay said.

"Because I didn't kill your friend," Casey said. He pointed at Max's truck. "But one of the things that did is stuck in the grill of that truck. Parts of him, anyway."

Doubt colored Jay's expression, but he cautiously walked over to Max's truck while keeping an eye on Casey. His friends stayed close, anxiously glancing between Jay's gun and Max, Casey and Anne. From what Casey could tell, they were as nervous as he was about the chance a shooting would happen. Jay might've been the leader, but the others clearly weren't on board with murder.

Jay leaned toward the grill of the truck for a split second before backing away in disgust, his fingers pinching his nose.

"Jesus Christ! That smells..."

He stopped, as if startled by his own thoughts. He leaned in again, daring to allow some air back through his nasal passage before quickly backing away again.

"Will," he said, pointing at the bespectacled kid. "What does that smell like to you?"

Will approached the truck warily, his face already twisted in anticipation of the disgust he would encounter. He sniffed and bolted backwards.

"Ugh. That's the smell from Bear's Track."

"Terry," Jay said.

Jay motioned with his head for his other friend to take a whiff, all while still holding his nose. Terry looked annoyed but took one step closer before sniffing in the truck's direction. He was still a good five feet away, but he nodded anyway.

"Yeah. That's Bear's Track, alright."

When Jay turned back to them, there was no longer any menace in his eyes, only determination.

"What is this thing? Some kind of Jurassic, man-eating skunk?" Jay asked.

"Don't be an idiot," Terry said. He turned to Casey. "He's being an idiot, right?"

"Not entirely. It's a lot closer than anything else I've heard people call it," Casey said. That drew a smug look from Jay as he elbowed his friend. "I suppose Jurassic skunk isn't that far off from a wendigo."

"Bullshit," Terry said.

"You've heard of them?" Casey asked.

"Is this a bad joke? Some kind of racist nativism thing?" Terry said. He was bristling, and Casey took Terry's reaction as confirmation of his heritage. "You read up on some Native American legends, and you think it's funny to pull some shit like this? You gonna ask me if I have big medicine next? Do a tomahawk chop? Our friend is missing, asshole. Come on, Jay. This is crap."

Terry pointed at Max and Anne.

"You guys actually made me think, just for a second, the rest of the world wasn't as backwards as this place. That maybe when I went to college, things wouldn't be so fucked up. I thought you were alright. But here you are, playing the same elaborate jokes on the dumb Indian kid they do at school. You can go fuck yourselves."

Terry started to walk back to the SUV. Jay and Will both followed behind, jogging to catch up, caught in the wake of Terry's doubt.

Casey struggled with the desire to call them back, to convince them of the truth. A part of him wanted them to go, to retreat to Manistee and stay safe, prowling neighborhoods where most of the time the biggest threat was running into a rival clique. While having backup would have been useful on the hunt for Luca – a few more people would disrupt any strategy Luca had devised to take on Max and Casey alone a second time – it was nearly as likely she'd use their presence to her own advantage.

They were just teenagers, after all. Only Jay had an obvious athleticism to him. The others could be bookish shut-ins for all Casey knew. Luca wouldn't hesitate to slice their throats just because they looked weak or uncoordinated. A scenario crowded into Casey's head, one where Luca could wound one of them and leave them somewhere they could scream for help, then wait in ambush.

But if there was one thing he'd learned in the last few days, it was that he'd been too quick to judge in the past. Max was as capable as a person got. Anne was more than an emotionally underdeveloped woman with an obsession with style. Jay wasn't a bully – at least, not the kind of bully Casey was familiar with.

The image of Janelle's flesh in Luca's hand flashed through his mind. The women he took home weren't faceless. And family wasn't always worth protecting.

He stepped forward, finally making up his mind.

"Jay, you had bacon and eggs this morning" Casey said. "Some toast with butter and strawberry jam. That kind with chunks of fruit. Probably local because I don't recognize the brand. It smells fantastic by the way. I'd like to know where you got it. Farmer's market?"

Jay's head whipped around so fast, Casey was worried he'd hurt himself.

"Will, you had raisin bran. You added sugar to it. A lot. It's probably the almond milk that makes it taste so bad. Is your mom forcing you to use it, or are you lactose intolerant?"

Will looked between Jay and Terry, confused.

"It-it's my mom. She thinks it's healthier."

"It's terrible for the environment. Incredibly so. You should tell her that. Maybe she'll let you use something else. Soy milk, maybe?"

"O-Okay."

He had Terry's attention now. He closed the gap between them, getting close enough to be as accurate as possible.

"Terry, you had polenta. Whoever made it must prefer asiago to parmesan. They use too much pepper for my taste, but the scallion garnish is a nice touch. You washed it all down with orange juice."

Even Max looked impressed by Casey's feat. The three young men looked as troubled as they did intrigued.

"That's a neat trick," Jay said warily.

"It's not a trick." Casey hoped the stress of the day wasn't clouding his good sense. He took a deep breath, preparing for whatever his next admission would bring. "I'm a wendigo, too. I could smell a squirrel's passing ten days after it crossed a stream. Not even a bloodhound can beat this nose, and, if it tried, I have some tricks up my sleeve to rig the race in my favor."

"The dogs," Will said, his eyes growing wide. He pushed his glasses up his nose. "That's why they acted weird. You did something to them."

"Not me," Casey said. "But I'm hunting the ones that did."

Everyone was quiet as the news sunk in. For better or worse, they all believed in the creatures now.

"Wendigos eat people," Terry said.

There was accusation in his voice – accusation and a little fear.

"They do," Casey agreed. "The only reason I don't look like some eldritch horror to you right now is because I never have."

"How does that work, exactly?" Terry asked.

Casey could see from the squint in Terry's eyes that he wasn't sure whether to trust him or not. His options were limited. He could show the tattoo on his back, but it might mean nothing to Terry, and assuming it did might anger him again. He couldn't mention where he went and who he saw to help him cure himself of the hunger, for fear just speaking of them further might provide a path for whatever evil inhabited him.

"Somebody helped him, Terry." Max said. Her fingers squeezed Casey's shoulder reassuringly. "Someone who believes if it's known who he is, the thing that makes Casey a wendigo will find them. Will hurt them."

She took Casey's hand. She was better at talking to them than he was; it was instantly noticeable. The untrusting look in Terry's eyes softened.

"When I found him last night," she continued, "they were trying to kill him because he wants to stop them. He's on our side."

Anne seemed to think the matter was settled. She headed off into one of the motel rooms, and returned with a couple more bats in an earlier stage of completion. The copper wiring had been attached, and the tape on the handle had been applied, but the tasers weren't mounted to them yet.

"This is what Max used last night," Anne said. "It worked well enough. If you guys wanna help out, I suggest you take one. If you don't, you should stay here with me."

"What will you do here?" Will asked.

"If no one comes back..." She looked over at Max and bit her lip. "It'll be my job to convince people this is a real problem, and not just some crazy urban legend, or someone's bad trip. More voices won't hurt."

"Staying behind is a good idea," Casey added. "They almost killed me, and I'm like them. I'd rather less deaths than more, come what may."

The sound of the shotgun being readied drew all their attention.

"I'm good to go," Jay said.

"Not with that you aren't," Max said. "You're more likely to shoot one of us than one of them. They move too fast to shoot with your gun. These aren't deer, or grouse. They're beasts that were once human. They think like humans. Can speak like humans. Can strategize like humans. But they move like nothing I've ever seen before."

"Come on, Max." Jay grabbed the electrified bat from Anne and gave it a disgusted look. "A bat?"

Max crossed her arms and looked Jay in the eye.

"It worked for me."

The shame hit Jay square in the face. He hefted the bat in his hands before looking Max up and down again. Casey could almost hear the thought that had to be running through the beefy teenager's head - *If Max could do it...*

Jay turned his attention back to the bat. He investigated the weapon more thoroughly, taking particular interest in the tasers.

"What have you done to these? Where are the triggers?"

"I rewired them to toggle switches," Max said.

Jay suddenly held the bat more cautiously, a look of apprehension on his face.

"That's illegal, you know. My dad would arrest the shit outta you if he ever saw this."

"I guess we'll just have to make sure he doesn't see it," Max said.

The two of them shared a conspiratorial smile before Jay handed the bat back to Anne and nodded.

"I'll stay with Anne," Will said, interrupting the moment of solidarity. He fidgeted when everyone turned to him. "I don't think I'd be a help out there. Not much of a fighter."

"I'm going with you guys," Terry said, looking at Casey.

There wasn't a shred of doubt in his voice. Casey marveled at the bravery of the young men – even Will, who had chosen to stay behind. At that age, the impulse to take action and avoid being seen as weak at all costs was strong, even knowing that action was the wrong thing to do. It was a small comfort to see Will's friends didn't look any differently at him after he'd made his choice.

"I'll get the bats ready," Max said. "Should take a couple hours. You can change your mind if you'd like. Be sure what you want. Know that this is deadly serious."

The three friends nodded, but looked unsure of what they should do.

"You should relax a little," Casey said. The idea that this might be their last hours alive suddenly made him queasy. "Swim, or something. Call your friends and have a chat." He looked at Jay. "Your girlfriend?"

"No," Jay said. "Knowing won't help Jessie. Knowing won't help anyone. But the pool, that's a good idea."

They ambled off toward the pool leaving Max, Anne and Casey behind.

"Let's get to work," Max said.

TWELVE

Casey was mesmerized by Max outfitting the bats. She was sitting on a bed across from him, in one of the rooms with two queens – copper wiring, circuits and assorted other electrical doodads that Casey didn't recognize spread around her. She was meticulous, double checking every connection, testing the welding of the copper spikes. If the Max's bats were the only thing between them and death by mauling, Casey trusted they wouldn't fail.

"I still don't know how I feel about these kids coming," he said.

Max pulled one of the industrial rubber gloves over her hand and flipped a taser on. The blue electricity arced between several of the spikes. It reminded Casey of those old black and white movies on TV where a mad scientist would bring something dead back to life.

"You really think we're any more equipped to take down a wendigo than them?" she asked.

He raised his eyebrows incredulously when she looked up at him.

"Aside from you, of course," she added.

He thought it through. She was right – it wasn't as if life trained anyone for this type of thing. If anything, the younger, faster teenagers were more likely to survive.

"We have a better grasp of what's at stake," he said. "Kids always think they're invincible."

"I don't know if these kids do," Max said. "Their friend is dead. His girlfriend is dead. They accepted that long before the adults did."

"Maybe."

He wasn't sure there'd be any argument that could make him feel better. He tugged at a spool of copper wire, picturing Luca and Noah the day he left them in the cabin all those years ago. He thought they'd be safe, too.

"I just hope I'm not about to kill two more kids."

Max set the bat down and swung her legs over the edge of her bed, so she could reach him. She put her hands on his knees.

"You didn't kill Luca and Noah. Those things out there, they aren't your siblings. When you left them alone, you were doing the only thing you could. You can't second guess that decision. You'll go mad trying to redo the past to figure out what you did wrong. You did what you did because you wanted to save their lives. That's what matters."

Casey slid his hands over hers. He tried to see his decisions the way she did, tried to look at his past through her eyes. It helped. And yet, he couldn't stop thinking he was dooming Jay and Terry by encouraging them to come along.

"You were sixteen when you started hunting wendigo," she said, as if reading his mind. "What would you have said at that time if some adult, not even your parents, just some adult, told you to get lost?"

"I'd probably have told them to fuck off and done it anyway."

"Yeah. I'm gonna go out on a limb and say us telling Jay he needs to go home and stay safe would have a similar result." She reached up and touched his face. "At least this way he has you on his side, looking out for him."

"What about you?" Casey asked.

"I'll probably be saving all your asses. As usual."

Casey laughed, then joined her on her bed. He kissed her. The words were there, ready to come out. He'd wanted to say them since the night they'd spent together, but it sounded juvenile in his head. Saying it so soon after meeting made it feel unearned, like he was a teenager still trying on his emotions to see how they looked on him. You needed to know someone, really know them, to love them, he thought.

When he looked into her eyes, he realized he did know Max. He knew when he spoke his fears, she would comfort him. He knew when he told her about his past, she wouldn't pull away, disgusted. He knew she wouldn't mock his choices or belittle his sacrifices. He knew Max, in all the ways that truly mattered.

"I love you," he said.

She closed her eyes and pressed her forehead against his.

"You can't say that. Not yet."

"Why?"

"It makes this feel like the end. That's why I haven't said it."

"You don't have a better reason than that?" he asked with faux disbelief. "Seems rather cruel to keep it from me because of superstition."

"Shut up." She placed her hands on either side of his face and kissed him again. "I love you, too."

He blushed just thinking about the fact that she'd said it back to him.

"I feel like I'm the teenager," Casey said with a laugh.

"When it comes to this kind of stuff, we all revert back to our most awkward selves. At least we're not jumping on couches on national TV."

"I can't honestly say that I wouldn't, given the chance."

They held each other for a little longer.

"I should get these bats done," Max said, pulling away. "You wanna check on the others, make sure everyone is okay?"

"Not really." He sighed dramatically. "But if we're not gonna have sex, I suppose I will."

He left Max giggling on the bed, his heart both lighter and heavier in all the right ways.

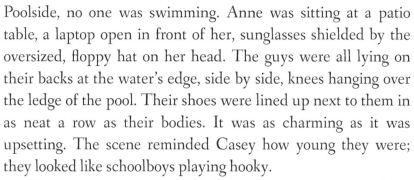

Poolside, no one was swimming. Anne was sitting at a patio table, a laptop open in front of her, sunglasses shielded by the oversized, floppy hat on her head. The guys were all lying on their backs at the water's edge, side by side, knees hanging over the ledge of the pool. Their shoes were lined up next to them in as neat a row as their bodies. It was as charming as it was upsetting. The scene reminded Casey how young they were; they looked like schoolboys playing hooky.

He sat across from Anne, a knot between his eyes and his thumbnail in his mouth. He bit at it until there was nothing left to bite anymore.

"Stop it." Anne's voice broke him from his stupor. "I dated a guy who did that. It's neither attractive or healthy. He always had swollen fingertips."

Casey dropped his hand, feeling as if he'd been scolded by his mother. He almost apologized before he remembered he didn't care all that much what Anne thought. That then turned into a self-reprimand, since he was trying to be nicer to her for Max's sake. The whole mental ordeal lasted less than ten seconds. But his annoyance over it? That he planned to mull on for the remainder of the time they had before they left.

Several snarky comments went through his head before he landed on something he could say that might help him puzzle Anne out without pissing her off.

"I'm sorry I wasn't trying very hard to get along before."

Anne looked over the top of her laptop and sunglasses.

"You're a wendigo," she said, as if that explained everything.

"Sure, but I'm a charming wendigo."

Again, the look came his way.

"I liked my sister's first husband," she said by way of explanation. Casey thought she'd leave it at that, just like her previous statement, but she went on. "I don't like you much. That probably means you're fine, because he was an ass in the end. And Max is right. I have terrible taste in men."

Casey tapped on the table absently.

"Does that mean you're okay with me now? I mean really okay, and not just pretending to be okay but secretly wishing I'd fall off a cliff."

"Wow," Anne said. She hit a key on her keyboard more forcefully than would ever be necessary. "You really think I'm terrible."

"Not terrible," Casey said. "People don't always get along."

"And in your experience, that means they wish death on them?"

"It was a joke. Ha, ha. You know, that thing with merriment."

Anne leaned back in her chair, the floppy hat shading her face so that Casey couldn't see her eyes behind her sunglasses anymore.

"I dated a guy like you once."

"You've said that before. This might be the third time."

"I mean, a guy who had, like, your personality. I'd forgotten how annoying he was. So full of smarm."

"You said 'charm' wrong."

"Yep. He was just like that," she said. She picked up her drink and sipped it before finally answering his question. "I'm okay with you. As much as I hate to admit it, you're over the moon about Max. It's probably why I hated you at first. I didn't want her to like you. I saw the way you looked at her when you first saw her. I didn't want to be stuck listening to you for years at family get togethers."

"Really?" Casey said. "Your dislike of me felt a lot more personal than that."

"Yes, really. I've answered your question. I'm done talking about this now." Anne spun her laptop around for Casey to see. She was on a site all about wendigos. "It doesn't say anything about the smelling thing."

Casey pulled the laptop toward him, ignoring the abrupt change in topic. If she didn't want to talk about how much she disliked him, he was good with that.

"I suspect that's because not many wendigos edit websites. Are you trying to find out something in particular?"

"I wondered if I could maybe pick up a strong-smelling perfume or something. Make a water balloon full of the trashiest scents. Mess up the other wendigo's noses. You could go in with a nose plug. It would be like when they use a flash grenade on people. Only for smells."

Casey blinked a few times in rapid succession.

"That's... That's actually..."

"Having trouble complimenting me?" Anne asked, snatching her laptop back. "It's alright. I'm not enthusiastic about talking you up either. And don't act so surprised. I'm surly, not stupid. Well, okay. I'm not great at math. And a little immature. But self-aware, so that means something to someone, I'm sure."

Casey didn't even realize he was smiling until she said something.

"What?"

"Nothing," he said. "I just—I can work with this. It's almost like we're siblings."

"I hate you so much right now," Anne said.

That only made Casey's smile widen.

"The smell thing, asshat," she said. "You have thoughts on that?"

"It won't work," he said. "I like what you're thinking, but it won't work."

"Why not? You said your stink is what gets the dogs all confused. Why can't that work on you?"

"Our... stink... is different. It smells like danger to animals, birds, insects even. It keeps them away. They're afraid of it. It isn't that the dogs can't track us. It's that they don't want to. They're frightened of it."

Anne looked at her screen. She pursed her lips then looked back at Casey.

"Is there a smell that means danger to wendigos?"

Casey's eyes went out of focus as he thought. It was another good idea, if only he could think of something that would fit. After a few minutes, he snapped his fingers.

"Do you have vapor rub?" he asked.

"You guys are scared off by menthol? Are you some kind of mutated chest cold?"

"It isn't for me. It's for Max and the others. To protect their noses."

"Yes, we have it."

"Then when it's time, we'll try your idea. Thanks."

"You're not gonna tell me what it is?" she asked.

"Not yet. I don't want to get people's hopes up. I want them to go into the woods thinking there's no secret weapon. I want them to be clear-eyed about the dangers. But I promise, if it works, I'll credit you."

A tiny smile rested on Anne's face for less than a second. Then a breeze blew across the patio, rippling the water, taking the smile with it before drawing their eyes to the boys.

"It's brave of them to go out there with us," Casey said.

"Or stupid," Anne said.

"Maybe."

The boys had been talking the whole time Casey had been sitting out by the pool. He was too far away to make out anything they were saying, but occasionally they'd break out in laughter. He was glad they could still laugh in the face of what they were about to do.

"They were pretty close with the guy who disappeared, I take it."

His probing was more to pass the time – a distraction from his own thoughts – than for any real purpose.

"George?" Anne shrugged. "I guess. We don't get involved with the town stuff too much. They aren't crazy about us."

This stirred Casey's interest. Several times now he'd heard

allusions to the motel's past. Now that he was sitting across from someone who wouldn't be likely to tell an embellished, sordid tale, he wondered if he could finally sate his curiosity. He hesitated, unsure the timing was appropriate. But then the timing would never be appropriate if the story was unpleasant, and he'd rather bother Anne with his prying than Max if it was a sore subject.

"Why is that?" he asked.

Anne scowled at the question. Perhaps it was his acknowledgement that she'd had a good idea. Or perhaps she, too, wanted to talk about anything other than the dangerous thing her sister was about to do. Whatever her reason, she didn't hold back.

"This place is a black mark to the people of Manistee. Max tell you my dad ran it?"

"She did."

"Yeah. He was never satisfied with what he had at home with us. He used to say shit about being 'just a community college professor' and how humiliating it was. Bullshit if you ask me. But he graduated from Princeton and was obsessed with prestige. He applied for work at big universities, ivy leagues. He couldn't get a foot in the door. It was his life's greatest embarrassment that he never became some mogul somewhere, or a renowned business professor. That he married a grade school teacher and had two mediocre children."

The disappointment in Anne's eyes was palpable. Casey no longer wanted to hear the story; it was too personal. For her part, Anne didn't mind telling him. She wasn't embarrassed or ashamed of it. She talked about it like it was a history of someone else's life.

"There were a lot of people who loved Mom, and us, who hated the way he talked about his life. And he constantly talked about it. How he never got his chance to be happy. How his family was dragging him down. Not in those words, but that's what they meant. He'd turn it around and talk about all the sacrifices he made. He took a job he hated, so that we would have a house, insurance, lives. He never went out with Mom, or ever did fun things like everyone else, because he was caring so much for his family. He used the word sacrifice. He meant burden. Everyone knew it.

"My uncle hated him. My mom's best friend hated him. Hell, Max and I even hated him sometimes. But my mom loved him, so she tried her best to make sure he was happy."

She waved her arms around, encompassing the motel.

"The Sunset was going to be his pride and glory. He was going to open it and become the premier vacation spot in Michigan. Get write ups in the *Detroit Free Press*. A feature in *Hour Detroit*. He'd leverage that success into investments into other boutique vacation spots. He used to call himself the Hilton, with a small h, of the quiet places.

"First few years he got into a lot of debt. The motel didn't make money. He didn't tell us, of course. But we knew. He didn't act like a man who was excited about his business. More like, he was afraid of it. None of us had been invited to see the motel. Not even for the opening. Mom asked, but he said it was bad luck. We snuck out one summer, the first year he had it, and drove by it, thinking we'd surprise him with balloons and stuff. We never got out of the car. We saw the place and knew immediately it wasn't going to be the premier anything of anywhere. We kept driving.

"But then, the fourth year he was in business, he asked me to come up here. It was weird and sudden, but Mom encouraged me to go. She thought maybe Dad had turned the place around and was testing out my reaction. I wish that she had been right.

"I got here, and he introduced me to some guy. Frank Campbell."

"Chief Campbell?"

"Yes," Anne said. "Though, he was just Officer Campbell then."

Her mouth curled up in a sneer.

"Dad introduced me as, 'the one you saw in that photo.' I didn't think anything of it at first. Then Campbell handed me a dozen roses. I was sixteen, in case you were wondering. Campbell was twenty-three. Fresh out of the academy and hired as a local police officer."

"Jesus," Casey said.

"No kidding." Anne plucked at her shirt. For the first time since she'd started talking, she looked uncomfortable. "He didn't make me do anything illegal. That makes it sound like I'm giving an excuse. I'm not. I'm just saying, I think he knew not to. That I'd say something to someone, and whatever deal he was making with Dad would be the least of his concerns. But I did go out with Frank on several dates. To the movies once. A couple times to a restaurant in town. I think he actually thought we'd hit it off, become a couple. We didn't. But still, the deal was struck, so my dad pressured me to do at least that much. Said Frank was a good guy, the kind of guy a dad would be proud to have as a son-in-law. Whatever."

Anne scowled at the pool, her expression of hurt and anger etched deep, coming from under the skin to surface. The look was familiar – she'd looked at Casey that way until Max had made her feelings clear. Her distrust of him felt more earned than it had before, if misplaced.

Anne looked up as the sun passed behind a cloud.

"In return," she said, "the police looked the other way when the motel became a place where dreams came true. If those dreams were having sex with exotic women from around the world – women who my dad contacted online and promised riches and a working visa if they came to be 'maids' at his motel. Women who barely spoke English and didn't really understand what they were getting into. Women who came from places so much worse than here, that the thought of rubbing down greasy men of middling income was not too high a price to pay for a shot at the land of the free and the home of the brave. Women who were easy to control, because they had so few options."

Her eyes met his for a fraction of a second before Anne looked away in shame. Casey couldn't imagine what shame she should feel over the situation. He wasn't sure it was his place to reassure her – coming from him it might make her feel worse, so he remained still as she went on.

"The police kept anyone from sniffing around. Apparently most of the officers were fine with that arrangement, so long as they got free samples. Campbell was the only one who wasn't interested in whores, as he put it. He wanted something wholesome. Someone who would be a nice wife and give him kids. Someone virginal and pure. And Dad was happy to provide that by having me stay and work the desk every summer until Campbell finally gave up."

Casey must have had a look of utter horror on his face, because, for the first time, Anne's voice became gentle when she addressed him.

"You're thinking too much about it," she said. "It helps if you don't. Trust me, I know."

"Anne—"

"Don't." She took a deep breath. "It's done. And Dad finally got what he wanted from it. The motel made money. Every summer that he came back here, the men, the important men, from Manistee, treated him like the big shot he always believed himself to be. They'd all come to the Sunset and have their fun, then go back home to their wives and families. He wasn't Hilton with a little h. He was a pimp with a capital P."

"Now I know why Janelle wouldn't tell me," Casey said.

"Yeah," Anne said. "It was a scandal when word finally got out. He'd been doing it for nearly two decades. The motel even became a rite of passage for the sons of the elite in town. They'd plan graduation parties out here.

"The motel kept making money, right up until the wrong people in town found out. When that happened, it all came crumbling down. And he couldn't take the thought of being plain ol' community college professor Martins again. So, he shot himself."

The bluntness with which Anne ended the story startled Casey into speechlessness. He pushed his hands into his hair, the weight of her words pressing down on him. The sun came back out and bathed him in warmth that struggled to sink into his skin, the cold depths of remorse in him fighting to keep it out.

"I'm so sorry, Anne."

He couldn't think of what else to say. Maybe there wasn't anything else worth saying.

"Thank you," Anne said. "It's probably better you heard it from me than Max."

Her cryptic words drew a questioning look from him.

"She had to clean up the mess." Casey's eyes opened wide and Anne shook her head quickly. "Not the body. The police found that. I mean, the motel, all the people involved, the staff. The women."

"What happened to the women?" Casey asked.

"When the news broke about what this place was, they lost all their customers. Which means they lost any income they were making. They couldn't stay here. The people from town treated them terribly. And all the reasons they stayed here didn't disappear just because Dad died. Max had to find a place that would help them. Somewhere that specialized in helping immigrants get on their feet. She wanted to give them all something, a nest egg of sorts, to help get them get started. She emptied out Dad's bank accounts and gave it all to them. Max and I didn't want any part of it, and Mom wasn't interested either. Max didn't even want to use it to fix the place up. She took out a loan to do that. She's hoping the sale of the motel will cover the loan. We aren't looking for a profit. We just want to get away from all this."

"What about the law?" Casey asked. "Aren't you worried about the government coming after you?"

Anne shrugged. The gesture spoke volumes about her weariness in having to deal with the motel.

"Dad paid taxes on everything he made, he just lied about how he made it, so at least the IRS isn't breathing down our necks. And Manistee managed to keep the scandal from breaking out of town, probably because so many prominent people are wrapped up in all this. So, the law hasn't come after us to capture profits or anything. At least, not yet. I suppose that could still be coming. One problem at a time, though."

She looked up at him with a wry smile.

"Saying it out loud, now it makes sense why she finds you appealing."

"Why's that now?" Casey asked, confused.

Anne's smile turned into a sneer.

"She can run off in the woods and be a wendigo, too. Leave all this shit behind. I don't blame her."

A vein pulsed in Casey's neck as he stifled a retort. Anne was mad – he accepted that. Her anger was directed outward, and he was just in the way of its blast. She went back to tooling around on her laptop, so he stood, leaving without comment, to go check on Max. By the time he reached Max's room, the itch that he felt in his brain, the one telling him to snap at Anne, had worn off. He was more than a little glad she'd be staying behind when they went to hunt Luca, though.

THIRTEEN

Max was showing Jay the basics of using her rigged bat. It was the fourth time she was going through all the motions. The first two times, he'd managed to electrocute himself, even with the lineman's rubber gloves Max had given him. His hair was frazzled and his face paler than before, but he was otherwise fine, and he'd learned to be careful with the bat at all times, keeping it away from his body or anything touching his body.

Terry had mastered the trick of wielding the electrified bat after being shown just the once. He was standing next to Casey, only half watching Jay practice with Max. Casey could feel the young man's eyes on him. He ignored it at first. They would be leaving shortly, and he didn't think getting into a discussion with Terry would help anyone. Finally, tired of being stared at, he turned to the teenager.

"What?"

"I noticed there are only three bats," Terry said.

"Yes."

"You aren't using one?"

"No."

"You'll be transforming then. If all this is true."

"Yes."

Terry turned to face him fully just as Jay and Max joined them.

"You're desperate enough to let us come along," Terry said. "Why not invite everyone in town? Up the odds. We could really corner them then."

"We can't do that," Max said.

"Why not?" Terry asked.

"They'll run," Casey said. "They'll smell the woods full of people and run. I'll have to start the whole process over again. I can't risk that. The last time I got this close was ten years ago. They've killed more than fifty people since then."

"You said you hurt one of them," Terry pressed. "Possibly fatally. Won't the other one stay behind, try to protect the wounded?"

Casey narrowed his eyes. He hadn't mentioned the wendigo were family. As far as he knew, Max hadn't either, taking her cues from him on what to say and what to keep quiet on. Yet, here was Terry, suggesting one wendigo might stay in harm's way to protect the other.

"We could take that chance," Casey said. "We could drag the rest of the town out here, hope we get into the woods before dark, hope the line of people is enough as we close in. But I don't see the wendigos sticking around for any reason once they're surrounded. And they only have to kill a couple to break the line. If it's just us going in there, they'll think they can handle it. They won't flee. They'll attack."

Terry looked unconvinced. The daylight hours were

dwindling, and Casey didn't have time to argue with the teenager about it.

"Stay here if you're concerned," he said. "I don't know if it's a good idea for you to come anyway."

"Don't worry about it, Terry," Jay said, jumping in. "I got this. You can hang with Will."

"You hit yourself with the bat, Jay," Terry said. "Twice."

"I'm good now," Jay said, flattening his frizzy hair. "Right?"

He turned to get confirmation from Max, but she couldn't muster a confident look. Jay grunted before looking back at Terry.

"I'm good," Jay said, providing all his own confidence.

Terry shrugged before heading to the SUV. The matter looked settled, but it didn't make Casey any more comfortable with the idea of the teenagers riding along. Max took his arm, linking it with hers, before guiding him to the car. They waved at Anne and Will, who watched from the doorway of one of the rooms.

The plan was for the group to drive back to the location where Max had found Casey. They'd have at least two hours of daylight left by the time they got there, and Casey would track down Luca, and possibly Noah if his injuries weren't as fatal as they suspected.

In theory, the plan was solid – wendigos holed up during the day, choosing to hunt at night when their preferred prey was most vulnerable. On top of that, if Noah was still alive, he'd need rest, lending credence to the argument that the twins wouldn't be roving about – they'd be holed up. And the group would have the benefit of being able to see.

There were a lot of little problems with the plan and one huge one – there wasn't time to address all the scenarios in which things didn't go well. If Luca was already hunting them, she'd have the drop on them. Luca was intelligent. Casey's approach to hunting her was based on what he knew of her movements – his strategy built on years of study. But Luca could easily have been watching him all these years, too. She might realize he'd go back to the last location he saw her and be waiting there for him. That was just one of the ways their plan could go wrong. But time was short, and they'd decided to forge ahead with the plan, flimsy or not.

They climbed into the SUV, Jay and Terry getting in the back, Max driving with Casey riding shotgun. Surprisingly, Jay hadn't balked when Max suggested she drive. The kid was a whole lot more compliant than Casey would have guessed, based on his previous encounter with him. He wondered if that night on the road was an aberration, until he remembered the convenience store clerk's assertation that Jay was, in fact, an asshole. There was too much conflicting information for Casey to be sure, either way. He'd seen both sides of the burly teenager. In the end, it didn't matter what Jay's personality was like; in an hour, they'd be facing down Luca. She wouldn't think twice about shredding the boy, asshole or no.

Without his realizing it, at some point Casey had taken Max's hand. All the old concerns came bubbling up again when he wrapped his fingers around hers. He couldn't take the noisy doubts in his head or the silence in the car. Maybe, he thought, if he talked to the kids he might be able to convince them to stay put; the car would be safer than the woods. This was his doubt taking charge again, but he didn't fight it this time. At the very least, trying to talk to them would crowd out the disturbing images his brain insisted on conjuring.

"You guys must have really liked George to do all this," he said.

"George was my best friend," Jay said without hesitation.

"Has been since I was eight. My dad is a cop. That's okay when you're eight. Kinda cool, really. But when you get to be twelve, thirteen, it starts to be a problem. Any party, anywhere, my dad was the one who broke it up. Got to be where everyone avoided me, wouldn't tell me shit, wouldn't hang. I couldn't score booze or... you know, whatever. George was different. He stayed my friend when everyone else cut me out."

Casey tossed a look over his shoulder at Terry, who was busy boring holes into the back of Casey's head with his eyes.

"You look like you're doing okay, now," Casey said. "You have friends. Even a girlfriend."

"Jess?" Jay scoffed. "Sure. She's likely to dump me any day now. I'm pretty sure she was just hoping to get closer to George. She's not even allowed to see me. That's probably the only reason she comes out with us. She can pretend she's being ballsy, and all her friends drink that shit up when she tells them what she's done."

He stopped and looked out of the window suddenly. The silence was so abrupt, Casey wondered if he'd touched a sore spot somehow.

"Sorry if that was too personal," Casey said. "I wasn't trying to pry. Just curious about you. I don't normally misjudge people so badly."

Jay snorted from the back seat.

"Misjudge? About me and Jess? You're not making any sense."

"I think he means us, Jay," Terry said. "Will and I. He sees you with us. He didn't know we were brown. He thinks it's weird your friends with brown people."

"Oh," Jay said. "Well, he's right."

"The fuck, Jay?"

Terry glowered across the seat at his friend.

"What?" Jay threw his hands up into the air. "You want me to lie? George is the only reason we became friends. You've said that a thousand times. Enough times even I can remember it."

Terry glowered for a few seconds before softening his posture. The kid had a chip on his shoulder, and Casey was sure it had been put there by the citizens of Manistee.

"I guess that's true. You were an asshole to us in fifth grade."

Jay nodded.

"George sounds like a good guy," Casey said.

"He's smart, too," Jay said. "He said Will and Terry were great, I just needed to give them a chance. I thought he was full of PC bullshit. Friending brown people for the sake of the community."

Terry looked annoyed again. Jay noticed and turned his tone around quickly.

"It wasn't that at all, though. I kept saying, dude, we don't do the same kinds of things at all. They aren't on football, unless it's in a video game or something. George was right, though. Will and Terry are great. They didn't care my dad was Chief Asshole. So, I gave 'em a chance."

"You weren't the only one given a chance," Terry shot back.

It was George's turn to look annoyed. Casey began to wonder if the fragile alliance between the big high school footballer and the two local outcasts would last now that George wasn't around to keep the peace. Normally, Casey wouldn't have tried to step into such a murky mess of a relationship. They were about to head into danger, however, and that took precedence.

"Friendships like that are rare," Casey said. He hoped the gentle reminder of their friend might smooth the friction breaking out between them. "I'm sorry for your loss."

His words did the trick. Both boys blushed guiltily before looking away. Jay was the first to break the tense silence.

"WWGD, right man?"

Terry chuckled, and the two smirked at each other.

"He wouldn't be doing this, I don't think," Terry said. "He'd call us both dumbasses."

Jay shook his head.

"No. I'm here because I know he'd be here." He turned to look at Terry and Casey. "George used to talk me down when I did stupid shit all the time. He wouldn't have let me get out of the car that night I saw you. He'd wouldn't have even let me stop. He was the good guy. He wouldn't have said this was stupid. If one of us was gone, he'd be here. I know it."

Jay blinked back what were obvious tears. Casey could tell Terry was trying not to look at Jay and embarrass him. Casey gave Jay a minute to collect himself before he asked his next question.

"What about that girl, Sarah? You haven't mentioned her. Aren't you going in these woods for her, too?" Casey asked.

That drew laughter from the boys. When they calmed down Jay leaned forward in his seat to look out the front window.

"Sarah didn't ever talk to any of us. She was there for George and no one else. Mayor's daughter. Couldn't hang with us. That would be gross. Wanted another checkmark for her list of 'Things popular girls are supposed to do,' book. She needed to date the quarterback of the football team. That was George. He liked her well enough, because that was just George. He liked everybody, and even if he didn't like her all that well, he would have gone in the woods after her. But she wouldn't have gone in after him." Jay leaned back again. "Not that I think that means she should've died. But that girl is trouble."

"Even after death," Terry mumbled.

"Right," Jay said. "Anyway, you don't need us to care about her. The whole town has that covered. We're here for the one they don't care about."

The car slowed as Max pulled off the road towards the tree she'd smashed Noah into. When the car stopped, they all sat still, waiting for the first person to make a move. Casey stared at the tree in front of the car. The bark was broken clear through to the meat of the tree. Thick, blackish blood sat in the grooves of bark that remained, making it look as if it was the tree that was bleeding.

"That it?" Terry asked.

Casey could only nod. He never thought it would be hard to see it in the daylight, but looking at Noah's remains, what little there were, pulled at him somewhere deep inside. He turned when he heard the door open, thinking it was Max, only to see her still sitting in her seat, staring in astonishment at Terry, who had left the vehicle and was closing in on the tree.

Casey hopped out and joined him. Terry was already kneeling when Casey got to his side, the teen's hands poking through the leaf litter around the base of the tree. His fingers came back with a tuft of fur, still attached to a not inconsiderable amount of skin, pinched between two of them.

"This is wendigo, eh?"

Casey smelled the air. There was no fresh sign of Luca or Noah, but his nerves were still on edge. She could be upwind, or even far enough away she could see them, but they couldn't smell her. He went over to the spot he'd been downed. In the daylight, the rock Luca had pounded his head against was easy to see. It wasn't buried like he thought. It stuck out of the ground three inches at least, the surface sticky with his dried blood. The handkerchief Max had dropped was still sitting in the dirt, untouched. He took off his shirt and rolled it up as Max and Jay got out of the car.

"Why are you getting undressed?" Terry asked.

Casey handed his shirt to Max. When she took it, she held his hands through the cloth until their eyes met.

"I need to change," he said, more to Max than to Terry.

He wanted her to be ready for it. She'd seen him before as a monster but watching him change was a different thing. The connection between him as a person and him as a creature of death would be laid bare.

"That shit on your back, does it protect us, too?" Terry asked.

"Protect us from what?" Jay asked.

"Becoming like him," Terry said. "That's how it spreads."

Casey started unbuttoning his pants. He stopped long enough to shake his head no, but Jay must not have seen him.

"It spreads?" Jay asked. "It isn't like werewolves? I don't have to be bitten?"

"Not from what I heard," Terry said.

"Heard?" Jay asked.

Terry shrugged. It looked like he regretted speaking up.

"It was just a story. An older cousin trying to freak out a little kid. It was probably bullshit anyway."

Jay walked up to his friend and gripped his shoulder.

"T, we're about to go hunting for some monster with baseball bats. Whatever you're gonna say can't be as fucked up as that."

Terry sighed, but relented.

"He told me about this cop his dad knew. The guy was like, an FBI agent or something. He hunted serial killers. He was close to this guy who ate his victims. He'd been hunting him for weeks. When he found the guy, it took more than a week to get a confession out of him."

Terry stopped and looked uncomfortably at Casey.

"That it?" Jay asked.

"No, dumbass. If that was it, I wouldn't have said anything." Terry kicked the dirt with his foot and shoved his hands into his pockets. "The guy, the cop, he killed himself a week later. Lit his house on fire and sat in a chair while it burned down around him. That's how they found him, all burned up, still sitting in the chair. When everyone tried to figure out why he'd done it, all they found was a notebook full of weird shit about a voice and how hungry he was. My cousin says the cop didn't find a serial killer, he found a wendigo. And the cop caught it and was afraid of what he'd do. So he burned himself."

Terry took a deep breath after he was done. He glanced over at Casey expectantly.

"So," Terry said, "does that crap on your back protect us?"

"You can read it?" Casey asked, surprised.

"No," Terry said. "I saw 'wendigo.' I guessed it meant something."

"It does. The tattoo keeps me in control. It also keeps it from spreading."

"How do you know?"

Casey was at a loss. He couldn't definitively answer the question. He looked up at Max guiltily, knowing his answer would have strong implications for her.

"I don't. Not for sure. I was told I was safe. I trust that was the truth. I do know it took months before I caught it from my father. Maybe years, even."

"Seems like you want a lot of trust from us," Terry said.

"Yes. But I also understand your doubt," Casey folded his jeans, leaving him only in his boxer briefs. "All I can say is, if you start hearing voices, I'll get you to the same guy who helped me. I swear it."

Terry circled Casey, examining the tattoo. Casey allowed the young man a moment to be at peace with everything that was about to happen; giving him a few seconds was the least Casey could do.

"How did those other two get it? The ones we're looking for?" Terry asked.

It was a good question. Casey couldn't help but smile at the teen's inquisitive nature. He'd have to tell them now. It was probably right they knew in any case.

"They got it the same way I did. From the same person I did."

Between the two of them, Terry was the first to realize what Casey's confession meant, or at least, he guessed what it meant, based on the change in his expression.

"Family?" Terry asked.

"Yes."

Casey could see the moment when Terry finally trusted him. It was a strange thing to witness. There was no obvious sign, no 'aha' expression, or a shoulder pat. It just happened; the air around him changed ever so subtly, his eyes lost their sharp edge, his posture softened when he looked at Casey. Terry made no further comment on the matter, just went to the SUV, opened the trunk and pulled out his bat.

"I'm ready," he said.

Casey looked from Terry to Jay, making sure they were both ready.

"Go on, then," Jay said.

Only one person remained to ask – the person who mattered the most. Casey took Max's hand.

"It's not gonna be pretty," he said.

"Sure it is," Max said. "At least... you are taking those underwear off first, right?"

He pulled her close, nervous laughter turning to a fervent embrace. He whispered close to her ear.

"Don't be scared."

"Never. I love you."

Her breath was barely a puff of air against his skin, but the power of her words carried farther than any shout. He pulled away and let his boxers drop. After handing his clothes to her, he closed his eyes and drew forth the hunger.

It roiled inside him, unwilling to bend to his desires. Casey wasn't used to it fighting him so hard when he wanted to bring it out. When he was pushing it down, it was a titan, clawing through him with reckless abandon. Now, it was as if the evil inside knew Casey's intentions, and was unwilling to be a participant in the events about to unfold.

He went to the base of the tree where Noah's blood still shone with wet. He got close, almost pressing his nose into the remains of his brother, inhaling the salty, metallic scent. The hunger churned – anger and sorrow mingling with the base desire to devour all those within reach. Casey mastered it quickly, reining it in and focusing his will to turn once again into the monster.

He fell to his knees from the agony of it. Compelling it back up so close to banishing it without sating its deepest need was grueling work. It came, but not without a price. Casey felt every bone that snapped into place, every piece of flesh it tore open, every snap of cartilage as it stretched to the limits his body could withstand more vividly than he ever had before.

Pain seared along his hands and arms as his fingers felt as if they were pulled apart, stretching into claws tipped with jagged bone. Muscles bunched, then tore violently through his legs and arms, as they were yanked and reformed into long, sinewy appendages. His jaw popped out of place and hung limp before resetting into a wide mouth, more fitting a snake than a person. His gums split open to allow the teeth to emerge, bony structures the look of which harkened back to something prehistoric.

Handfuls of his dark hair fell to the ground when his skull shifted and his skin molted. He shed the outer layer of skin violently, the searing heat blackening the surface of his body until it flaked away in ashen chunks. The dark, mottled skin that remained resembled that of a dog with mange, scaly and festering, stretched so thin the bones in his joints erupted through the surface, yellowed and cracked.

His insides created so many points of pain, they almost cancelled each other out. Something in his gut pulled like a taught rubber band; the sensation started as merely unpleasant before turning to a torture he'd never felt before. He screamed his throat raw as the pulling went on, his body like taffy, stretched to the breaking point.

Just as he thought he could take no more of it, the pain ebbed, leaving him curled on the ground, weeping into his claws. He felt someone's hands on him, warm and unwavering, and opened his eyes to find Max looking down at him.

"Is this how it always is?" she asked.

"No," Casey croaked. With her help, he was able to sit up. "It's never hurt this much before."

He heard retching and looked over Max's shoulder. Jay was nowhere to be seen, but Casey could smell the partially digested meal cooling on the forest floor and knew precisely where Jay was from that alone. Terry looked pale but was clearly using herculean effort to keep his last meal inside his body. Sweat was forming on the teenager's forehead.

Max helped Casey to his feet. He wobbled a few seconds but got it under control.

"Are you going to be able to do this?" Max whispered.

Her words were soaking in concern. Casey took a step, trying his muscles out. They were stiff at first, but when he took a second step, the power of his wendigo form flooded in.

"I'm good." He turned to the others. Jay was just rejoining Terry. "But this next part might be even harder for you."

"It gets worse than that?" Jay asked.

He groaned and leaned against the car.

"I need to spread my scent onto all of you," Casey said. "Saying it will be unpleasant is an understatement of epic proportions."

Even Max looked pained at this idea. Casey moved to the back of the SUV where Max had stashed a bag of first aid supplies. It was hard not to notice the way Jay and Terry kept about ten feet away from him. Rummaging through the bag of supplies took more time with his claws. The tips kept catching on gauze and tape. Max had made her way around the car and was just about to lend him a hand when he found the plastic blue jar he was looking for. He held it out to Max.

"Put it under your nose. It'll help. Some."

Several minutes went by while the group passed around the vapor rub, dabbing generous amounts under their nostrils. Jay looked as if he'd dipped his entire nose into the jar, gobs of it as high up as the bridge of his nose. When they were all done, Max tucked the jar into her pocket and nodded at Casey. She did not look confident in the power of the cold medicine.

"Right," Casey said. "I'm going to rub my scent onto you. It's going to be really strong and very terrible. But I think it just might be the thing that keeps my brother and sister away from you."

"This is a crazy idea," Max said.

"You can thank Anne for it," Casey replied. "She thought of disguising your scents. This won't do that. Luca and Noah would be able to smell you, even if I covered you head to toe in it, but it does mean they'll think I'm with you, and won't be able to figure out who to go after. They'd usually try to isolate us, then pick us off one at a time. But with my scent on you, they won't know where I am without actually seeing us, which will make it hard for them to determine who to target first."

The group looked anxious about the whole thing. When no one stepped forward, Max took the initiative. She cleared her throat and nodded.

There wasn't a great way to spread his smell on them; Casey was sure they were all imagining the worst as well. Fortunately, he didn't need to spray them down like a skunk. He flexed his forearms as if he were clawing a tree, forcing the glands in his palms to ooze out a secretion.

Max must have been able to smell it, even over the thick vapor rub under her nose. Her lips pressed together so hard, they turned white. Casey could even hear her stomach churning. But she managed to keep from retching, even as Casey rubbed her arms with his palms, spreading the sticky scent onto her skin.

"That should do it," he said.

"Okay," she croaked, before giving a thumbs up to Jay and Terry.

"Aw, man," Jay said in reply.

Terry was next up. He approached, his movements stiff, as if his body was actively fighting against his decision to subject himself to such a stink. It was the first time he'd come within reach of Casey since he'd transformed. Terry managed to keep from wrinkling his nose, though he had broken out in a sweat so heavy that, by the time Casey was done, the pits of Terry's shirt were soaked through.

"Sorry," Casey muttered when he was finished.

"It's fine. It's a good idea. If it gives us an edge, it's worth doing."

Jay was the only one left. He stayed put, unwilling to step forward when Casey motioned for him to come. It was hard to blame him – he'd had to accept the presence of wendigos, see someone change before his eyes, and finally, have one smear him with its stench before they all headed off to a fight that had a good chance of killing them.

"It has to be done?" Jay asked.

A whiny sound tinged his voice.

"You could go as is," Terry said. "I think that would mean you'd be the first taken, since we'd all smell like something a lot more dangerous than a human with a bat, electrified or not."

Jay walked forward without any further complaint.

"Will it wash off?" he asked.

"Yes. Don't worry. It's strong enough to last a while out in the elements, a warning to keep most things away, but even a moderate rain will dilute it enough that it loses its power. Add in some soap, and it should be hardly noticeable."

"Should?" Jay asked.

"Hardly?" Terry chimed in.

"I... haven't done this before," Casey said. "I just know when we leave a mark on a tree, nothing will come near the spot. The smell frightens everything away. After a rain, whatever is in our stink that frightens everything away, doesn't work anymore. I can still smell it, but the other animals don't seem to. Or care if they do. I don't think it's like a skunk, though. I've gotten it on my clothes, and a good washing gets it out."

Casey lifted his claw to spread the smell on Jay when the

bulky teenager made a halting gesture. He took off his letterman jacket and tossed it on the hood of the car.

"Okay."

When Casey was finished, the combined stench of them all was rough even for his finely tuned nose. They donned their rubber gloves and triple checked their equipment before heading out into the woods.

Casey led, tracking Luca's every stop through the forest. For the first mile, she'd run full out. Something must have happened after that point, because there were places along the trail where she must have sat for nearly an hour. It was at one such place that Casey stopped to investigate.

"What is it?" Max asked.

Casey reached down and touched the tiny splash of blood at the base of the tree he was investigating. He cocked his head at a thought.

"There should be more blood." He looked further ahead into the trees. "I think we're close though. I can smell the den."

The tension among the group trebled. Casey kept moving forward, but at a significantly slower pace.

"What are we looking for?"

Terry's question was whispered hoarsely. Casey didn't bother to tell him that Luca would smell them long before she'd hear them.

"A cave?" Jay asked.

"There aren't any caves around here, dude," Terry said.

"He's right," Casey said. "They'd have had to make do with what there is here. A cave would have been preferable, but they go where the food is. They've hunted here before, so they felt safe, even without caves to hide out in during the day."

The feeling that something wasn't right increased ten-fold as Casey scented something rotting. He recognized the smell –

its familiarity was far from comforting. Somewhere, nearby, Janelle's body, or what remained of her body, was decomposing. It meant that the den was close.

"Why haven't we been attacked yet?" Max asked.

The question was ripped right out of Casey's head. He continued forward, until he found the source of the smell. Janelle's upper body was hanging from a limb in the air, like a gruesome party banner inviting them to a soirée. Her entrails were dusty and blackening with rot, dangling from just below her ribcage like streamers. Casey was barely aware of the sounds of retching behind him.

Under the gruesome sight, a bower nestled. Saplings had been bent and entwined to form a natural roof. Dead trees had been drug from around the forest to form further support. Mossy branches and vines made up the rest, making the whole thing, if not for the rotting corpse hanging above it, look like nothing more than a natural pile of forest compost. The size of the pile of branches and trees would be a curiosity, but most people would pass it by, thinking it a bear den that should be avoided if they noticed it at all – and that was without the smell.

"Why would they do that?" Max asked.

Her question drew Casey's eyes back up to Janelle's remains.

"It's like they're advertising they're here," she finished.

"It's a message for me," Casey said. He got closer to the entrance and inhaled. "They want me to see who it is. That it's someone I know."

He glanced around the woods, desperate to know what it was Luca was trying to tell him. Something from within the bower smelled all wrong.

"Watch the trees," Casey said. "Yell if you see something."

Max took a defensive stance just outside the bower's

entrance while Casey crawled inside. He could hear the muffled arguing that erupted between Jay and Terry. He waited for his eyes to adjust, the last of the daylight filtering in through small gaps in the structure, casting everything in a hazy green glow. When he could finally make out what was in the center of the bower, he fell to his knees in shock.

Flowers and colorful fungus were placed around Noah's body. He was no longer in his wendigo form. The sight of Noah, as a human, was only part of the shock. He was emaciated to the point that he was more bone than skin or muscle. His face was all shadow and no light. His bones were badly broken, his legs twisted garishly, knees scraped raw, hands missing fingers. None of that mattered – Casey could only see the kid brother he'd lost.

Noah had been posed, probably as best as Luca could manage without further damaging his body. He looked to be at rest - a small bundle of moss and flowers cradled in his arms. He couldn't remember ever going to a funeral as a kid, but if he had, this is how he'd imagine the body being laid out.

Casey leaned over Noah, cupping his head in his claws. He'd never seen his brother as a man. It felt even more painful for Casey to get a glimpse of the person his brother might have become had he been given the chance. He wept, his tears falling onto his brother's sunken body. He would have never guessed a wendigo, and one as far gone as Luca, was capable of such a display of grief.

Another smell brought him out of his pain and back to the present. It wasn't wendigo. It wasn't his brother. It wasn't Luca. It was distinctly human.

He turned his attention to the bundle – the source of the smell. He pulled back the blanket of moss to reveal a baby. It was young, weeks old at most. He was too startled to be horrified. How had a baby gotten into the bower?

It was thin, as if it had gone hungry. Casey pulled the moss lower, exposing its belly. The cord had been chewed through, and the baby hadn't even lived long enough for it to heal fully. He looked around the bower, searching for any clues that would explain what had happened. He found a wooden bowl, crudely carved from a chunk of long dead tree. In it was a mash of dried blood and bits of human flesh. A tiny spoon, silver like the ones in Janelle's kitchen, sat in the middle of the mess of pre-chewed human flesh.

Fresh horror flooded through Casey. He tossed the bowl away. He started to back out of the bower, but something in the center of the dead baby's forehead caught his eye. It was a single, yellow gem. He crashed through the entrance, running smack into Max. She turned to look at him, and immediately grew concerned.

"What is it? What did you find?"

"She's not here. We have to go. Now."

FOURTEEN

Anne and Will sat on a bed playing slapjack. She wished it could be any other game, but slap jack was the only card game she'd ever learned. It was so incredibly dull, she'd purposefully lost the last two rounds of the game. Will attempted to teach her something else, but there were only so many two player card games, and Anne didn't have the patience for any of them.

Her thoughts persisted in going back to Max in the forest with that monster. Up until the last hour, she'd been checking her phone every five minutes for news. She'd had to force herself, and William because he was no better, to put it in her pocket and leave it there for at least an hour before checking again. It hadn't helped all that much. Try as she might to distract herself, and she'd tried – she'd imagined herself as a famous star in a movie portraying her harrowing ordeal, she'd imagined herself on a talk show discussing the best wendigo repellent techniques, she'd imagined herself at a book signing –

it didn't matter. Her mind was willful and determined to make her as anxious as possible.

Max was out there, fighting a thing that shouldn't even be real, and she was sitting in a motel room playing a card game for six-year-olds. It was enough to make Anne scream in frustration. She hated that she felt so useless all the time. She never blamed Max – or at least, she tried not to blame Max. Sometimes she couldn't help but feel bitter that Max had her life in order when she didn't. Never married, nearing forty and no job of consequence – it was a far cry from success.

She tossed the last card down from her hand and waited while Will flipped until he slapped the next jack from his hand. He gathered up the cards and started to shuffle them when Anne put her hand on his knee, unwilling to subject herself to another game.

"Let's take a break. I'm thirsty. You want a drink?"

"You're not going out of the room, are you?"

Anne tried not to sigh. Will had made some comment under his breath earlier, probably thinking she hadn't heard it, about how often she sighed. She couldn't help it though. If there was ever a time for excessive sighing, it was when you were trapped in a hotel room with a teenager and a wendigo was on the loose.

"No. I filled the cooler, remember?"

"Oh," Will said. "Okay. If there's root beer in there, I'd take that."

Anne started toward the cooler.

"Or a cream soda! Actually, I'd like that more."

Anne nodded and kept going.

"Wait, no. Root beer."

This time Anne did sigh.

"Sorry. I'm nervous," Will said. "It's getting dark. I can't help thinking about them."

"It's all right," Anne said. "Maybe we should try some TV instead of cards."

"Okay. Hey, a new episode of—"

Anne ran to the bed so fast she almost knocked Will over. Her hand clamped across his mouth as she looked at the motel room door.

"Shh," she said. "I heard something."

Will nodded from under her hand and she let him go. There was only one lamp on in the room. Anne crept toward it and flipped the switch, casting the room in darkness. She took Will's arm and led him to the bathroom, pushing him in.

"If it's trouble, I'm coming back here," she said. "We'll lock the door and wait it out."

"Okay," Will whispered.

The curtains were thick, the kind that blocked out most of the light, but a sliver of blue tinged light from outside splashed on the carpeting beneath the window. Anne checked her phone. Somehow, they'd played right up to dusk without realizing the sun had gone down. She tip-toed to the window and rested her cheek along the wall. Crooking her pinky finger, she started to pull the curtain slowly open to look outside.

A banging noise sent her sprawling backward. She pressed her hands to her mouth to keep from screaming. Her brain moved like lightning, planning escape routes and attack vectors. She couldn't run from this thing; it had the nose of ten bloodhounds and from what she'd read - if any of that could be trusted – speed unlike anything she'd ever seen. Locking themselves in the bathroom might be the best bet. The door was the solid kind, thick, heavy and industrial. The lock was nothing to write home about, but the door swung inward, meaning they could hold it shut. Perhaps between the two of them it would be enough to keep the creature out.

She'd just started toward the bathroom when the banging came at their room's door. She couldn't hold the scream in this time. It flew from her mouth as she ran toward the bathroom. She crashed into Will, completely in a panic. The two of them fell to the bathroom floor in a heap, tangled up in each other's limbs, elbows cracking into the floor and wall.

"Is it here? Oh my god it's here," Will said.

"It's... Shut up. Let me listen."

The pounding started up again, this time Anne could hear a voice accompanying it.

"Anne? Is that you? I'm coming in there if someone doesn't answer this door!"

Anne felt her teeth grind together involuntarily. She groaned as she pushed herself up, not out of pain, but from annoyance. Of all the times for Frank Campbell to come sniffing around, he had to come tonight. She helped Will up then went to the door, opening it just as Frank was about to ram it with his fist again.

She stared out at him angrily.

"I heard screaming," he said.

His hand was on the butt of his gun, the snap already undone on the holster. His partner, Mike something – Anne hadn't bothered to remember his last name – was behind him, gun already drawn.

"You can put your guns down," Anne said. "I screamed because you freaked me the fuck out, banging on the doors after dark like you're some kind of commando."

Frank kept his hand on his gun and pulled a flashlight out, shining it into the room behind Anne. She moved to stand in front of the beam just as it caught Will in the face.

"Who's that?"

"None of your business," Anne said.

"Anne," Frank said.

"Don't you 'Anne' me. I'm tired of this shit. I didn't come back here because I missed you. Or was I somehow unclear when I told you to buzz off all those years ago. I'm not interested. I've told you that as plainly as possible. If you keep harassing me, I'll have to file an official complaint."

"I didn't come here for you, Anne. I came here to bring Casey Pierson in for questioning."

Anne crossed her arms while Frank tried to look over her shoulder again.

"Why? Didn't his story check out?"

Frank lowered his flashlight and sighed.

"I get Max protecting this sleazebag. She's always had a soft spot for smooth talkers."

"Don't you talk about my sister," Anne started.

She didn't have much chance to continue as Frank just talked over her.

"Why do you care about him? He's a drifter. We may not be friends, but I know he's not your type."

With his last words, he tried once again to peek over Anne's shoulder. She heard Will move around in the room behind her. He tripped over the cooler in the dark.

"Go away. He's not here," Anne said.

Anne was suddenly very glad she'd talked Max into parking her truck behind all the cargo containers on the other side of the motel. There was no way she'd get Frank to leave if he saw the busted-up vehicle.

"Where have they gone?"

"They?" Anne asked.

"Max's truck is gone. I knocked on her door first. No answer. I assume wherever he is, she is."

"They went into town, maybe." Anne threw her hands up in the air. "I don't know. I'm not my sister's keeper."

Frank looked annoyed, but Anne wasn't feeling any of it. She was tired of him thinking he had any right to any part of her life. After a few more tense seconds of staring at each other, Frank finally gave in and re-snapped his holster.

"You need to call me," he said. "If you hear them come home, you need to call me. This is serious, Anne. People are missing."

"You don't need to remind me how serious this is," Anne said. "Trust me on that."

She turned to head back into the room, the door about to close when she smelled it.

"Mike?" Frank said.

He pointed his flashlight back at the squad car. Anne, despite the fear inhabiting every inch of her skin, followed the cone of light.

"Mike? You're supposed to be backing me up. This is not protocol. Mike? We talked about this."

"Frank," Anne said.

"Just a minute. I have to find my dumbass partner. Mike!"

The light flashed around the trees surrounding the lot too fast for Anne to follow. Frank started toward the car.

"Frank! You have to—"

He was half way to the car when something slammed into him. He didn't even have time to scream. But the wendigo did.

Chunks of Frank's flesh still in its mouth, it turned to Anne, blood dripping from between its teeth like drool. It opened its mouth and screamed at her, just as she slammed the door shut, sliding the lock into place and backing into Will.

"It's here," he gasped.

Anne's eyes darted from the heavy metal motel room door to

the huge plate glass window beside it. Her mind bucked her control and began to critique the idea of a secure door when a giant window was all a killer would really need. Despite her fear, she silently berated whoever came up with that design. She felt the tug on her sleeve as a shadow blocked the line of light beneath the door.

"Here," Will said. He pulled her to the door to the adjoining room. "You can open this, right?"

Anne got control of herself. She looked at the door, then nodded as she opened the first of the two doors separating the rooms. The knob on the door leading to the parking lot rattled.

Anne's hands shook as she pulled out her key ring and found the master key. It took too many seconds to fit the key in the handle, seconds where the thing outside moved from trying the knob to testing the strength of the door. If Anne could see the flaw of hiding in a motel room, the beast was sure to see it soon.

When the second door to the adjacent room clicked open, there was a brief moment where she felt like cheering. The tiny victory gave her hope, even as insurmountable as their odds looked. She pushed Will through. She started after him but turned to the bathroom door with a sudden thought. She closed her eyes in silent hopes that she wasn't going to get killed over a stupid idea, before running to the bathroom. She pulled off her sweater and tossed it inside the bathroom, then turned the lock on the handle so that when she closed the bathroom door, it would be locked up tight. She tested it to be sure, just as the wendigo screamed and slammed into the door leading to the parking lot. Anne shuddered, but the motel room door held. She darted back to the adjoining room door and slipped through, quietly locking it.

"Why'd you do that?" Will asked.

"Maybe it will buy us time. It might think we're hiding in there."

She shivered, now only in a tank top, as she looked around the room. They were in Max's prep room, wires and tools still spread out all over the bed. The shotgun was leaned up against the wall. Both Anne and Will looked at it, there eyes glued to it as soon as they saw it.

"I have never shot a gun before in my life," Will whispered.

"I have," Anne said. "Once."

She approached the gun with hesitance. She had shot a gun once; it just wasn't a shotgun. She was about to leave it on the floor when the sound of shattering glass came from the next room over. Fear overtook her reticence and she snatched up the shotgun. There was nowhere else she could think to go, so she pulled Will into the bathroom before locking the door and shutting it.

"Should we turn the light off?" Will whispered.

The walls rattled as the wendigo slammed into the bathroom door of the room they'd just left. Anne shook her head as she looked over the gun.

"I don't think being blind will help us."

She examined all the pieces of the shotgun. She found the safety easy enough, it was clearly marked. But the rest of the operation of the beastly weapon was less obvious.

"You have your phone?" she asked.

"Yeah. Why? Should we call Jay and them?"

"No. Not yet. Look up how to shoot a shotgun."

"Oh, fuck."

Every second that went by while Will fumbled with his phone felt like an hour. With each sound of the wendigo tearing up the room next door, Anne flinched. She backed into the wall of the bathroom without even realizing she'd done it. Something finally gave in the room next door announced by the sharp crack of splintering wood. Then the wendigo screamed again.

"Here, I found something," Will said.

Anne could hear the wendigo at the doors between the rooms. The thing was checking them, twisting the knob and finally pressing its weight into it to see how solid it was. Anne heard the metal groan under the weight, even in the bathroom, but it held. It would be harder to break through than the bathroom door – the doors separating rooms were the same type as the heavy doors leading out to the lot. She turned her attention to the phone as Will hit play. The man in the video had a shotgun similar to the one Anne was holding.

"What the fuck," she cursed as the man asked viewers to like and subscribe. "I hate this shit on the best of days. Fucking go forward!"

"I can't," Will said. "It'll have to rebuffer. Trust me, it'll take even longer if we do that."

The wendigo was no longer testing the door to the adjacent room. The pause before a second crash of glass was brief, the beast using what it had learned in its previous break-in to speed up the process. The stench began filling up the small space of the bathroom before the light coming from under the door was blotted out.

The man in the video pulled down the stock of the gun, locking it into place. Anne nervously copied his movements as he checked the safety and the slide lock. The only thing of note she remembered from the one time she ever shot a gun, was the kickback. She carefully lodged the stock against her shoulder and leveled it at the door, just as the first blow came against it.

"Oh my god," Will whimpered.

Anne's fingers grew sweaty in an instant. She risked wiping them on her jeans for fear of them slipping when she needed them most. The door shuddered again, drawing a gasp from Will.

"Should I call them now?"

"Can't hurt," Anne said.

The door cracked in half, causing Anne to panic and pull the trigger. The blast in the tiny bathroom rang in her ears. She opened her eyes, not remembering when she'd closed them, to see dust heavy in the air. The tiling around the door had been shattered by her blast. The door was in pieces, but she and Will were both still alive. The wendigo was another matter – it hadn't shown its face yet.

She shook her head in a futile attempt to stop the ringing, when her nose warned her they weren't done yet. She looked up to see the wendigo, none the worse for wear, peering in through the splintered mess. She wasn't sure if the thing had a grin on its face, or if that was how the beast always looked, but it hardly mattered – it was terrifying either way.

Anne pumped the shotgun again, barely able to hear, when the beast started to tear through the rest of the door to get to them. She heard a faint pop, and the wendigo went sideways. She looked down at the shotgun in puzzlement. She hadn't pulled the trigger yet.

The fuzziness of her hearing started to fade, and she heard two more pops, only this time they were clearer – gunshots. The wendigo screamed and headed out of sight toward the sound. Through staggered breaths, Anne pulled Will toward the door.

"What are you doing? That thing is out there!"

"And you think we're safe in here?"

Anne pointed toward the splintered door angrily. As if it was waiting for a cue to fall, a piece of splintered wood dropped from the upper hinge. It was all the convincing Will needed. He allowed himself to be pulled along behind Anne as she dragged him from the bathroom, turning away from the door outside.

She ran to the glass doors leading out to the pool and flung them open so hard, they derailed from their track. She didn't think about closing them, instead running full on toward the other side of the pool where the laundry room was, only to be once again slammed by the scent of the wendigo.

She reeled back in fear as the creature rounded the corner of the laundry area and came barreling toward her. Without thinking on it, she raised her shotgun, finger on the trigger. The creature darted so fast, her eyes were unable to track it. It was in front of her before she could react, grabbing her on either side of her body in such a way it caused her to drop the shotgun. She was sure the next thing she'd feel was its teeth as they sunk into her throat. When she heard Casey's voice, she lost all composure and started crying.

"Where is she, Anne? Where's Luca?"

FIFTEEN

The SUV slid across the gravel roads with every turn. Casey was sure Max would end up in a ditch, but she not only kept control of the vehicle, she also made better time than he'd thought possible.

"Do you do off-roading?" he asked as he struggled not to be tossed about in his seat.

"Used to," Max said. "SUV is not my vehicle of choice for it. Way too top heavy. But my ex loved that kind of stuff. And really, we're in Michigan. At least a quarter of the time you're on a road going anywhere, it turns into an off-road adventure. Especially in the winter."

As if to illustrate her point, a series of large potholes forced her to weave the car back and forth to avoid them, careening the passengers into each other. Casey looked at his seatbelt wistfully. He'd be more likely to slice the thing in two than manage to buckle it. The two guys in the back, however, both clicked theirs into place as soon as they regained their seats.

"Are you sure your sister wasn't in those woods?" Jay asked.

"She wasn't. I'm sure," Casey said.

"How do you know?" Terry asked.

Casey fidgeted and accidentally sliced open the leather in the front seats. He surreptitiously covered the damage with his clawed hand, before looking up to see a smirk on Max's face.

"She left me a message."

"A message?" Max asked.

"One of the gems from that old phone of Anne's. The one you gave me. She left it on... in plain sight. I know my sister. I've been tracking her for years. I know what it means."

"She's gone after Anne?" Max shook her head in disbelief. "Why?"

Casey wasn't sure the best way to explain it to them. He wasn't about to go into the details about what he'd found in the bower – that would take too long to explain, and he wasn't even sure if he truly understood it himself. He had a hunch, but that wasn't enough for him to open that particular can of worms just then. It was the kind of detail that could wait, if he survived the night.

"She would have smelled Anne on me when I fought her. She would have smelled you, too," he said, looking at Max, "but you showed up in that truck ready for battle. She won't think you showed up uninvited. She'll think you were meant to be there. You had a weapon and knew how to use it."

Casey looked out the window at the rush of trees they passed. He dove into Luca's perspective, and viewed the scene as she would have.

"I don't usually have anything personal on me," he said, thinking aloud. "My license, but that's not unusual. Luca, somewhere deep in her brain, wouldn't think an ID was anything of note. But she'd have seen that phone. It would be weird to her, stand out. Not just because it was covered in sparkling plastic, though that wouldn't help. I've been following them, but they are aware and have been watching me as well. That's been obvious to me for a while."

He couldn't help but wonder if that was why he never truly lost them. Over all the years, he'd never spent more than a couple weeks without some sign they were still out there and hunting. He'd started to question the timing of some of his finds – days when he'd been at his wit's end looking for some clue, only to find a blatant leaving. Perhaps they'd been searching for him, in their own way, as much as he'd been searching for them.

"The phone was Anne's," Casey continued. "Luca would have smelled her scent all over the gem. She would assume that person was precious to me."

"I still don't get it," Jay said. "Why not Max? Max was the one who saved you, right? I don't get why her being there makes her less important to you than someone who didn't show up."

The smell of the bower came back to Casey. He shook his head before the memory of the tiny malnourished body could stick around.

"She doesn't think like that. Things that are precious to her, things she'd want to protect, she wouldn't bring into danger. She'd leave them behind."

"How can you be so sure?" Max asked. "That's an awful lot of guesses based on a single plastic gem."

"If it was you she went after," Casey said, "you she wanted to hurt to send a message, she'd have left your handkerchief for me to find in the bower. The one you took off when you were looking for something to stop the bleeding. But it was on the ground where you'd dropped it. Untouched. Luca would've had to hunt for that gem."

Max's knuckles whitened as she gripped the steering wheel. She gunned the engine, pulling onto the paved highway, kicking rocks and dust up in her wake. The car's occupants were silent, the strained sound of the engine doing more than enough to indicate the mood of the group.

"I'm sorry about your brother," Max said quietly.

Her sudden condolences brought Casey back to the bower again. He looked out the window and tried not to think too much about it. The sound of the vehicle racing along the pavement only aided his concentration, focusing his mind on what he'd seen rather than banishing it from his head.

The baby couldn't have been Luca's. It wasn't possible. Wendigos weren't built for procreation, only death. Even if they had found some way to pair, the baby smelled human, right down to its core. Perhaps she'd found it somewhere. Runaway teens were one of Luca and Noah's favorite prey. They were easy to hunt and plentiful, often passed out from drugs or alcohol. Maybe one such victim had a child with them. Maybe they were pregnant. The image of the chewed umbilical cord haunted Casey.

Something about the baby kept Luca from killing it. It was impossible not to see humanity in the act. Why else would Luca spare the child if not because there was still something human inside her? He didn't want to believe it; he needed to kill Luca, and the already difficult task would only be made more arduous if he had to imagine his sister was still inside the monster.

"Something's bothering you," Max said.

"It's nothing."

Max turned onto the final road before the Sunset. She flipped off the lights and decelerated to make less noise as they approached.

"We have about five minutes, Casey." Her voice was calm but concerned. "We won't get a second chance at this. I don't think she'll let us this time. Whatever it is you're thinking, it's best to let it out."

Casey's tongue felt thick. Max was trying to help him, to give him a chance to voice his doubts. He didn't think he'd be able to.

"I wonder if she's still in there somewhere."

Max didn't answer at first. Casey thought she might not say anything at all.

"If she were," Max began. "If there was something left in there, would that change how we deal with this?"

Casey shook his head.

"Only how I felt about it after."

Max exhaled slowly, and her hands loosened on the steering wheel. She reached out to him.

"Whatever you feel. However long it takes you to feel it. I'll be with you."

Casey took her hand into his claw, carefully enfolding it. He kept hold of it until the Sunset came into view, red and blue flashes strobing out from the parking lot near Max and Anne's rooms.

"Shit," Max said. "We'll park on the other side."

"Why?" Casey asked.

"Dude," Jay said, "you look like some shit crawled out of a nightmare. If they see you, they'll shoot first and ask questions later."

Casey took the advice to heart. He ducked down in his seat as Max pulled around to the far side of the motel, near all the cargo containers and dumpsters. They climbed out of the car, grabbing their gear as they went. They'd taken three steps when a shotgun went off somewhere in the vicinity of the motel.

"Come on," Max said, running.

Casey bolted ahead of them, skidding around the corner of

the motel. More gunshots rang out, this time from a pistol. He sprinted past the laundry room just in time to see Anne and Will clambering out the sliding doors of one of the rooms. Anne was carrying a shotgun and dragging Will behind her. Casey took off in their direction, only to have Anne level the shotgun at him. He jumped, purely from instinct, dodging her aim and landing in front of her.

The gun was a danger; he couldn't risk her using it. He gripped her arms on either side of her body as hard as he dared, causing her to drop the shotgun. He flinched when it hit the ground, afraid it would go off. Anne looked terrified, as if she was prepared for him to eat her face. He didn't have time to calm her down.

"Where is she, Anne? Where's Luca?"

Anne broke down then, sobbing, just as Max made it into the courtyard, Jay and Terry close behind. Anne looked past Casey and then shoved him aside to get to Max.

"Oh my god! You're still alive!"

The two sisters embraced, Max pulling away first to look into the open motel room. The breeze picked up, blowing straight through the room and causing the thick, rubber coated curtains to drift outside the door.

"Wait here," Casey said. "Stay together."

His feet made a tapping noise as he crossed the cement patio, the claws scraping every time he lifted them. He could smell blood, lots of it, coming from the room. Campbell was in there. Alive or dead, Casey couldn't be sure, but he was inside. Luca was close. Casey didn't like leaving the others behind, but he hoped Luca would see the five of them as more of a problem if he was left alive. She'd want to take down the toughest opponent first, so as not to be taken by surprise.

The room was a wreck. The door to the bathroom had been

torn apart so violently, splinters of wood were embedded in the wall across from it. He stepped past the bathroom toward the front door. Glass covered the floor while a few huge shards of it still held onto the window frame, the curtain around it in tatters. Blood soaked the carpet and bed. Casey heard a gurgling noise coming from the other side of the bed. He slunk past the mattress and looked down to see Chief Campbell, dying.

His insides were a mess. Casey wasn't sure how the man wasn't already dead. He could see bile leaking out from the large, continuous wound in Campbell's body. The gurgling sound was coming from his chest cavity, which had been ripped wide open, one of the lungs shredded, thick bubbles of blood forming and popping with every attempted breath.

There was still enough of Campbell's mind present for him to look up and become terrified again. Casey heard a repeated clicking. He moved part of the bedspread that was draped over Campbell's shoulder to reveal his arm, the gun still in his hand, his finger desperately pulling the trigger. It was horrific and distressing, but Casey didn't have time to put an end to the man's misery. He found that out as Luca slammed into him.

They landed with a thud against the wall, splitting the drywall right open. Luca was stronger than when he'd last fought her, rage filling her eyes with hatred. He pushed against her, trying his best to catch a breath as she pressed into him.

"Hey," she said.

Then she clamped onto his hand, crunching down with all her strength. He felt his bones snap and his tendons tear. The howl that flew from his throat only encouraged her to bite down harder. He raked her chest with the claws in his free hand, and she finally backed away, taking several of his fingers with her. She screamed at him, her mouth still wet with his blood. Something primal surfaced within him, and he screamed back.

"Casey!"

Max's panicked yell drew Luca's attention. He grabbed Luca's head and smashed it into the wall, sending bits of drywall and paint flying. She kicked him, and he landed in the TV, knocking it to the ground and snapping it in half. Luca got between him and the sliding doors. She grinned maliciously before she darted past the curtain toward the courtyard.

"No!" Casey yelled.

He sprung to his feet and bounded through the room, taking only two steps to cover twenty feet. He came out to the pool area to see Luca standing about forty feet away from Max and the others. Max was holding her bat aloft, her heavy-duty gloves on, blue sparks leaping from spike to spike.

Casey thought they'd be safe, until Luca leapt the fence to the pool and picked up one of the wrought iron patio tables. She'd learned from her last encounter – she couldn't get close to Max, but that didn't mean she couldn't hurt her.

Luca tried to throw the table, but the steel cable tying it to the fence kept it from going far. Casey had a second of indecision, trying to pick who to run to – Luca, to stop her from finding a projectile to launch, or to Max and the others, to shield them from whatever was coming. He hesitated a moment too long. Luca pulled the table hard enough that the bar it was attached to bent inward, finally releasing the table from its anchor.

A satisfied sound escaped Luca right before she launched the table through the air at an alarming speed. Casey was unprepared and forced to jump into its path to intercept it, using his body to stop it instead of trying to deflect it with his hands. He was successful, but only just. When the table hit him, it broke several of his ribs. When he landed, he realized the blow had also shattered his hip. He hit the ground in immense pain. Every time he tried to rise, it was pure agony.

He fell back to the ground, helpless to aid them any longer. He still had one thing he could try – he was the only one who knew Luca, the only one who might be able to talk to her.

"Luca," he shouted.

She turned to him, her hand halfway to another table.

"Please stop. You have to be in there somewhere. I know you do. I saw what you left for me. I know that wasn't the monster. Please."

Luca's claws hovered over the table. But if there was anything left in her, anything that cared what Casey had to say or what he thought, it was gone faster than it surfaced. She punched her claws through the top of the table to get a grip and started to pull against the tether. Her eyes told Casey this time she was aiming for him. There was no way he'd be able to dodge the throw.

He heard a grunt from Max and turned to see her bat flying toward Luca. All the tasers had been turned on, and the bat sparked and crackled as it flipped through the air. The throw was accurate and hit the iron table. Luca yelped as the pulse of electricity from the bat travelled through the metal and hit her. The pain caused her to pull away as the bat bounced off, landing in the pool.

The lights in the pool flickered, then turned off. The constant hum of the filter went dead. The pool went dark, and the slight ripple above the outflow jet died, making the surface smooth as glass as the now defunct baseball bat sunk to the bottom of the pool.

Luca snarled at them, sniffing her burnt hands. Max ran to Casey and tried to pull his arm around her shoulder. Casey attempted to push her away, afraid she'd be caught up in Luca's next barrage of attacks, but Max wouldn't let him. She held him tight. It wasn't the gesture of someone who thought they still had a chance; the look in her eyes told Casey she was unwilling to leave his side, even if this was the end.

Luca abandoned the table and started toward the group. The sound of another bat firing up drew her attention. Terry took up a position in front of the group, defiantly staring the creature down. The electrified weapon gave Luca pause enough to consider what she'd do next. Her thoughts were practically projected on the wall of the motel as she looked around at all the patio tables.

"She has more tables than we have bats," Will said. "She'll either crush us that way, or we'll run out of weapons and she'll tear out our throats."

They all seemed to come to the same conclusion and huddled together behind Terry. All except Jay, who was eyeing the gate to the pool.

"I've got an idea," Jay said.

He flipped on his bat and stood next to Terry while Luca started yanking another table, trying to free it. Casey grunted as he turned toward the teenager.

"No more ideas," he said. "You all need to run. Maybe she'll be happy killing me. Maybe she'll leave you alone. Just run."

"No," Max said.

"It's alright, old man," Jay said. "I know what I'm doing."

"Jay," Terry's voice was tense. "What the hell are you thinking? You electrocuted yourself just earlier today. Maybe the guy is right. We regroup. Get more people out here."

A wrenching metal noise interrupted them. Luca's yanking had pulled one of the iron spikes free of the fence. She dropped the newly freed table to inspect it. With a gruesome grin, she launched it at them like a javelin. Casey had just enough time to pull Max to the ground to avoid them both being impaled. The fence spike struck the side of the motel, sinking in more than a foot.

"I thought the tables were a problem," Will said.

"Shut up, Will!" Terry said. "You're not helping."

While they were bickering, Jay had moved into a crouch, his body aimed up for the gap in the fence.

"Terry, take care of Will, okay? George would've wanted us to look out for each other."

Terry turned to Jay, a protest dying on his lips as Jay put his hands down on the ground.

"I never met a quarterback I couldn't sack," Jay said.

Casey reached forward to stop the kid, but it was too late. Jay jumped up and charged, shoulders forward, head tucked in and low. Luca was picking up the table she'd freed from the fence and turned to see Jay. Casey would never know what she was thinking. Everything moved so fast, yet his thoughts were almost languid as the events played out.

Jay's bat was turned on to full, every taser pumping out fifty thousand volts. When he crashed into Luca, the bat was sandwiched between them, locking up their muscles into an embrace. They tumbled into the pool, the table on top of them. The surface of the water became foamy as the two bodies twitched violently for a few seconds before finally stopping. Then, succumbing to the weight of the table, they sank to the bottom.

Casey tried to move, only to violently heave forward in pain. The hunger was leaving, without warning. He wasn't sure how or why, but it sunk back into his core and left him to transform back into his human body, each tug of muscle worse than the last as his shattered hip shifted under the strain. When he was finally able to unfurl from the fetal position, he looked down at his human hands. He was missing three fingers on his left one. He tried to stand up, but just grunted in pain as he leaned against Max.

"Stop. It's over," she said.

"I need to see her to be sure."

Max lifted him. It was slow going but she managed it with Anne's help. They hobbled over to the edge of the pool and looked down, taking care not to walk through any water. Two bodies rested at the bottom of the pool, weighed down by the heavy table. Jay's fingers were still curled around the bat. Casey tore his eyes away from the brave teenager to look at the second body. He gripped Max tightly as he saw the pale face of his sister – gaunt, aged, but still her. He buried his face in Max's neck, too in pain to cry. It was over.

Their moment of solace was brief. The sound of sirens interrupted the night, lights joining those already coming from the parking lot. Max turned toward the others, confusion on her face.

"I called them," Will said.

"Will!"

"I'm sorry, Anne. It made more sense to call the police than Max or Jay."

Their words started to ebb in and out, as the last of Casey's adrenaline wore off, and he collapsed into Max's Arms, the sound of the swing set blowing in the wind was the last thing he heard before he passed out.

SIXTEEN

Casey woke to a bang. He groaned as he rolled over.
"I thought you were going to tell those guys they couldn't start work until at least seven."

He reached out, but his hand was met with a tumble of blankets. Max wasn't there. A second groan escaped him as he glanced at the red numbers on the cheap motel clock – nine thirty. Despite having slept in, he felt like he'd just gotten up from an ill-conceived nap of twenty minutes – just long enough to make him more tired than when he'd gone to sleep.

He slid out of bed and pulled on his boxers, trying to blink away his tiredness. It didn't work, but he tried. Several minutes after he'd pulled on a robe, he was still standing in front of his door, daring himself to open it and begin the day. He heard the key in the lock and stepped back just in time.

"Oh, you're up." Max looked him over. "Have you been standing here in front of the door?"

"Yes?"

She gave him a funny smile and leaned in for a kiss. When

she pulled away, his lips lingered in the air hoping for something more. He was too slow and tired to catch her up, though he tried, his arms coming back empty as she breezed past him into the bathroom.

"Come back here," he said lazily. "I want a proper morning snuggle."

She flitted past him again, tossing him jeans and a shirt.

"Come on. The sign's done."

"It is?"

He dropped the clothes on the floor and followed her out of the room. The cement was cool under his feet, and he found himself missing the summer already. Warm cement under bare feet was one of life's greatest pleasures, especially in the morning. He forgot the thought quickly, though, as he followed Max all the way to the office. He came up behind her, resting his chin on her shoulder, as they both looked up.

The sign stretched up into the sky, all the marquee letters lit up bright yellow, each buzzing quietly as the gas inside them was agitated by electricity – Sunset View Motel.

"That's it then," he said.

"That's it."

They stood there quietly for a few minutes before Anne's voice pierced their solitude.

"Hey. Scott's on his way to take possession. Any minute now." She looked pointedly at Casey. "You should get dressed."

She disappeared back into the office before Casey had a chance to respond. It would have been nice to bask in a job completed for a little longer, but he was ready to go in any case. It was time to leave the Sunset.

Max and Casey linked arms and headed back to their room. The pile of clothes was where he left them, and he gathered them up to get dressed. He sat on the bed to pull on his pants while Max wheeled a suitcase closer to the door.

"You think the mayor will actually get anything out of this place?" Casey asked. "I mean legitimately. No illegal gimmicks, no cooking the books. Just people booking rooms."

She came over and joined him, the bed bouncing a little as she sat on it.

"My dad couldn't. But maybe he was a terrible motel manager."

The question Casey wanted to ask next was delicate enough he wasn't sure he should ask it. He'd been holding onto it for a couple months; it was the last time he could ask it before it would be too late. Now might be too late, he thought, but he'd never found the right time before. There was no good reason to keep the worrying thought from her; Max had insisted he could talk about anything with her, and this counted as anything.

"You aren't worried he'll just start things up again? The way your father had?"

To Casey's relief, Max wasn't fazed by the question.

"Terry and Will said they'd keep watch. If something fishy starts up here again, they'll let me know. And questions be damned, we'll let the authorities know."

"Will you be ready for that?"

Max took Casey's left hand in hers. She raised it to her mouth and kissed the smooth nubs where three of his fingers used to be.

"If you are, I am."

"Good," Casey said.

He pulled on his shirt and stood.

"Let's bid farewell to the Sunset then."

The day was unremarkable. That wasn't to say it was unremarkable when compared to other places on other days – it was unremarkable for northwest Michigan in October. For the peepers who came down the highway with some regularity, it was a glorious day. The sun was shining, the air was cool and crisp, and the trees were displaying their full range of colors, from blistering red to sunny yellow and everything in between. Casey was used to the gorgeous tapestry. He'd spent many falls in the upper Midwest – too many to take special note of it.

There was one difference this day, though, and it wasn't the scenery or the pleasant weather. Normally, the coming winter would fill Casey with dread. He'd have lost another year without finding his brother and sister. They'd hunker down for the cold months, usually finding some long-abandoned cave somewhere, and slumber through the darkest months of the year. He'd lose their trail, and the long wait for the first murder would begin. Winter was when Casey usually felt the lowest, the most like a failure, and the most regret. On this mid-October day, he finally felt at peace.

The three of them sat on a bench outside the motel office, Max sandwiched between Casey and Anne. Casey's heart was full in a way he never dared dream. He wasn't heading out to find a place to live for a few months, ready to scrape by on the change he got from odd jobs and snow shoveling. He was going somewhere he hadn't gone in more than twenty years – home.

Scott Linkman, mayor of Manistee and local businessman, pulled up in a shiny car. The vehicle, Max had remarked once, cost more than most homes in the area. Linkman hopped out of the car with a spring in his step. He crumpled up a sizable fast food bag and dumped it in the trash outside the office, complete with his own swooshing sound, like he was a kid on holiday. It worried Casey just a touch.

Linkman hadn't been happy the night he was called to the Sunset not two months prior. Policemen had been killed, another teen was dead, and a whole slew of new questions and problems had arisen from the whole scenario. Casey had been barely conscious during the discussions of what to do about everything. When Linkman announced they wouldn't be calling any outside authorities, it shocked Casey, even through his haze of pain. Two police officers were dead, after all. That was never a thing that was met with indifference, no matter who the police were.

But Scott Linkman somehow made everything go away – the questions, the bodies, all the sordid details had been swept up. The matter of the motel was trickier. Linkman's only condition for his assistance was that Max and Anne leave and never come back. In order to facilitate this request, the mayor bought out the motel.

It was a deal that made Linkman furious enough to turn red. Casey could only guess that the mayor was more involved in Max's father's motel than anyone previously had known. It was the only thing that would explain why Linkman would continue to handle things despite his anger.

Something had happened in the last week, however. Linkman began to express true interest in taking ownership of the property. Casey harbored concerns there was another scheme cooking in Manistee regarding the motel, but he'd mostly kept those concerns to himself. It was hard not to think his suspicions were right when Linkman approached. The mayor looked positively cheerful.

"Here are the keys," Max said.

She held up a ring of keys, mostly the same – masters for all the staff Linkman would presumably need to hire to get the place up and running.

"Thanks!" Linkman said. "You fixed the place up nice, Max. I really do appreciate it. Makes my job a whole lot easier."

"Sure," Max said.

Casey knew her well enough to feel the tension in her voice. She picked up a ledger from between her and Anne and handed it to Linkman.

"These are the financials. My father kept good records, if nothing else."

"This is all of it?" Linkman asked as he started flipping through the pages hungrily.

"Yes. Though the years of pertinence to you will be the first three. That was from before he... before his new business model took over."

Something about the tone of Max's voice finally caught Linkman. He looked up and smiled reassuringly at her.

"Those are the ones I'm interested in. Don't worry."

"Hmm," Max said.

If she was thinking anything else, which Casey strongly suspected, she didn't voice it. Casey briefly considered taking her aside to mention his suspicions again and suggest they take more time to find another buyer. He changed his mind after seeing the look on her face. He couldn't take that relief away from her. And besides, he thought, Terry was just a phone call away. He'd promised to keep an eye on things. If the mayor was going to do something they didn't like, they could always send an anonymous tip.

"I think that's it for us then," Anne said. She got up and hauled a designer purse over her shoulder. "Max, you guys drive safe, okay?"

"You know I will," Max said. "See you for lunch tomorrow?"

"Absolutely. I can't wait for Mom to stop asking me questions about Casey and start asking you."

"She could ask me now," Max said.

"I tell her that every time. And yet."

The two sisters grinned at each other and hugged. Anne waved once more before she got into her car and pulled out onto the highway. With one last look at the motel, Casey and Max got into their new red truck. They rolled down the windows at the same time, each reaching out and waving. Linkman waved back at them, clearly mistaking their gesture as aimed at him. They shared a laugh, then drove off, putting the Sunset in the rearview mirror.

Scott waved awkwardly at Max and her outsider beaux before they pulled out of the lot. He was glad to see them leave. They were trouble, and if covering up all the mess they were involved in got them out of his town, then he had no problem with that deal. Once they'd pulled out of sight, he opened the ledger again, flipping to the last five years.

Sales had dropped in the waning days of Sam's business. But the old guy hadn't kept the place up. Scott remembered lying on the yellow bedspread waiting for Natasha to get out of the shower. The rooms were garish, smelly and uncomfortable. Sam had the right idea, that was obvious by the numbers in the ledger. Scott's eyes opened wide when he read through some of the figures from the Sunset's heyday. Sam's problem wasn't his original idea – it was that he let it go stale.

Scott would remedy that. He had new ideas, fresh ideas, ideas that could put Manistee back on the map. The Sunset would be the start. He wouldn't do anything that would be as morally outrageous as importing girls, but why should he? The girls in Manistee were perfectly fine. And unemployment being what it was, they'd rush for the opportunity to get a high-paying job. Rooms with a view, and a complimentary massage – it was legal, so long as the girls kept it quiet if they did anything extra. Scott was sure they would once the money started rolling in.

He got up, phone in hand, ready to call a select group of business partners to let them know it was time to move on this opportunity. He had the phone open and ready to dial when his stomach growled in complaint.

"Oh, fine. We'll eat first."

He got into his car, shoving aside the mountain of food containers littering the seat, and headed to the nearest fast food place he could think of.

A NOTE FROM M.M. PERRY

Hi, and thanks for reading my book. I hope you enjoyed it! I wanted to take a moment to ask if you'd consider leaving a review.

One of the best ways to support independent authors, besides buying our books, of course :) , is to leave a review. Independent authors don't have the deep pockets of big publishers and can't spend thousands on advertising to get our books in front of the eyes of possible readers. That's why when our books do land in front of someone, it helps if those potential readers can look up opinions on the book and see if it's the right fit for them.

I hope you'll consider leaving a review. Thank you for your purchase! I love hearing from readers. Send me a line at:

authormmperry@gmail.com.

START A NEW ADVENTURE FROM M.M. PERRY!

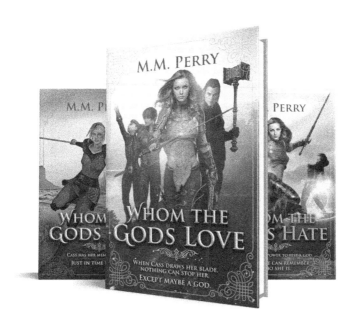

Grab *Whom the God's Love* FREE from your favorite retailer!

"I'm a huge fan of mythology and this book certainly plays to that love. You can immediately tell that this book is well thought out, well laid out, well written and extravagantly loved." — reviewer on Amazon

"Tons of adventure and the author created a wildly imaginative world that I want to visit again." — reviewer on B&N

"I love a story where a strong female can be a warrior as well as a woman." — reviewer on B&N

"I must say that M.M. Perry is unarguably a very talented writer, but more than that she genuinely impressed me with the thorough world-building and sheer creativeness on many levels. All too often I read works that feel clearly derivative of other books, and although I appreciate literary influences (as is mildly felt here on occasion as well), when something this original comes along it is a refreshing change of pace!" — Reviewer on Goodreads

"Just a wonderful world of mystery... can't wait to find out what happens next" — reviewer on B&N

"The final page left me waiting for the next book in the series." — reviewer on B&N

"wow, I'm actually surprised by how much I loved this book! Fantastic fantasy adventure suitable for adults and mature teens." — reviewer on B&N

"The characters are appealing and well drawn (I especially liked the new slant on the motivation of warriors) and the author has created a mythology with gods misbehaving much like Greek or Norse deities." — reviewer on Amazon

"Yo inez is the best." — reviewer on B&N

Get the story of Cass and her fellow adventurers with the complete trilogy, 30% off the standard price.

ALSO BY M.M. PERRY

Of Gods and Mortals Trilogy

Whom the Gods Love (Book 1)

Whom the Gods Hate (Book 2)

Whom the Gods Fear (Book 3)

Mission's End series

The 13

The 12

Chain of Deceit

The Arbiter

Molly's Tale

The Dream Merchant

Enchanted Legacy

Voro

Coming Soon!

The 11

Keep up to date with new releases and exclusive bonus content by signing up to the M.M. Perry Readers newsletter on authormmperry.com.

ABOUT THE AUTHOR

M.M. Perry has published twelve books. By day, she is an expert cat and dog wrangler, a nacho connoisseur, and writer of fantasy, science fiction and horror. By night... she does the same things. She is hard at work getting her next book edited and published. She's equally busy teaching her pug to sing along to the Muppets. She is known for saying, "No task involving a pug is impossible, just highly improbable."

For more information:
Authormmperry.com
authormmperry@gmail.com

CPSIA information can be obtained
at www.ICGtesting.com
Printed in the USA
FSHW022058191119
64307FS